A CHRISTMAS KISS

BOOK 4 IN THE LIFE ON THE MOORS SERIES

ELIZA J SCOTT

LANGUAGE

This book has been edited in British English (BrE) and therefore uses British spellings.

To the wonderful book community with all my love x

1

THE FRIDAY BEFORE CHRISTMAS
Zander

ZANDER THREW THE PHONE DOWN, rested his elbows on his desk and pressed his fingertips against his forehead. 'How the bloody hell did I ever get into this mess?' He was reeling from a call from Melissa, his girlfriend of three years. Make that his *needy, self-absorbed* girlfriend of three years. His emotions were veering from anger to feeling utterly fed-up. How could she do this, today of all days?

He glanced at the clock on the wall; it had just gone five-thirty – just gone five thirty on the evening their Christmas plans were supposed to spring into action. The evening Zander had been looking forward to for months and, up until two minutes ago, he thought Mel had been, too. But, thanks to the verbal hand-grenade she'd just lobbed smack, bang in the middle of them, everything had gone tits-up. 'Bloody woman!' He'd spent the day at Runswick Way Practice where he worked as a GP, making sure he was caught up on everything; he'd sent off referrals, drafted letters and signed prescriptions, leaving him free to go on holiday content in the knowledge that no work-related niggles would suddenly ping into his mind and trigger a cold sweat in the middle of the night.

'Right, let's get this over and done with.' He snatched up the phone and started scrolling through his contacts list, looking for his parents' number. Just then, there was a tap at the door and Noah peered around it, his hair a vivid ginger in the artificial light.

'Bad time?' Noah grimaced.

'No, come in.' Zander put the phone down and dragged his hand down his face. 'It's just ... just the usual crap.'

'Ah, by that I assume you mean Mel?' Noah flopped into one of the patients' chairs beside the desk.

'Got it in one: Mel.' He sighed, nodding slowly. Noah and Zander went back a long way – to university in Newcastle in fact. And Zander had always had the feeling that his friend wasn't exactly enamoured with Mel.

Noah looked at his watch. 'Listen, we'll be closed up here in half an hour. Fancy going for a beer after?'

'Sounds like a plan. I should be organised by then – with work, that is.' *And there's not exactly any need for me to rush back now,* he thought. 'Though, I'm driving, so it'll just be a shandy for me.'

'Yep, same here; I'll give you a shout when I'm ready. In the meantime, the dreaded Mrs. Wilkinson awaits ...'

'Not *the* Mrs. Wilkinson?'

'The very same. I, it would appear, have drawn the short straw and she's been added to my list today.'

Zander couldn't help but smile. 'Unlucky, mate. What complaint will it be this week, I wonder?'

'Hah! It's anybody's guess, but her notes make interesting reading. She must be going through some great tome of medical complaints, convincing herself she's got everything listed in it and is doomed to be dead within three years.'

'One of life's classic time wasters.' Zander shook his head. 'She doesn't realise how much better off she'd be by just getting on with her life, instead of worrying she's got every complaint under the sun; she'll outlive all of us that one.'

'And would you like to tell her that?' Noah smirked.

'Hmmph. Not particularly.' His words came out sharper then intended. 'Sorry, just ignore me; I'm still smarting after Mel's phone call.'

'No worries, mate.' Noah got to his feet. 'Right, well, the sooner I see Mrs. Wingebag Wilkinson, the sooner we can consider it the weekend and go for that shandy.'

Once the door clicked shut, as if on cue, Mel's words leapt back into Zander's mind.

'Sorry, Zandie, but two weeks in the French countryside in the middle of winter with your family just doesn't do it for me – especially that frosty sister of yours; I know she doesn't like me – and before you try to deny it, we both know it's true. It's unfair of you to expect me to have to deal with it at any time of the year, but over Christmas, even you would have to agree it's a bit much. On top of that, it'll be as dull as ditch-water. I want to have fun while I'm still young, and I most certainly don't want to behave like a boring middle-aged old fart. You'll be getting a pipe and slippers next; sipping port in a woolly cardigan, having a mug of cocoa before bed. In fact, that's sorted out the headache I had trying to think of a Christmas gift for you; a pipe and slippers would be perfect: "The Middle-Aged Man's Survival Kit!" Haha!' Mel cackled loudly at her own joke when she finally came up for air.

Zander winced.

'I'm only thirty-six, Mel – four years older than you – I hardly think that qualifies me for middle-age.'

'Ha! But you're old before your time, Zander Gillespie, always have been. In fact, I'm sure you were born aged forty-five.' Though her tone was jokey, he could sense the thinly-veiled snipe.

He picked up a pen and started doodling on his notepad. 'What, because I don't want to go clubbing every weekend, and would rather have a romantic meal at a nice restaurant, eating decent food with my girlfriend? I thought you liked that, spending quality time together?'

'Not *all* the time, Zander, and don't get me started on the walks in the country with that smelly old Labrador of yours … yawn, yawn, yawn. Sometimes, I actually think you care more about that mutt than you do about me.'

Zander felt himself bristle; she was always having a pop at Alf, and she knew he didn't like it. He and the black Labrador went back a long way – seven years, in fact – and were there for each other when nobody else was. As far as he was concerned, Alf was the best buddy a man could have – and if he was completely honest, he did have the biggest chunk of Zander's heart.

He swallowed down his niggle; he wasn't going to get drawn into an argument about Alf. Zander had been looking forward to their break, getting away from it all and relaxing. In fact, he couldn't remember a time when he'd needed a holiday more. Not to mention the effort he'd put into getting a pet passport for Alf.

'You could've said something before now, Mel. What am I going to do about your ticket?'

Her impatient sigh lost none of its impact down the phone line. He could picture her pouting, rolling her expertly made-up blue eyes and flicking her long blonde hair over her shoulder, before focusing her attention on her latest expensive manicure. A manicure he'd paid for along with a pamper session as a pre-Christmas treat.

'This is like a bolt out of the blue, why didn't you tell me you didn't like doing those things? Actually, come to think of it, I don't remember forcing you to do any of them. And the holiday's been planned for months, Mel, you've had plenty of time to tell me you didn't want to go.' In fact, she'd done a pretty convincing act of letting him believe she was keen to see his parents' newly-purchased chateau. Her eyes had lit up when he told her it was in Carcassonne in the sunny south of France. And she'd practically salivated when he'd shown her the pictures of the luxurious six-bedroom, six-bathroom property. Something must have happened to change her mind. And, if he knew her like he thought he knew her, he suspected she'd had a better offer.

'I'm sorry, Zandie; I didn't realise I didn't want to go until recently.'

Why did he get the feeling she wasn't telling him everything? 'So what are you going to do with yourself while I'm in France, Mel? Surely you're not going to just sit and stew at home?'

'Zander, since when have I ever done that?' she snapped. 'I'm not a *sitter*, I'm a *doer*, always busy, busy, busy and, for your information, I've had an invitation from Anna to join her and Pete ... and some, er ... friends at her sister's house in London.'

Ah, he was right; and that pause was interesting. 'And you just leapt at the chance without giving a thought to how I'd feel at being backheeled by my girlfriend while she trots off to spend Christmas with some people she's only known for five minutes?'

'Oh, don't be so miserable.' Her tone had developed a petulant edge. 'It's not like I'm leaving you all on your own; you've got your whole family to spend all of Christmas and New Year with. I can't believe you're being so selfish. What's wrong with you spending the festive period in the way that *you* enjoy, while I spend it in the way that *I* enjoy? It's hardly unreasonable. In fact, I think it's more unreasonable if you expect me to give up this opportunity. Anna thinks so, too.'

'I don't care what Anna thinks, Mel. But if that's what you want to do, then I'm not going to stop you. Will I see you before you go? Get a chance to give you your Christmas presents?'

'Er, no ... er, no need to worry about the presents, that's all sorted and er ... and we're getting the train down to London tonight, it's all booked, we're going First Class.'

'Right ...' His mind was scrambling over the subtext of her words; it might not be out of character for Mel to be self-ish, but it was totally out of character for her not to be both-ered about presents. At Christmas and birthdays, she was usually up at the crack of dawn, tearing the paper off her gifts like an over-excited child. Telling him not to worry about the presents just didn't fit. Realisation dawned; if they'd got First Class rail tickets this close to Christmas, they must have been booked a while ago. Mel had clearly been planning this trip for some time. He was getting fed up of her selfish attitude and sly ways; they were exhausting. He exhaled noisily. 'Okay, have a good time.' With that he'd ended the call.

2

LIVVIE

Livvie Weatherill pulled on her raspberry-red overcoat and wrapped a moss-green scarf around her neck before slinging her handbag over her shoulder and gathering up her cluster of shopping bags. 'Now I know what a packhorse feels like,' she said to herself, distributing them evenly between both hands. 'I'm off, Bry. Hope you have a good weekend,' she called.

'Ooh, you too, petal. Hope it all goes well.' Bryony rushed out from the depths of the kitchen at the back of the shop, pulled Livvie into a tight hug and planted a kiss on her cheek, rubbing it in for good measure.

'Thanks.' Livvie smiled at her best friend. They'd met at Blushing Brides wedding gown shop in the small town of Rickelthorpe just over four years ago and had hit it off straight away, sharing the same sense of humour as well as love of Prosecco and all things chocolate, and a loathing of the tyrannical owner Mrs Harris.

'Haven't you brought a hat?' Bryony's eyes flicked over Livvie's thick auburn hair that was gathered in a messy "up do" on top of her head.

'No, I'll be fine, I don't have far to walk.'

'Rather you than me; I can't bear having cold ears. Ooh, and don't forget this.' Bryony swiped up Livvie's mobile phone from the counter and popped it into the top pocket of her friend's coat.

'Oh, thanks, Bry; I'm such a scatter-brain.'

'No worries; and you're not. Anyway, I hope Donny appreciates all the effort you're going to.'

'I hope so, too.' Livvie ignored the little niggle at the back of her mind that hearing her boyfriend's name had triggered.

'Hey, what's not to love about tornado rossini followed by stiffy tockee pudding?' Bry chuckled at the name they'd given to sticky toffee pudding after Livvie had ordered it at a restaurant – a Prosecco or two too many jumbling her words, making the waiter laugh. The name had stuck ever since.

Her friend's joke temporarily chased Livvie's doubts away, and a smile lifted the corners of her mouth. 'Yep, when you put it like that, what's not to love? I just hope he gets his work finished early. Debbie –the woman from the flat next door – is being a bit of a pain with all the plumbing problems she needs fixing; they're always urgent, too. She's only been there for six weeks, but she's definitely made her presence felt.'

'Uhh, she sounds very demanding.'

Just then the brass doorbell above the door jangled and two women stepped in on an icy blast of cold air. 'Will you be able to manage?' Livvie always felt guilty about taking time off work, even if she was only leaving a couple of hours early.

'Two women doesn't make a stampede, Liv. Looking at the weather, I doubt we'll get many more in. Go on, get yourself home.' Bryony made her way over to the door, holding it open for her friend. 'And hurry up about it, we're letting all the warm air out.' She smiled.

'Okay, see you Monday night.'

'Yep, if you pop round for six thirty, that should be perfect.'

'Looking forward to it. And are you sure I don't need to bring anything?'

'Nope, just bring your gorgeous self, Liv; and Donny, of course.'

Bryony and her boyfriend Josh were hosting a party at their flat. Ordinarily, Livvie would be looking forward to it, but a nagging doubt at the back of her mind told her that Donny would be reluctant to go; he never liked to do anything with her friends and always seemed to engineer an argument so he didn't have to go.

She mustered up a smile. 'Okay, will do; have a great time tonight.' She leaned in to Bry, lowering her voice. 'And enjoy the thought that we don't have to be here and put up with Mrs Harris for a whole two weeks.'

'Bliss.' Bry grinned. 'Now go.' With a laugh, she pushed Livvie through the door.

'Alright, I'm going.'

Every year, the shop closed for the festive period from the Friday before Christmas until the Saturday after New Year's Day, while Mrs Harris and her husband took off to join their daughter and son-in-law in the Canary Islands. She claimed there was a lull in wedding dress shopping at this time of year and it was a waste of time the shop being open, but, meanly, insisted that Livvie and Bryony take two weeks from their annual leave to accommodate it, leaving them short of days to use over the summer.

Once outside, Livvie noted that the sky had taken on an

unusual shade of gun-metal grey tinged with a bruise-like purple. That, in Livvie's experience, usually meant snow was on its way. She hurried along the pavement, dodging other shoppers and a group of merrymakers who'd obviously started their Christmas celebrations early. 'Oy, sweetheart, how about a kiss under the mistletoe?' A man, looking rather worse-for-wear loomed over her, waving a pathetic-looking piece of berryless foliage. Livvie took a step back, holding her breath; he was radiating boozy fumes so strong, she feared they might melt her eyeballs.

'Leave her alone, Dave,' called one of his friends, dragging him away. 'Take no notice of him, love.'

Livvie breathed a sigh of relief and hurried off, regretting losing her gloves as the heavy carrier bags dug into her frozen fingers. Soon, she was at her little silver banger of a car, grateful that she'd managed to get a parking place so close to work that morning. After a quick rummage for her keys, she dumped her shopping in the boot and squashed what wouldn't fit in the footwell behind the front seats.

'Brrr. I can't believe how cold it is.' She shivered and flicked the engine on, turning the vents onto the windows that had already started to steam up. Hopefully, it wouldn't take long for the car to start generating a bit of warmth.

Just as she'd fastened her seat belt, her phone rang, reminding her it was still in the top pocket of her coat. She fished it out and smiled to see Donny's number. 'Hi, babe,' she said, waiting for an answer. 'Donny? ... Hello ... Donny, are you there?' There was no reply, but she could hear a muffled mix of background noises. *He must've butt dialled me by mistake.* She laughed softly to herself and was just about to hang up when she heard a woman's voice; a woman's voice that was vaguely familiar and it was saying her boyfriend's name. Livvie listened on, her brow furrowing at the collection of unpalatable groaning sounds that followed.

Her heart lurched and panic began to swirl in her gut as realisation dawned. She'd had her suspicions for the last couple of weeks and she didn't have long to wait for them to be confirmed when the woman asked Donny to do something toe-curlingly explicit; something you definitely wouldn't ask of a plumber who'd called round to fix a leaky tap.

Tears welled in Livvie's eyes, as hurt seeped up inside her. All the planning she'd done to prepare for this dinner, the amount of money she'd spent on getting the best ingredients to make tornado rossini, Donny's favourite meal. Not to mention having to use up a day's holiday when she only needed to leave work a few hours early. Mrs Harris was a dragon and had refused to budge on letting Livvie leave early if she made the hours up by working over-time. If it wasn't for Bry, Livvie would have left there years ago.

In a moment, anger quashed her sadness and she snatched the tears from her eyes. Throwing her phone down, she flicked the indicator, pulled out of her parking place and made her way home, her heart thudding angrily as her head filled with the words she planned to hurl at the pair.

Livvie tucked her car around the corner from the converted Victorian villa she shared with Donny in the less salubrious part of Rickelthorpe; she didn't want to alert him to her early arrival. As she walked towards the building, she spotted Donny's scruffy white van parked on the road in front of it. The lights were on in their flat; surely they weren't having their sordid little rendezvous there? Anger jostled with hurt, urging her forward and giving her a much-needed blast of courage to confront him.

With her heart pounding even harder in her chest, Livvie slotted the key into the lock of the large black front door, made difficult by fingers that were still numb with cold. Carefully, she clicked it shut and tiptoed over the tiled hallway that led to the broad staircase. She made her way stealthily up the stairs, avoiding the ones with the tell-tale creak – though the runner was threadbare in parts, it still did a good job of muffling her steps. Alighting silently on the landing, Livvie steadied her breathing and pressed her ear to the door of their flat. A wave of nausea washed over her; they were there.

Before she knew it, she found herself pushing the door open and following the voices to the living room; wanting to catch her boyfriend out, yet not wanting to face the truth. She was conscious of her mouth falling open as she took in the sight of Donny, his blond hair sticking up in tufts, and their neighbour Debbie en flagrante on the sofa. *Her* sofa, the one she'd saved for ages to buy.

'You bastard!' Livvie tore across the room and kicked Donny hard up the backside. 'You bloody cheating slime-ball.'

'Arghh! Arghh! You caught my bollocks, you stupid cow!' Donny fell to the floor, rolling around, groaning in agony.

'Good! You bloody-well deserve it!' Adrenalin raged around her body. She turned to Debbie. 'And you can get your slaggy arse off my sofa and get out of my flat.' She picked up a pile of discarded clothing and threw it at the woman, who desperately tried to cover herself. 'Go on, get out!' Livvie was surprised at just how good screaming at her felt.

'It's my flat too, and keep your voice down, the neighbours will hear.' Donny was still bent-double.

'Well, that hardly matters, does it? The neighbour's sodding-well here, screwing around with my boyfriend of the last two years.' She watched as Debbie, her face a picture, struggled to pull her dress over her head.

'It's all her fault; leading me on. What d'you expect me to do when it's offered on a plate?' Donny went to push himself up, his face puce and still crumpled with pain.

'What do you mean, offered on a plate? You were the one who came on to me with your sad little cheesy pick-up lines. But you needn't bother wasting them on me anymore and besides, you're not that great.' Debbie snatched up the remains of her clothing from the floor and looked at Livvie. 'And don't think I'm the first; all he's done is brag about his conquests and how you're too stupid to even notice.' With that she flounced out of the room, slamming the door behind her.

Livvie's mind was reeling as she turned her attention back to Donny. Debbie's last words had stung, but they were enough to elbow the tears that had begun to well in her eyes out of the way. She took a fortifying breath. 'I think you should go.'

'Go where? This is my flat, too, you know; we rent it together.' His blue eyes had lost their usually playful expression, replaced with one that was cold and challenging.

'Shame you don't always remember that when it comes to actually paying the rent and the bills, isn't it? And I think you'll find it was me who paid the deposit.'

'I pay what I can; you know that. There's just not that much work around at the moment.' It didn't escape Livvie's attention that he seemed reluctant to make eye-contact as he pulled on his clothes.

'That's probably cos you're spending half your time shagging around!'

'Well, you've only got yourself to blame. When was the last time we had sex, eh? Answer me that. Two weeks ago? Three weeks ago? It's so flaming long ago, I can't even remember.'

She flinched; if her reckoning was right, it was closer to four weeks ago. She'd been sensing her feelings change towards Donny as a succession of little niggles had started to creep their way into the back of her mind, pushing an invisible wedge between them. Returning home late, smelling of other women's perfume, stale beer on his breath, not to mention finding the back of an earring in their bed a couple of weeks ago; a bed she'd only just changed that morning.

At that thought, Livvie suddenly found herself making her way towards their bedroom.

'What're you doing? You don't need to go in there.' Donny followed her down the hall, pulling at her arm.

'And why would that be?' She took in the sight of the crumpled sheets of the bed she'd left made that morning, the decorative cushions cast on the floor. 'In our bed, too? You total slime-ball.'

'Yeah, well, like I said, you've only got yourself to blame.'

'And when did you last initiate anything between us? It's been down to me that last couple of times.'

Donny's expression changed to a spiteful sneer. 'Well, maybe if you took a look in the mirror, you'd see why; see what I have to look at. You've let yourself go, Liv, piled on the weight, especially on your arse, and as for those thunder-thighs, they're like a couple of massive tree-trunks. It's no wonder I don't want to come anywhere near you.'

His words plunged into her heart like the blade of a knife, but she wasn't going to let him see he'd hurt her. She fought with all her might to hold her tears back. 'I think that says more about you than it does about me; you're a nasty, spiteful individual, and I think you should go.'

'Don't worry, I'm not hanging around here tonight, listening to your crap. I'm off out.' He strode back towards the living room and grabbed his keys from the bowl on the sideboard. 'And don't forget what I said about looking in the mirror.' He threw the words over his shoulder as he left the flat.

Livvie's heart twisted. She hurried over to the window, watching as Donny climbed into his van and drove off. Only then did she let the hurt take hold and the hot tears flow.

3

ZANDER

'WANT TO TALK ABOUT IT?' asked Noah. He and Zander were sitting at a small table in the corner of the pub, by the large Victorian fireplace that housed an electric "roaring" fire. Already the Queen's Head was buzzing with people in a party mood, the festive music from the speakers slowly being drowned out by the increasing volume of the revellers' high-spirited voices.

Zander took a long, slow slug of his shandy before he answered. 'There's not a lot to say, really; I thought I was about to go away to Carcassonne for Christmas and the New Year, take Mel so she could get to know my family better, and they could get to know her. But now it's all off.' He shrugged, wiping the condensation from his pint glass with his fingers. 'Simple as that.'

'Doesn't mean you can't still go, though.'

'I know, but I don't think I could stand all the sympathetic looks from my family; you've no idea what it's like being the only unmarried offspring. Steff's been happily married to John – who, incidentally, is the "perfect" son-in-law – for what feels like forever.

'I thought you liked John?'

'I do, he's a really good bloke; I didn't mean to sound sarcastic. And Toby's still on cloud nine after getting hitched to Jo last year. Which leaves me, at the grand old age of thirty-six, who doesn't seem to be able to hang on to a partner for more than five minutes, doomed – in their eyes – to a life of singledom.' Zander puffed out his cheeks and sighed. 'I'm dreading making the call to my parents, telling them we won't be going.'

'I still think you should go, the sympathetic looks wouldn't last for the whole break – and you never know, you might meet a nice French girl.' Noah hooked an eyebrow at him.

'Er, I'm still in a relationship with Mel – at least I think I am – and the thought of having to explain, face-to-face, why she isn't with me; seeing the pity in their eyes, catching them whispering about me ... ughh!' Zander was still unsure of how he should broach the subject of Mel when he went to collect Alf from Steff's later that evening; the interrogation, though well meant, would be intense and he didn't know if he was up to it. He was seriously considering not mentioning it. He could get round it by explaining the situation to his mother over the phone; he knew she'd be disappointed at first, but she'd have the grandchildren to take her mind off it. And the fact that she could break the news to everyone was, he had to admit, very tempting. It may be the coward's way out, but deep down he knew what Steff's reaction would be, and he knew she'd be absolutely right. 'Trust me, Noah, having Christmas dinner, just me and Alf, is the easy option.'

'I take your point. But, if you want my opinion – and I hope you don't think I'm stepping out of line here – it might be a good time to have a think about where your relationship with Mel is going. It's just, you seem to have a lot of hassle with her; nothing seems straightforward. And it's been a while since I've seen you look properly happy.'

Zander gazed into his glass; his friend was right, there had been umpteen times recently when Mel had scuppered their plans and blown him off for doing something with her trendy new friends. As for feeling happy, now he thought about it, that wasn't something he'd felt around Mel for quite some time. 'Yep, maybe I will; we can't go on like this forever.'

Noah paused for a moment before his eyes suddenly lit up. 'You could always come to us for Christmas dinner; it's our turn to host this year – last count I think Jess said we had eleven coming; that's fifteen including us and the kids, you could make it a nice even number. And it goes without saying that Alf's welcome, too.'

'Thanks, buddy, that's a kind offer but the last thing you need is my miserable face putting the dampers on the day.'

Before Noah had chance to reply, their attention was drawn towards a group of women – clearly on the other side of a few egg nogs. They were giggling loudly and looking in the direction of Zander and Noah's table. The giggles increased in shrillness and volume once they realised they'd got their quarry's attention.

Zander groaned as the loudest of the group started to weave her rather tipsy way towards them. 'Great,' he said sotto voce. 'That's all we need.'

Noah snorted into his pint.

'Hi, I'm Bex, and me and my friends were just wondering if anyone had ever told you that you look like that Henry Cavill bloke?' Swaying precariously on a pair of dangerously high heels, she peered at Zander, twirling the ends of the tinsel she had draped around her neck.

'Er, yeah, once or twice.' He felt his heart sink. He daren't look at Noah who he could sense sniggering beside him.

'Thought so.' The swaying continued as she peered more closely at him. 'Your eyes aren't half blue.'

Zander just nodded.

'Well, if you fancy buying us a drink and getting to know us a little better, Henry, we're going to be over there for the next half hour or so. Mine's a Porn Star Martini.' She arched her eyebrows suggestively at him. 'Your friend can come too, if he fancies.'

'Thanks,' said Noah.

'You're welcome, Ginger Nuts.' Bex turned on her heels, almost losing her balance, and headed back to her chums amidst shrieks of laughter.

'Nice,' said Noah. 'Tempted?'

'I'd rather stick pins in my bollocks,' said Zander.

'Ouch!'

Zander raked his fingers through his short dark crop. 'How come I always attract the wrong sort of women?'

'I don't think it's the attracting part that's the problem; the choosing part, however, is a different matter.'

Zander thought for a moment, his mind briefly parading his girlfriends of the last ten or so years before him. Hmm. Noah had a point; there was definitely a theme going on.

'If you think about it, all of the women you've had a relationship with – apart from Clara – have been the glamorous, high-maintenance, self-centred, dolly-bird type who think appearance and material things are everything; I'm sorry to say it, but you have an affinity for shallow birds, mate. Whereas, those of us who don't have your film-star good looks, well, we don't have that problem; that type of women seem to by-pass us – not that I'm complaining. I've got my lovely Jess, who's beautiful, kind and easy-going.'

'Yep, you're a lucky bloke.' Zander nodded. A memory of Clara who he'd broken up with seven years ago popped into his mind; he quickly shooed it away.

Noah pulled a face. 'Sorry, that sounded a bit smug, didn't it? Didn't mean it to; but you get where I'm coming from?'

'No worries, mate, I know you didn't and, yes, I'm beginning to realise what you mean.'

Zander glanced around; the pub was filling up with a sea of happy-looking people, all ready to get into the festive spirit and have a good time. 'Right,' he said downing the dregs of his shandy, 'time to go and collect Alf from Steff's. Can't say I'm looking forward to the questioning; nothing gets past that big sister of mine.'

Noah checked his watch. 'Yep, time I was heading back, too. Good luck, and remember, if you change your mind, you're always welcome to join us for Christmas.'

'Thanks, you're a good mate.' He reached across and tapped Noah on the shoulder before getting to his feet. It triggered a burst of cheering from the group of women at the bar.

'Ooh, decided to come and join us, have you, Henry?' The woman's screeching tone was like chalk down a blackboard, making Zander grit his teeth.

He pulled on his dark tweed coat, shaking his head. 'Sorry, ladies, I'm afraid I'm going home.'

'Well, let us know if you'd like us to come and join you,' Bex said, making her friends cackle.

He smiled politely and turned back to Noah. 'You have a fantastic Christmas; give my love to Jess and the kids, and I'll see you in the New Year.'

'Yep, you too. And don't forget what I said.'

'I won't.'

Zander headed towards the door, ignoring the whistles and leers from the women at the bar. Outside, he paused for a moment, the icy air nipping at his ears and nose. A gust of wind suddenly blasted down the street; it carried with it the inimitable hint of snow. He pulled up the collar of his coat and headed towards his car, wondering just how he was going to explain to Steff that he wasn't going to be joining them in Carcassonne. No longer bolstered by Noah's chat and the Christmas vibe in the pub, he felt his heart plummet right down to his brown brogues. *Bloody Melissa*.

STANDING at his sister's shiny, pillar-box red front door, Zander took a breath and braced himself. Postponing the inevitable, he took a sudden interest in the large wreath that was hanging from the door-knocker. Made of thick, glossy branches of pine, it was adorned with fresh, rosy apples, deep purple baubles and sprigs of holly sporting vivid red berries. Trimmed with a rich burgundy bow and woven with warm white fairy lights; it's festive aesthetic wasn't wasted on him. But now wasn't the time to admire Steff's handiwork; he had a Labrador to collect and an explanation to give. 'Best get this over with,' he said to himself as he pressed the doorbell.

Its melodic chime triggered a babble of excited children's voices, followed by barking from Alf and Cynthia – the family's wire-haired dachshund – as the four of them raced down the hall. Moments later, the door was flung open, and the dogs shot towards him, Alf's tail wagging furiously and Cynthia running circles around him on her stumpy little legs.

'Woah. Hello there.' Zander ruffled his Labrador's ears.

'Hi, Uncle Zandie, Mum's making some mince pies and we've been helping,' said his nephew Joel, whose face was smeared with the proof.

'And I rolled out the pastry on my own and cut out the shapes.' His niece, Annabel beamed proudly.

'Sounds like you've been having fun. And have you been helping, Alf?' Alf responded by wagging his tail so fast, his whole body shook.

'Alf's been trying to eat everything,' said Joel.

'Sounds about right.' Zander smiled at his faithful dog who was gazing up at him with adoring, gentle brown eyes.

'Stand back, you two, and let your Uncle Zandie through the door; you're letting all the warm air out.' His sister bustled down the hallway, wiping her hands on a tea towel, her shiny black hair escaping from its ponytail. 'Come in, Zandie; it's freezing out there,' she said above the Christmas music that was wending its way down the hall and out into the neat front garden.

The children scurried back towards the kitchen, with Cynthia in hot pursuit, allowing Zander to step into the warmth. Alf stuck close by, sniffing at his dad's trousers. 'Thanks, Steff, it's pretty nippy out there now; I wouldn't be surprised if it snowed before the night's out.'

'Well, it's forecast, though I do wish it would hang on until we're all safely over in France.'

Oh, Lord. His stomach clenched as he followed her down the long hallway, past a wicker basket full of shoes. He stopped momentarily to hang his coat on the newel post of the staircase, being careful to avoid the pine garland, trimmed with fairy lights that was wrapped artfully around the bannister.

'Smells good in here.' He looked around the post-baking detritus of the kitchen. There was a dusting of flour on the floor, with soggy patches where Alf and Cynthia had tried to lick up any sticky bits of stray mincemeat – *That explains why Alf's beard is suddenly greyer than when I dropped him off this morning.* On the pine dresser, Emma Bridgewater pottery jostled for space with a collection of Christmas cards, party invitations and a variety of festive decorations – some clearly this year's handmade offerings from the kids. The final flourish was a further pine garland that ran along the top, twinkling with warm white lights.

Zander loved to spend time at his sister and brother-in-law's home; it was chaotic but homely and cosy. All squashy sofas and plump cushions, the term shabby chic could easily have been coined for it. And there was always a trail of delicious smells emanating from the kitchen which was definitely the beating heart of the home here. He'd always hoped he'd have somewhere just like this himself one day, filled with love and happiness ... and a gaggle of children. An image of Mel suddenly popped into his mind, jarring with his thoughts. In fact, whenever he thought of her, his mind conjured up sharp corners and hard edges; nothing soft or homely. She was cold and shallow. Vapid, even.

'We've been in a last-minute mince pie baking frenzy; I hadn't realised we were heading off to Carcassonne when I offered to bake thirty of the blimmin' things for the school Christmas Fayre. And I'd clean forgotten all about it until one of the mums reminded me at the school gates tonight. I'm going to drop them off with her first thing in the morning before we set off.' She feigned mopping her brow. 'Panic averted.'

'Look, Uncle Zandie, I made these all by myself.' Seven-year-old Joel held up some suspicious looking offerings that could only just pass for mince pies.

'Wow, they look amazing.' Zander smiled at the eager expression on his nephew's face.

'Here, have one.' Joel thrust one of the heavy lumps into Zander's hand. 'They're super-yummy, aren't they, Mummy?'

'They most certainly are, darling.'

'Thank you, they look it, and Alf certainly seems to think so, judging by how much he's drooling.' Zander took a bite – watched closely by Alf – wearing an expression that said they were just as Joel had described. 'Mmm mm.'

'And I only picked my nose once while I was baking, Uncle Zandie. Just once.'

Zander's face dropped and he stopped chewing, at a loss for what to do with his mouthful.

'You picked your nose loads more than that, Joely,' said Annabel. 'I saw you. And you ate some of it, too.'

Zander glanced across at Steff, who was trying but failing to suppress a giggle.

'I did not! Well, only two times at the *very* most.'

'Coffee, Zander?' asked Steff. 'Help wash your mince pie down.'

He swallowed his mouthful. 'I think I better had. Thanks for the warning, by the way.'

'Sorry.' She filled the kettle and set it on the Aga. 'If it's any consolation, every time I caught him with his finger up his nose, I made him wash his hands.'

'Good to know.'

'Watch this, Uncle Zandie.' Joel patted him on the arm.

Zander turned to see his nephew touching the tip of his nose with his tongue.

'Bet you can't do that,' he said proudly.

'Hmm. I don't think I can.' He attempted to copy his nephew. 'Nope, can't do it.'

'Boys are so *disgusting*,' said Annabel.

'And that's not all; wait till you see this, Uncle Zandie. Wait, wait, wait you're going to totally love it.'

Zander watched with morbid fascination as Joel stuck out his tongue and popped the tip first in one nostril, then the other.

'Impressive.' He gave Joel a thumbs up.

'Urghh! That is so gross,' said Annabel.

'None of my friends can do that.' Joel wiped his nose with the back of his hand and grinned.

'I'll bet. It's some party-piece you've got going on there, young man; you're going to be quite the hit with the girls when you're older.'

'Urghh!' Annabel and Joel chorused.

'And where've you been taking my nephew to learn such tricks?' Zander asked Steff.

'Gets it from his father.' She gave a mischievous grin.

'Ah.'

'Oh, while I remember, Alf's had his tea.' At the word "tea" the Labrador's ears pricked up. 'Just with you being late back, he and Cynthia were looking at me, sucking their cheeks in, trying to convince me they were starving.'

'Sounds about right – and sorry for being late, s'just—'

Steff splayed her hands. 'Hey, no problem, I just thought I'd better let you know in case Alf tries to con another meal out of you.'

'Wouldn't be the first time, would it, buddy?'

Alf replied with a wag of his tail.

'Come and sit down, Uncle Zandie, then you can have a look at my baking – you can have some, too.' Annabel pulled out a chair at the scrubbed pine table and patted the seat. Zander did as he was bid and she set a tea plate in front of him. He smiled, she was definitely a chip off the old block. "Gently bossy" is how their mum used to describe Steff, which suited her perfectly; and now Annabel, too.

'You can have a mince pie with a star on the top, one without, or one with some icing – it's lemon flavoured,' she said pointing to a range of wire cooling racks with the pies set out on them. 'And I've sprinkled edible glitter over them, so they look extra Christmassy.'

'They look very professional, Bells. Are you sure your mum didn't make them?'

Annabel's face flushed with pride. 'Nope, I made all of them; Mum hardly helped me at all, did you, Mum?'

'That's right, Bells did pretty much all of it herself. I think we've got a little Mary Berry on our hands. She made the Christmas pudding a couple of months ago, and the Christmas cake.' Steff placed a steaming mug of coffee on the table in front of her brother. She grabbed one for herself and flopped onto the patchwork cushion of the slightly battered armchair that sat beside the Aga. 'Phew!' She blew a straggle of hair out of her eyes.

'Which one would you like to start with, Uncle Zandie?' asked Annabel.

'Erm, I quite like the sound of the one with lemon icing, thanks.'

While the children were distracted, Zander quietly slipped Joel's mince pie into his trouser pocket. It popped out straight away and was quickly hoovered up by Alf.

Before he knew it, half an hour had passed and Zander still hadn't mentioned that he wouldn't be joining the rest of the family in Carcassonne; the more he thought about it, the more he was dreading the inevitable grilling from Steff. He knew what she'd say, and he knew she'd be right, but he just didn't have the strength to hear it.

'So are you all packed up and ready to leave first thing in the morning?'

'Er—'

At that moment, John arrived home, setting the dogs and kids chasing down the hall in great excitement. It didn't escape Zander's attention how Steff's face lit up and her eyes sparkled as her husband walked towards her, pulled her to him and pressed a kiss to her lips. Zander felt a sudden pang of – what? Loneliness, self-pity, envy? *No,* he thought. It was none of those, it was despair at himself, his crap choices and his pathetic life. And it was time he did something about it.

'Right, that's my cue to leave.' After the initial flurry of hellos, Zander took a last sip of his coffee.

'Don't rush off on my account,' said John. 'You're more than welcome to join us for dinner.' He set his briefcase down and unfurled his scarf.

'Yes, why not stay, there's plenty of beef casserole and dumplings to go round,' said Steff. 'And there's a massive apple crumble for afters.'

Zander felt his stomach rumble; his sister was a fabulous cook and always made enough to feed an army. And her apple crumble was to die for; all soft apple with the perfect tang of tartness and a hint of cinnamon. As for her custard; thick and creamy, speckled with vanilla, and there was usually a trickle of toffee sauce, too. *Mmm.* He almost succumbed when he realised he'd be quizzed about tomorrow.

'Please stay, Uncle Zandie,' said Annabel.

'Yes, please stay for dinner. I'll even let you have another one of my mince pies,' said Joel.

Zander did his best not to laugh at the face Annabel was

pulling behind Joel's back. 'Much as I'd love to, I really need to get back.'

ONCE OUTSIDE IN the crisp evening air, Zander gave a sigh of relief, his breath hanging in a plume of condensation, suspended in the glow of the lamp above the door. That was one hurdle over and done with; the next was telling his mother. He wasn't looking forward to that. 'Right, young man, it's absolutely freezing, let's get you home,' he said to Alf. 'Time to put plan B into action.' The pair made their way down the path and out onto the street. In the time he'd been indoors, a thick frost had crept over the gardens and footpaths, making them sparkle in the soft light of the Victorian street lamps.

The pair headed towards Zander's car. 'The only thing is, I don't have a bloody plan B.'

4

LIVVIE

LIVVIE GLANCED up at the clock; it had been just over an hour and a half since Donny had left. In that time, she'd taken herself into the kitchen – the only room that had no evidence of his indiscretions – where she'd sobbed and sobbed until she had no more tears left to cry. Now, her head pounded and her heart ached with an unpalatable combination of hurt and humiliation; his cruel snipe about her weight before he left still smarting.

What had happened to the fun-loving Donny she'd fallen for; the one with the permanent smile and boyish charm? When they'd first met, she'd been drawn to him like a moth round a flame, eagerly anticipating their dates, her heart thrumming with excitement. Though from this vantage point, it was hard to believe there'd been a time when her face had ached with laughter because of his seemingly endless supply of jokes and funny anecdotes. They'd dried up long since, fast becoming a distant memory, along with the permanent smile. The Donny she was familiar with now was a colder, coarser version of himself, and Livvie didn't like him one bit.

With a sniff, she pulled out another tissue from the box and blew her nose, just as a text pinged through on her iPhone. It was Bryony in her usual cheery tone, hoping everything was going well. She'd signed off with a mixture of happy, party emojis. Livvie felt her throat tighten as fresh tears threatened. She resisted the urge to call her friend and pour her heart out, not wanting to put the dampers on her evening. Bryony had been excited that Josh had booked them a meal at the new fancy restaurant that had opened up in town, followed by VIP seats at the cinema for a viewing of the latest blockbuster starring Nicole Kidman and Keanu Reeves. She'd been bubbling away about it for the last couple of days and there was no way Livvie could throw a bucket of icy-cold water over that; she knew that Bry would feel torn between wanting to go out on her date with Josh and the urge to comfort her best friend.

'What a mess.' She pushed her phone out of the way and heaved a sigh. To say the day hadn't exactly panned out how she'd hoped would be an understatement. By now the preparations for the meal should be well under way with delicious aromas of chopped onions, garlic and mushrooms for the duxelles floating around the flat, the table should be set for a romantic dinner for two, while Michael Bublé's smooth tones would be playing gently in the background. The wine should be chilled to perfection; ready for her to pour a glass for Donny who was due to burst through the door at any minute. She'd even bought some new under-wear for the occasion; he regularly grumbled about her usual choice of trusty M&S knickers, so she'd pushed the boat out – and her self-consciousness to the back of her mind – and picked up some of the tarty stuff he seemed to prefer.

Instead, here she was, five days before Christmas,

sobbing her heart out, hardly daring to face the future. Her spirits slumped along with her shoulders. If she was honest with herself, Livvie had known she and Donny had been drifting apart for a while; that their relationship had been hanging on by a tiny thread that had been getting stragglier by the day. The cheeky-chappy banter she'd once found funny had begun to grate and it had gradually begun to dawn that he was using her. In fact, she couldn't remember the last time he'd contributed to the rent or the household bills; he'd bring in a four-pack of beer and some family-sized bags of crisps, referring to them as a treat for her as his way of distracting her from the fact that he barely dipped his hand into his pocket and paid his way. She'd let it pass; not wanting it to cause an argument.

One evening, when she'd worked late owing to a private viewing by a local minor "celebrity", she'd returned home, hoping that Donny would at least have brought something in for dinner. But, true to form, there he was, sprawled on the sofa, beer can in hand, watching the football, grumbling at the length of time he'd had to wait for his food. When she'd commented that he could at least have made beans on toast, he'd flown off the handle.

'It's not just you who goes out to work you know, Livvie. I've been flogging my guts out today, doing proper stuff, not swanning around in a frock shop, fawning over stupid women like you do.'

'There's no need to shout; I know you work hard, but I don't just swan around, there's much more to working in a wedding gown shop than you think. I have to—'

Donny held his hand up to silence her. 'Spare me the details. Anyway, you've totally spoilt the surprise; I was going to order a takeaway from your favourite restaurant, save you having to cook and do the washing-up.'

That comment had irritated her on so many levels; he was a chauvinist of the highest order. But Livvie was too tired for an argument. Instead, she pushed down her annoyance and focused on the more palatable part of his words. 'I'm sorry, that's really thoughtful of you. Just ignore me, Mrs Harris has been a right old bag today, treating Bry and me like dirt in front of the customers.' She flopped down on the arm of the sofa. 'A Chinese takeaway would be lovely.'

A little victorious smile hovered over his lips. 'Yeah, well, the number's on the sideboard; I'll have sweet and sour spare ribs, duck spring rolls and chicken egg fried rice. Oh, and tell them to chuck in some of them prawn crackers, they go well with beer.' He leaned forward and slurped noisily from his can.

Livvie cringed inside and, difficult as it was, she resisted the overwhelming temptation to grab his beer and tip it all over him. Silently seething, she stalked over to the sideboard, snatched up the menu and called in the order. *How much longer can I put up with this?*

Half an hour later when the doorbell rang, it was obvious that Donny had no intention of moving from his place on the sofa. 'That'll be the takeaway,' he said, his eyes never moving from the TV screen.

'I'll get it, shall I?' *Seeing as though your arse has taken root there.*

'Yep, you be a good little woman.' He followed that up with a loud belch.

Ughh! Revolting pig! To this day, Livvie didn't know how she hadn't run over and jumped up and down on his nuts. Instead, she bit her tongue and went to fetch the food. 'I'll pay for it, too, shall I?' she said to herself as she stomped to the door.

Yep, looking back, the rot had well and truly set in some

time ago. She'd been fooling herself, trying to hang onto a failing relationship that she hadn't been happy in or felt comfortable with for, well, easily the last year. Turning a blind eye to things that had really started to niggle her. And, no doubt, Donny was feeling the same. Actually, who was she trying to bloody-well kid; of course he wasn't happy, why else would he be screwing around with any women daft enough to let him get into her knickers. She'd been a mug; but not anymore.

The thought of Christmas day suddenly loomed in her mind, making her heart sink. They'd been invited to her sister and brother-in-law's house for dinner. 'Ughh!' That thought made Livvie's blood run cold. Cheryl and her smarmy husband Gavin had the sort of house that made you feel it didn't want you there. As soon as you stepped through the front door, the off-white walls and cream carpet screamed OCD at you. It was a shoes off at the door type of home, with the said shoes being exchanged for slippers from a box that was kept tucked out of sight in a cupboard under the stairs. Livvie wasn't keen on wearing footwear that somebody else's sweaty feet had been in – and there was no way Cheryl would offer the same courtesy at her flat which made Livvie even less inclined to do it – so she'd started to take her own fold-up party slippers; Cheryl's face was a picture the first time Livvie had turned up with them.

'No slippers for me thanks, Chez, I've brought my own.' Livvie produced a velvet pouch containing a cute pair of velvet slippers from her bag, waving them at her sister.

'Oh.'

As Livvie slipped her feet into them, she was aware of Cheryl's eyes burning into her; she'd be dying to snatch them off her so she could give them a thorough inspection before granting a seal of approval. Livvie wrestled with a smile; was it wrong to get so much pleasure out of telling her sniffy sister she didn't need her stupid slippers? No, she told herself, this was way too much fun.

'And you know I don't like "Chez".'

'Sorry, I forgot.' Livvie bit back the urge to use "Chezza" instead; Cheryl liked that even less. *Chezza, Chezza, Chezza!*

That was the most Livvie had ever smiled at her sister's house. As a rule, from the very moment she arrived there, her carefree spirit was sucked out of her and replaced with a tightly knotted ball of anxiety. Everywhere gleamed and sparkled like it was a freshly decorated show home; not a thing was out of place. Livvie regularly wished she'd perfected the art of levitation as she tiptoed down the hall into the pristine living room. Even sitting on the sofa, with its precisely placed cushions that managed to ping up every-where as soon as she sat down, brought her out in a sweat. And it was clear that Cheryl couldn't relax with the slightest hint of disorder and itched to drag Livvie off the sofa and plump the rogue cushions back to perfection before re-aligning them – Livvie often wondered if she used a ruler and a spirit level to do it.

She marvelled at how her ten-year-old nephew Ryan managed to survive in such a hostile environment when it seemed to bring out a clumsy side of Livvie she only ever had when she was there. It was so bad, she'd even wondered if the house was deliberately booby-trapped to make things go wrong for her. Like the last time she'd been given the "royal approval" to visit and the handle had dropped off the teacup she was drinking from, sending tea splashing all over the newly-fitted cream carpet. Though it clearly wasn't her fault, the expression on Cheryl's face said otherwise; it still made Livvie shudder.

'Oh, God, I'm so sorry.' Livvie felt distraught as the hot liquid soaked into the thick pile of the wool carpet.

'Funny how that hasn't happened to anyone else.' Cheryl's expression was tight as she watched Gavin rush off for a bowl of soapy water.

'But I didn't do it on purpose, look, the cup separated from the handle, which I'm still holding.'

'Well, all I'm saying is that I don't see how it could be the fault of the cup when it's from a very expensive set and it's never happened before.'

Oh, of course it would be bloody expensive, God forbid you had anything in your snooty house that the rest of us common folk would own. 'All I did was hold it, heard a crack and then the cup ended up on the floor. You and Gavin saw it for yourselves.'

'Yep, Liv's right, we both saw what happened; the cup's obviously faulty.' Gavin earned himself a frosty glare from his wife.

There was always so much tension in the air; no wonder Ryan hardly ever ventured down from his bedroom.

'Ughh.' Livvie had another thought: their mother – Delia – would be spending Christmas day there too, with her never-ending comparisons of her two daughters; Livvie never came out of those looking good.

'I honestly don't understand it,' Delia had said the previous year. 'I've brought you girls up identically and yet you're so different.' They were sitting around the table at Cheryl's house after Christmas dinner.

Oh, Lord, here we go. Livvie's heart went into freefall straight down to her velvet slippers.

'There's our Cheryl with her beautiful, immaculate home, a good job as a legal executive, married to a *very* successful solicitor, and on top of all that, they've given me the most adorable grandson. Anyone could say she's living the perfect life.'

Adorable, my arse, thought Livvie, *he's a spoilt little brat!* She could hardly bear to look at her older sister, who was sitting opposite with a smug expression on her face. *As for "the perfect life", it's about as far removed from perfect as I can imagine. There's nothing homely or happy about this place.*

'And then there's Olivia.' Her mother turned, fixing her youngest daughter with a steely glare. Delia was on the wrong side of half a bottle of sherry and was sporting the tell-tale signs: a flushed face, glassy eyes and a vicious tongue.

Livvie groaned inwardly and braced herself. *Here goes, I've got a feeling I'm not going to like this.*

'What can I say?' The disappointment in her mother's voice made Livvie's heart twist. 'Who'd have thought the two year age gap between the pair of you could make such a difference. But it does. Livvie's the complete opposite to Cheryl, with her chaotic flat, her dead-end job in a little frock shop, and that waste of space she calls a boyfriend, with not even a glimmer of hope of starting a family – not that I would recommend that with *him*, mind you. Honestly, Liv, anyone would think you made such terrible choices deliberately, just to upset me.'

Livvie could feel her face prickle with anger. 'Do what to upset you, Mum? Not live the life you want me to?'

'Mum does have a point, Liv,' said Cheryl, barely concealing a smirk. 'You could make more of an effort with your life choices. Take Donny, for example, why isn't he here with you, celebrating Christmas day with his girlfriend?'

Livvie's eyes were drawn to the supercilious expression on Gavin's face; that and his bulbous nose that had turned a vibrant shade of puce thanks to today's generous quota of claret. 'I'm afraid I have to agree,' he said.

'What is this, "Pick on Livvie" time? For your information, Donny's having Christmas dinner with his gran over on the other side of town.'

'That's what he tells you,' said her mother. 'And have you met this grandmother in question? Hmm? And why weren't you invited to join them?'

Panic reared in Livvie's stomach. 'Not yet, no; and I wasn't invited because Donny knew I was coming here.'

Gavin held up his hands. 'Hey, no need to sound so defensive, we're just looking out for you.'

'Gav's right. We don't want to see you hurt, and even you would have to admit that Donny comes across as a bit of a freeloader.' Cheryl was visibly smirking now. But deep down, even a year ago, Livvie knew there was more than a hint of truth in what they were saying. Yet, despite this, some perverse part of her couldn't help but defend him.

'Look, I know Donny's not everyone's cup of tea—'

Gavin snorted. 'You can say that again.'

Livvie ignored him – and the urge to kick him under the table – and continued. 'But I know he cares for me; and he does all sorts of thoughtful things I don't tell you about.' In truth, she couldn't remember the last time he'd done anything thoughtful for anyone other than himself. 'And you're right, Mum, Cheryl and I are different but – and don't take this the wrong way, Cheryl – I wouldn't want to be like her with her high-pressure job and perfect home, or wear my hair and clothes so ... so ... precisely.' Livvie tiptoed around the words she'd really like to say – *She walks around all buttoned up and covered up, with a face that would sour milk, and she's so uptight, she looks like she's got a broom stuck permanently up her arse!* – but she kept those thoughts to herself.

She braved a glance across at her sister whose smile had dropped and who was now glaring at her.

'And I most certainly wouldn't want to dress like you, or wear my hair like you.' Cheryl arched a combative eyebrow.

Livvie puffed out her cheeks and sighed, wondering if there was any point in continuing to defend herself. It never got her anywhere and it looked like today wasn't going to be any different. She was just going to have to try and get used to being constantly compared unfavourably to her sister, and accept that she was the black sheep.

Though they shared the same hazel eyes and thick auburn hair, that's where the similarity ended. Where Livvie's locks were a mass of unruly curls – and usually piled haphazardly on top of her head – Cheryl's were cut into a precise, blunt bob with a heavy fringe and straightened to perfection. And, unlike Livvie who embraced her natural curves, Cheryl was stick thin, thanks to her strict adherence to whatever trendy diet she was following. It resulted in her face being bony and sharp; some would say it looked cruel. As far as clothes were concerned, Cheryl's capsule wardrobe of beige, black and white stood in stark contrast to Livvie's passion for bohemian clothes in bold, vibrant colours, many that she'd made herself.

'All I'm saying is that our Livvie could do with taking a leaf out of our Cheryl's book; the way she—'

'I think Livvie gets the point,' said Gav, topping up his glass of claret. 'Now dinner's all finished, I think I'll head into the lounge. He stood up and left the table, taking his glass with him; he'd clearly had enough of the bear-baiting and was keen to get started on his usual Christmas tradition of drinking himself stupid for the rest of the day – much to his wife's disapproval.

5

ZANDER

ZANDER PULLED into the driveway at the side of 4 Milton Gardens. Mel's car had gone but lights blazed from every window of the smart Victorian villa he'd called home for the last eight years. It rattled him that she had no regard for global warming or taking care of the environment, or even wasting money; he'd lost count of the times he'd mentioned that she could perhaps consider turning a light off when she left a room she had no intention of returning to for a while. He felt his mood dip as he recalled her words. 'Stop being such a Scrooge, Zander; you're always nagging, "turn this light off, turn that light off, turn the heating down, put this in the recycling bin, put that in the recycling bin", nag, nag, nag. There's more to life than constantly worrying about the environment, you know. You're becoming a real bore'.

Zander was pulled back to the present by a whine from the back of the car, followed by a snort as Alf stuck his nose through the dog guard. 'Yep, you're right, fella, time to venture inside; see what chaos awaits us.'

With a feeling of dread, he pushed open the front door and stepped into a wall of warmth. 'Bloody hell, it's stifling!'

The temperature stood in stark contrast to the biting cold outside. Typical Mel, always had to have the radiators bouncing hot; she'd sooner open a window than turn the heating down.

He unravelled his scarf and took in the mess of the hallway which was littered with an assortment of discarded shoes – mostly Mel's, but there appeared to be an unfamiliar pair of male ones. Alf gave them a thorough sniffing before trotting along to the kitchen. Zander followed. 'Mel,' he groaned. The room reeked of stale cigarette smoke and was littered with the detritus of a hastily prepared meal – evidently his girlfriend hadn't been alone if the amount of cups and crockery was anything to go by, or the small bowl that had been used as an ashtray. That annoyed him more than anything; she knew he didn't like her smoking in the house, never mind inviting some stranger –or strangers – to join her. He went over to the island in the centre of the room. Something vivid and sticky had been spilt down the full length of one of the cupboard doors; it looked like it would leave a permanent stain. Her disrespectful attitude was really beginning to grate on him.

The living room was no better. Zander's eyes were drawn to a little dish he'd brought back from a holiday in France; it was perched precariously on the arm of one of the leather sofas, and was now full of cigarette butts. He tutted as he went to pick it up, noticing what looked like a splodge of nail varnish on the seat next to where a pile of clothes were strewn – had they been put there to hide it, he wondered? On closer examination, it would appear that someone had tried to pick the nail varnish off, taking the top layer of the leather with it; presumably that's why they gave up, he thought. To top it off, there was what looked like a cigarette burn in the carpet.

Fuming, he shook his head. 'What a bloody mess, eh, Alf?' The Labrador stopped his exploration of the new scents in the room and looked up at him, his tail wagging ten-to-the-dozen. 'That woman must take me for a fool.'

'RIGHT, that's it. Time to relax now, Alf.' Zander had spent the last hour trying to restore some semblance of order to his home. The first thing he'd done was to turn the radiators down and throw open a couple of windows. The bedroom and en-suite bathroom had been as he'd expected: full of Mel's chaos. He'd started at the top and worked down, pushing her clothes and shoes into bin bags and dumping them in the utility room. The kitchen had proved quite a challenge and, once all of the washing-up was done and rubbish thrown in the bin, he'd taken a closer look at the stained cupboard door; it would need to be sanded down and painted over. But the biggest disappointment had been the living room. The cigarette burn was in a very obvious place and he suspected the leather of the cushion would be permanently marked by the nail varnish and would need to be replaced. 'This has got to stop.'

Pouring himself a glass of wine, Zander, closely followed by Alf, headed for his study where he fired up his laptop. He was feeling restless, too restless to sit in front of the television and watch TV or a movie. But he had the overwhelming urge to get away. Get away from this large, empty house that only served to remind him of the bad choices he'd made. He found himself thinking of Clara again. Quiet, gentle, easy-going Clara – on the face of it, at least. His family and friends had all loved her; everyone had expected him to marry her. Not do what he did. His stomach

clenched at the thought. How would things have been if
they'd stayed together?

The thought that he still needed to call his mother ran
through his mind, triggering an involuntary sigh. He'd been
putting it off, trying to find the right words, building up the
courage to pick up the phone.

He clicked on the mail icon of his laptop and watched
the emails slide into the inbox. Amongst the mix of junk,
newsletters and adverts, an email from "Quaint Country
Cottages" leapt out; it was the company who managed the
rental of his holiday cottage in Lytell Stangdale in the
middle of the North Yorkshire Moors. He clicked on it,
hoping it wasn't telling him of some problem or other.
Thankfully, it was a round-robin, informing their clients of
their festive opening hours.

Zander sat for a moment, drumming his fingers against
his chin. 'Lytell Stangdale. I wonder...' Alf looked up from
his position, curled up by his dad's feet, and wagged his tail.
'You thinking what I'm thinking, buddy?' He reached down
and rubbed the Labrador's ears, which increased the speed
of the tail wagging.

EARLIER THAT YEAR, Zander had been visiting his cousin,
Beth, who was a GP at a surgery in Danskelfe, the next
village to Lytell Stangdale. He'd been sitting in the Sunne
Inne on the Saturday lunchtime, enjoying a pint of local
beer, absorbing the community spirit of the place, when
he'd found himself roped into a local fundraiser – he hadn't
realised when he'd agreed to it that it would involve him
taking his clothes off for a calendar shoot, but that was by-
the-by. He smiled at the memory.

He'd been visiting the area to check on the property he'd purchased with a view to renting out as a holiday let. Dale View Cottage was an achingly beautiful thatched long-house, typical of the area, and, despite the fact that it had needed a massive amount of work doing to it, Zander had fallen in love with it on the spot. Indeed, it had been a labour of love restoring it to the standard it was today.

He had fond memories of that weekend and, despite having to get his kit off, he'd been tempted back several times since, struck by how friendly and welcoming the locals were. Each time he'd found himself laughing and chatting in the pub with Jimby Fairfax – whose idea the fundraiser had been – and Ollie, who was Jimby's best mate. Camm, whose looks betrayed his gipsy heritage, had been a regular, too, as was local architect Robbie. Yeah, they were a great bunch of blokes and Zander felt like he'd known them for years. His mind roamed over the memories of his visits there; he'd always thought Jimby's sister Kitty was cute, but she was off-limits, being married to Ollie. 'Shame,' he said aloud, his mind moving on. Kitty's friends were hilarious; sassy Molly whose wicked sense of humour always made him chuckle; he didn't wonder that she lived with someone as easy-going as Camm. Then there was glamorous, purple-haired Violet who was a dead-ringer for a young Elizabeth Taylor; she was recently married to Jimby. On the face of it, Zander thought you wouldn't put the two of them together, yet the reality was that they complemented one another perfectly. Yep, he mused, they were a nice bunch of down-to-earth folk.

Before he knew it, Zander found himself looking at the "Quaint Country Cottages" website and, in particular, the listing for his own property. His spirits suddenly lifted. 'Perfect!' Thanks to yesterday's cancellation of a booking that took in the whole of the festive period, the property was empty. He pushed up his shirt sleeve and checked his watch, his mind racing over an idea that had started to bloom out of nowhere. He glanced out of the window, remembering that Steff had said snow was forecast; it hadn't started yet.

'Alf,' he said, flipping down the lid of his laptop, 'pack your bags, buddy, we're heading off to the North Yorkshire Moors.' Alf jumped up and trotted after Zander who had headed to the spare bedroom where his suitcase, all packed for Carcassonne, sat on the bed. 'Right,' he said rubbing his chin. 'I only need to make a few adjustments to this, then we're good to go.'

Knowing he couldn't put it off any longer, Zander called his mother who, though disappointed, took the news much better than he'd expected. She tried very gently to talk him into changing his mind, but didn't push when she realised she wasn't going to persuade him. If he'd thought about it, why should she be surprised, when, thanks to Mel, he'd cancelled other things at the last minute. The last time sprang into his mind. The pair had been en-route to a Bonfire Night party at Toby and Jo's when Mel had suddenly thrown a wobbler about not wanting to be there. She'd had an offer from her new friends and was kicking off about not being able to spend the evening with them, doing what she wanted.

'You're so selfish, Zander. Why do we always have to do things with your stupid family?' she'd yelled at him, pouting like a spoilt child.

'You could've said you didn't want to go when I first mentioned it to you.' She was unbelievable.

'Well, I didn't know about this party at the time, did I? She'd shaken her phone at him. 'And it sounds amazing;

much better than spending a boring evening at your brother's.'

The argument had got so heated, Zander had ended up turning the car round, dropping Mel off at her friend's party and heading home; he hadn't been in the right frame of mind to celebrate and didn't want to bring the mood down at his brother and sister-in-law's get-together. And, out of some misplaced loyalty to Mel, he didn't want them to judge her if he'd turned up alone. Deep down, he knew they thought she wasn't right for him, but good manners always prevailed and she was always made welcome whenever she deigned to accompany him on a visit. But Zander was growing tired of it.

He ended the call with his mother with a sense of relief, and, before he knew it, his suitcase was on the back seat of his four wheel drive, his wellies were thrown in the footwell and Alf's large, squishy bed was pushed into the roomy boot. Alf, seemingly up for the adventure, leapt up, wagging his tail and wearing an expression of 'Ready when you are, Dad'.

'Looks like you're all fired up for a road trip, buddy.' Zander laughed and rubbed Alf's head. 'We'll have a great time, just you and me, won't we? Who needs women?' Alf's tail beat faster, thudding against the back of the seats.

As they pulled out of the drive and made their way along Milton Gardens, the prospect of spending Christmas tucked away in his cosy cottage in the middle of the North Yorkshire Moors suddenly made the world seem a much brighter place.

6

LIVVIE

THERE WAS no way Livvie could stay at the flat over Christmas and there was *definitely* no way she could face going to Cheryl's on Christmas day. There'd been radio silence from Donny since he'd stormed out a couple of hours earlier, but Livvie didn't expect otherwise, though she did wonder if he'd be back later that night. He was unpredictable at the best of times, and no stranger to spending the night who-knew-where, offering only a vague excuse for his absence on his return the following day.

What a mug I've been.

The thought of seeing him again, of listening to his crap, made her stomach swirl with nausea. Livvie put her head in her hands, closed her eyes and tried to weigh up her options. It didn't take long to realise that she had very few of those; there was no large welcoming extended family of cousins and aunts who could offer her a place to stay in her time of need. If she called Bry, she knew she'd say she could stay at her flat, but there's no way Livvie wanted to intrude on her friend's Christmas with Josh, or play goosegog for that matter.

The urge to get away from it all started to gnaw at her. She needed to escape from here, escape from her judgemental family and her loser of an ex-boyfriend. The thought of going somewhere where nobody would know her was suddenly very appealing, particularly so the romantic idea of swapping her flat for a quaint little cottage in the country. 'That's it!' she said, sitting up straight. 'I'll book a holiday cottage for over Christmas.'

Before she knew it, she'd booted up her laptop and googled "quaint country cottages", ignoring the little voice at the back of her mind telling her she'd left it a bit late in the day. The first website on the list was for a company called exactly that: "Quaint Country Cottages". It offered her a tiny glimmer of hope and she grabbed tight hold of it. 'That sounds promising.' She clicked on it, gasping as the screen began loading images of stunning cottages of all shapes and sizes. The blurb informed her it was a small, family run company that specialised in the area around the North Yorkshire Moors, which was, she reckoned, the perfect distance away from her flat; not too close and not too far.

She began scrolling down and hadn't got far when her eyes landed on the sweetest little thatched cottage she'd ever seen. *It's so beautiful, it's bound to be fully booked.*

Livvie hovered the cursor over the calendar and clicked on that day's date. 'Oh!' Her heart leapt; it was available! In fact, it was available right up to the week after the New Year, and even offered a reduction in the fee owing to a last-minute cancellation. Her mind scrambled over the information; that covered the time Blushing Brides was closed. It was perfect; fate was talking to her. Before she had chance to think about it, she hurried off in search of her purse and her bank card.

Within minutes of her filling in her details and pressing

send, a couple of emails had landed in her in-box. One was a booking confirmation, the other included directions, information about the cottage and the code for the key safe, which was apparently on the wall by the door. Livvie hastily printed everything off and raced to the bedroom to dig out her suitcase.

Her heart rate had gone into over-drive and she was consumed by the urge to move quickly; she didn't want to risk Donny coming home and find her halfway through packing. She'd had enough experience of him worming his way into her mind, talking her out of doing things he didn't want her to do, and she knew he'd do his best to talk her out of this. Or worse, talk her in to telling him where she was going. She didn't want to think about that.

An image of his smug face loomed into her mind, firing up her anger towards him once more. She threw the suitcase on the bed and began hurling her clothes in with little concern for creases or space-saving, her heart pounding with every item.

She was almost done when she heard the main entrance door of the building slam shut. She froze, her heart thudding even harder, nausea swirling in her stomach as she held her breath, listening intently. She sensed footsteps and the sound of movement coming up the stairs and only when they passed the door to the flat and she realised it was the tenant from the flat above could she breathe again. 'Oh, my God, that was scary!'

Quickly, she headed to the bathroom where she grabbed her toothbrush and cosmetics; she threw them into a washbag then scurried back to the bedroom where she stuffed them into her already bulging case, her pulse thrumming in her ears all the while.

Next, she peeled off her work clothes, throwing them in the direction of the washing basket, before pulling on her jeans and a warm bottle green jumper dotted with cream stars. 'Boots,' she said aloud, hurrying to the cupboard by the door to the flat where she found her black biker boots.

'Right, that's it.' She had one final check round, making sure she'd got everything she'd need, and before she knew it she was dragging her suitcase down the stairs and out into the street.

It may have been a good idea to park around the corner from her flat when she was trying to catch Donny unawares, but her case weighed a ton and kept toppling to one side thanks to a wonky wheel. It made her wish she'd had the foresight to move her car once he'd gone. It didn't help that every time she heard a car approaching, panic reared up inside her, fearful that it was Donny. And despite the sparkling frost, which made it slippery underfoot, she was sweating buckets.

Livvie was almost at her car when the familiar sound of a rattly engine sent a chill down her spine. She glanced up to see a white van heading down the road, in her direction. Donny's. 'Bugger!' Quickly, she bobbed down beside the nearest car, holding her breath until he passed. Hearing the engine slow down as he pulled into the parking space on the drive, she moved as quickly as she could, dragging her case onto the road and squatting down in the gap between two cars. Not daring to move, she waited, the sound of her breath amplified in her ears. She heard the slam of his van door, the crunch of his shoes on the gravel, then the jangle of his keys as he fumbled for the lock. And he was whistling. *After what happened, how could he be whistling?*

Livvie waited to hear the main door of the flats close

behind him before she tentatively stood up. She released a
noisy sigh which billowed out in a mushroom of condensation in the chilly air. As she pulled her case onto the pavement, the dodgy wheel caught on the curb, causing it to fall
against the car she'd been hiding behind. The impact set the
vehicle's alarm shrieking out into the darkness, sending a
ginger tom cat racing from beneath it. 'Arghh! No!' Livvie's
heart had never pounded so fast in her life. She mustered all
of her strength, heaved her case onto the pavement and
dragged it as quickly as she could, not daring to look back
until she'd rounded the corner to where her little car was
parked.

'Oy, what the effing hell d'you think you're doing?'
Donny's voice carried down the road. Livvie froze, her
breath caught in her chest.

'S'alright, mate. It's just me checking my car. I just saw a
cat shoot off down the road; think it probably jumped on
the bonnet, set the alarm off.' She recognised the voice as
belonging to their neighbour from five doors down.

'Oh, righto, John. Just thought I'd better check; you
never know these days.'

'Aye, you're right there.'

'Well, see you later, then.'

'Yep, see you later.'

Livvie slowly released her breath; she was shaking as she
very quietly opened the rear passenger door and hefted her
case onto the back seat of her car, only daring to close it
when she heard Donny retreat.

It wasn't until she was on the main road out of Rickelthorpe that she could relax. And, only when she felt she
was safely out of Donny's reach, did she pull into a little side
road and tap the address of the holiday cottage into her
sat nav.

As she drove along, her tiny car eating up the miles, she was pleased to find that fear was slowly receding and excitement taking its place. Even if it meant she'd be spending Christmas day alone, Livvie had no doubt she'd made the right decision.

7

LIVVIE

THE JOURNEY to the moors had been fairly straightforward, with the main roads being well-gritted and frost-free. But it was a different matter once Livvie headed deeper into the countryside, with its narrow, twisting lanes, some with sheer drops down vertiginous valley sides. A few of the roads had been gritted by the local farmers, but that was patchy. To make matters worse, it had started to snow; sleet at first, but it had become increasingly heavy and the flakes had grown larger with every mile. Livvie was shocked at how quickly the road was disappearing under a thickening blanket of snow. She was unused to driving in such inhospitable conditions and, even though she was taking it slowly, her car still managed to skid around a bend, making her stomach clench and her knuckles blanch as she gripped tightly onto the steering wheel. She took a moment to steady her nerves, thankful that the roads were quiet and she'd managed to avoid colliding with a dry-stone wall that had loomed threateningly close before she'd ground to a halt.

It didn't take long for her to realise that the sat nav's directions had become unhelpful and were sending her on a wild goose chase; her tyre marks had been covered by the snow, but a stone marker she could have sworn she'd seen twice before appeared on the roadside once more. 'Bugger!' She looked out onto the moor where tiny dots of light from farmhouses blinked back at her. Could Dale View Cottage be one of them? She had no idea, so she tucked her car into a pull-in place and reached for her road map.

'Oh, why don't they include the little roads on these things?' she said to herself. As she was trying to make sense of it, she was startled by a loud scraping sound and the bright lights of a tractor illuminating the road. It came to a halt beside her. Feeling slightly anxious, Livvie lowered her side window as the driver leaned across and opened the door of his cab.

'Woah!' The bitingly cold wind slapped her in the face as it leapt into the warmth of her car, hurling snowflakes everywhere.

'You okay?' asked the tractor driver. Livvie noted he had a friendly face and a mass of dark curls escaping from the brim of his thick, woolly hat.

'Erm, I'm a bit lost, actually.' She wiped snow from her eyes.

'Where do you need to be?'

'Dale View Cottage; the address I've been given just says it's on the Dale Road in Lytell Stangdale, which seems to have confused my sat nav and it's started sending me round in circles.'

The friendly face laughed, a twinkle in his eyes. 'You're not the first person to say that about sat nav round here. That's Zander Gillespie's holiday cottage you're looking for. You need to be up along the road by Tinkel Top Farm, then past Fower Yatts Lane; it's not far from here, but it can be tricky to find. I'm heading that way, so you can follow me while I clear the road ahead of you if you like?'

'Oh, right. Okay.' She paused for a moment, listening to her gut that was telling her she could trust him. A sudden memory of the said gut-feeling she had when she first met Donny flashed through her mind, telling her to steer well clear of him. Turned out it was right; shame she hadn't listened to it then.

'I'm Camm, by the way; I live at Withrin Hill Farm just over there.' He nodded behind him. 'And I've just taken on the contract with the local council to keep the roads clear of snow in the winter.'

'I'm very pleased to meet you, Camm. I'm Livvie.'

'Right, Livvie.' Camm looked around at the snow that had started falling much more heavily; large flakes were now swirling around in the wind that had been gradually gaining strength. 'I think we'd best get you there before the drifting gets too bad. It'll only take five or ten minutes. Stick in a low gear, no hard braking and you should be fine.'

'Okay, thanks.' She smiled, relief washing over her at hearing how close she was to the holiday cottage; she'd barely driven in snow before and had never had the need to fit winter tyres to her little car. She wound her window back up, thinking how nice it was to see a friendly face. The kindness of strangers, she mused; what a contrast to her family.

Camm eased his tractor along the road, Livvie following slowly behind him. Her heart leapt into her mouth a couple of times when her tyres lost their grip on a stretch of road that was on a worryingly steep incline and spun alarmingly. Luckily, she'd managed to right herself and gripped onto her steering wheel for sheer life, her heart banging against her chest, until they'd reached the top. After that, they took a left and headed down a long, narrow track which led into nothing but inky darkness. It crossed her mind that she was in the middle of nowhere, following a total stranger to who-knew-where. For all she knew, he could be a crazed serial killer who would chop her up into hundreds of tiny pieces which wouldn't be found until the snow had thawed in the spring. Then she remembered his warm smile and his kind eyes and told herself she was being ridiculous. *Trust your instincts,* she reminded herself.

Before she knew it, the warm glow of lights from a cottage reached out onto the track. Camm turned right beyond the building, then reversed back out, turning the tractor so that it faced in the opposite direction. He tucked in and came to a halt, before climbing down from the cab and making his way over to her car. She opened her door and stepped out, the harsh wind catching in her throat and the icy snowflakes stinging her cheeks.

'We're here; Dale View Cottage.' He nodded towards a long, low house that appeared to be huddling into the hillside. In the garden, a Christmas tree decorated with fairy lights swayed in the wind, while another one twinkled from behind the glass of a mullioned window. 'The area I've just cleared yon side of the house is the parking place; if you drive in there, it'll get your car off the track.'

'Oh, okay, thanks.' She climbed back into her car and did as she was bid, glad to get back into the warmth.

In a moment, Camm was standing beside her. 'I'll give you a hand with your bags if you like?'

'Oh … I … er … I think I'll be fine, thanks; I don't have that much.'

'Well, if you're sure. I could just carry them to the door and leave them there so you could take them inside yourself.' He gave her a reassuring smile and she felt a pang of guilt, hoping she hadn't made him feel that she doubted his intentions.

'Actually, it would be really good if you could help.' She remembered the troublesome wheel on her suitcase. 'I honestly haven't brought that much. I left in a bit of a hurry; it was a last minute booking and I wanted to get here before the snow arrived.' The snow part might be a tiny white lie, but Livvie felt it added to her explanation of lack of luggage and stopped her having to explain any further; she didn't want to look like a pathetic case.

'Lucky you didn't leave it any later. Here, let's get this thing inside.' Camm reached in and pulled out her suit-case. Livvie grabbed her bag and snatched her mobile phone from the seat beside her, following his large foot-prints to the cottage, her head bowed against the savage wind.

He pushed open the wooden gate. 'At least the path's been gritted; Zander's got a good team looking after this place,' he said, stopping outside a low, wide front door that was sporting a large festive wreath; it too twinkled with fairy lights.

Camm dumped the case on the doorstep while Livvie reached inside her bag and retrieved the piece of paper with the code for the keysafe, thankful of the glow from the outside light by the door.

'Right, I'll go and get the rest,' he said.

'Are you sure you don't mind?'

'Course not. But I'll get this in first, before it gets soaked.'

'Oh, okay.' Livvie released the key from the small metal safe and wriggled it into the lock, the cold biting into her exposed fingers, making her wish she'd found her gloves. She pushed open the door to reveal a cosy hallway, softly illuminated by a table lamp on an old oak coffer. Camm lifted the case inside, being careful not to step any further than the doormat, then headed back to the car.

'Wow!' Livvie took in the old flagstone floor, covered with a large Persian rug, the low-beamed ceiling and the delicious aroma of Christmas, no doubt thanks to the festive pot pourri that sat in a large blue and white bowl the centre of the coffer. There was another door of similar proportions directly opposite the front door, and a further two leading off from the hallway – one each on either side of the front door. The one to the left was set in an uneven stone wall, while the one on the right was set in an ancient, oak partition that had darkened to a rich, deep brown with age. Swags of fake pine branches, decorated with deep red baubles and more fairy lights were draped along the length of it. Her heart pumped with excitement; she'd never been in a house like this before, the sort you usually only see in magazines. 'Oh, this is beautiful.'

Already, this trip felt right.

'That's the lot,' said Camm, armed with the shopping bags from the boot of her car; the ones she was carrying when she left Blushing Brides earlier that afternoon, full of delicious ingredients for her romantic meal with Donny. The contents had cost her a fortune and there was no way she was going to let them go to waste. 'And looking at the weather, it's just as well you came prepared.' He gave a hearty laugh.

'Yes, it is … and thank you so much for this, and for helping me get here.' She was beginning to feel very guilty; the poor man was absolutely covered in snow.

'Hey, it's no problem; I could hardly leave you abandoned by the roadside.' He paused for a moment, making her feel a little awkward. 'Listen, here's my number, if you need anything. It's our landline – you'll find that mobile phone signal can be a little, er, unreliable round here.' He reached inside his jacket, pulled out a small business card and handed it to her. 'If I'm not in, Molly – my partner – might answer or her son Ben or his girlfriend Kristy.'

'Thank you, that's really kind.' She glanced quickly at the card, noting the word "campsite". 'Though, I think I've put you to too much trouble already.'

'Don't be daft, it's what we do out here, help each other out.' He grinned, rubbing his hands together. 'Right, time I was getting back to road clearing. Looks like you'll be toasty enough in there.' He nodded up to the chimney where the wind was pulling smoke one way, then the other.

She stepped out and looked up. 'Ooh, a real fire.' The thought sent a wave of happiness through her as her mind conjured up an image of flames dancing in a large grate.

'Aye, that'll be down to Mrs Hoggarth who looks after the place and gets it ready for guests.'

'Well, I'm glad she could get here! And thanks again for all your help, there's no way I'd have been able to find this place without it; or even get here for that matter.'

'No worries; you get in where it's warm. Enjoy your stay; and you know where we are if you need us.'

Livvie headed back in and closed the door, shutting out the cold, suddenly aware that her feet felt like blocks of ice and were soaking wet. Her boots might look stylish, but they were hardly practical for wading through inches of moorland snow. She heeled them off, then tugged at her soggy socks, leaving both by the front door. 'Ooh.' Delicious warmth from underfloor heating seeped through the soles of her feet, making her skin tingle.

Carefully, she pushed open the stripped pine door to the left, revealing a scene of utter cosiness. Soft lighting courtesy of table lamps dotted around bathed the room in a warm glow, along with fairy lights from the Christmas tree she'd spotted from outside. Livvie took a deep breath; she loved the smell of a real Christmas tree, something she hadn't had since she'd moved in with Donny. He didn't like them, claiming they were a waste of money, insisting they had an artificial one instead.

'They're nothing but a bloody nuisance, and an expensive bloody nuisance at that,' he'd said. 'And it'll be muggins here who'd have to carry the sodding thing up the stairs to our flat, then have the problem of dragging it back down, with needles dropping off everywhere. No, you can make do with an artificial one; they look just as good but without the hassle.'

'Sod you, Donny!' Livvie said aloud.

She pushed him out of her mind as her eyes roamed around the rest of the room. Just like the hallway, the ceiling was low and heavily beamed, with the lower part of a thick cruck-frame pushing up through wide elm floorboards, though instead of flagstones, in here the floor was covered by a rustic sisal carpet. To the immediate right ran an ancient wall of dark oak panelling which extended to roughly six feet. Livvie walked beyond it to see a wooden settle built into the other side, it sat directly beside a huge, low inglenook which housed a sturdy log-burner. Thanks to Mrs Hoggarth, flames danced merrily behind the glass while logs were stacked neatly beside it. 'Ah, so that's where the smoke was coming from.'

A large, squishy sofa, piled with plump cushions and a tartan rug over each arm faced the fire. It was flanked by two equally comfortable- looking armchairs. Livvie felt a smile tugging at her lips as she pictured herself stretched out on it in her PJs, a hot chocolate topped with marshmallows perched on the coffee table in front of it, while she lost herself between the pages a good book. *Oh, bliss!* On the subject of books, her eyes were drawn to a large book-case at the far end of the room, stuffed with a variety of colourful spines. She made her way over to it and was thrilled to see several titles by her favourite authors and some by ones she'd never read before, but had always intended to. Now would be the perfect time to put that right, she thought, pulling one out. 'This is just getting better and better.'

The windows were adorable; set low with deep sills. She'd never been in a house with real stone mullions, though she noticed one had been replaced with a Yorkshire sliding sash, its small Georgian panes glinting in the light. It added a quaint and quirky air to the room.

At the far end, a grandfather clock was keeping time by an L-shaped staircase, it's ticking low and rhythmic. At the right of the stairs, was another door that had a small sign with the word "snug" written on it. 'Wow, a snug,' she said to herself. She flicked on the light switch and peered around the door to find a sweet room fitted with twin beds covered in matching patchwork throws. It too, had an inglenook fire-place – though on a much smaller scale to the one in the living room – but it was currently unlit and the warmth in here appeared to be courtesy of the underfloor heating. This room, too, had a stone mullioned window. Livvie went across to it and drew the curtains. '"Snug's" the perfect name for this room.'

The kitchen could have been straight from Country Living magazine, thought Livvie, thrilled to find the ubiqui-tous cream Aga – in her dreams, she had a cottage in the country with a large Aga, where she'd cook mouth-watering casseroles and bake huge fluffy scones. Though the room was sympathetically decorated to suit the age of the house, with its tasteful handmade kitchen and the odd piece of polished copper dotted about, there was no short supply of mod cons, including a fancy coffee machine – which, she noted, also had a setting for hot chocolate. Livvie clapped her hands gleefully; she'd be trying one of those just as soon as she'd looked around everywhere.

She headed back into the living room and made her way upstairs. On the landing, a small table set with a lamp and a scattering of magazines was tucked under the eaves, a neat leather chair beside it with a checked woollen blanket thrown over its back. She soon discovered that there were two good sized bedrooms, with cathedral-style ceilings and the upper half of the sturdy cruck frames that reached upwards, meeting in the middle of the ceiling, held together by huge oak pegs. The windows were sweet dormers that would no doubt have amazing views over the countryside during daylight hours.

The bathroom took her breath away. Like the kitchen, the décor was sympathetic, but was furnished with everything you would find in a contemporary space. And though the room was an awkward shape, thanks to the sloping roof, it had been planned with great attention to detail; it appeared that not a millimetre had been wasted. On one wall was a large roll-top bath with chunky claw feet, above which was the biggest chrome rainfall shower head Livvie had ever seen. While a gleaming white sink was sat on top of a purpose-built vanity unit, next to which was a wicker chair in a delicious shade of duck-egg blue that matched the walls. Shelves in what looked like driftwood housed toiletries and trinkets, and paintings with a seaside theme added a tasteful finish to the walls. Livvie released a happy sigh, the sadness of the day's earlier events temporarily pushed from her mind. She couldn't wait to have a soak in the bath. 'Hot chocolate first,' she said, drawing the blue and white ticking curtains before making her way downstairs.

Getting her suitcase up the stairs had been interesting, but she'd managed, and heaved it onto the case-stand in the bedroom she'd chosen; the slightly bigger one that boasted two dormer windows. 'Right, I just need my jimjams and a pair of fluffy socks; I'll unpack properly later.' She rummaged around amongst the messy bundle of clothes and pulled out what she needed.

ARMED WITH A CREAMY HOT CHOCOLATE, Livvie headed to the bathroom, where steam and the delicious aroma of lavender spilled out thanks to the complimentary bubble bath she'd found on one of the shelves. She peeled off her clothes to a stream of Christmas songs that blared out from the music system she'd spotted downstairs and put into use; she figured as she was in the middle of nowhere, she was free to play it as loud as she wanted.

With her mug of hot chocolate perched on the vanity unit, Livvie fixed her curls more securely on top of her head, then stepped into the bubbles. Her body groaned with delight as she slipped into the soothing warmth of the water. 'Ahh, bliss!' she said as it lapped over her. She lay her head back and closed her eyes, allowing the joyful spirit of the songs to wash over her, refusing entry to thoughts of Donny.

8

ZANDER

THE WEATHER HAD TAKEN a turn for the worse as Zander headed towards the North Yorkshire moors. What had started out as sleet was now falling as thick, feathery snowflakes, quickly settling like a dense blanket on his windscreen. As soon as the wipers swept it away, another one took its place. 'Bugger,' he said as he increased their speed. 'Let's hope we actually get there, Alf, buddy.'

On hearing his name, Alf sat up and pushed his nose through the dog guard, his wagging tail thudding against the boot. Zander smiled, wondering if there was ever a time when Alf wasn't happy. The thought was quickly intruded upon by a reminder that, yes, there was a time when he was sad; sadder than he'd ever seen a dog. Zander pushed the horrible memory away; he still couldn't bear to think of it.

As his car ate up the snowy miles, he was relieved when road signs for Lytell Stangdale and the surrounding villages started to appear. 'Nearly there, young man.' He pressed on with renewed vigour.

He took the junction for Lytell Stangdale and carefully made his way along the isolated road, full of twists and turns. 'It's a different world out here, Alf,' he said, taking in the rapidly growing snowdrifts that were lining up in the more exposed parts of the moors. By now the snow was really hurling itself at him. 'Thank goodness the roads have been ploughed; and fairly recently too, by the look of things.' He didn't have far to go, but Dale View Cottage was set in an isolated spot on its own out on the moors and Zander was concerned the little lane that led to it would be impassable.

He didn't encounter another car as he drove through Danskelfe but as he left Lytell Stangdale, he noticed the lights of a tractor climbing steadily up the steep incline of Withrin Hill. 'It's clearly a local farmer who's clearing the roads, Alfie. Keep your paws crossed he's done the little side-roads, too, fella.'

Alf gave his usual reply of a whimper and a wag of his tail.

'BLOODY HELL, am I pleased to see that.' Zander had finally reached the turn off for the lane to Dale View Cottage but the icy climb hadn't been without its scary moments; at one point, he'd found himself sliding backwards towards a sheer drop. Luckily, the four wheel drive had come into its own, finding traction on a stretch of grit and heaving itself forwards, continuing up the hill with dogged determination. 'I think we owe that farmer a pint; it looks like he's ploughed along here, too.'

He wondered at the reason for the lights being on and the Christmas tree being lit up in the garden – a sight which, he had to admit, warmed his heart. He glanced upwards to see smoke billowing out of the chimney and blowing down the dale. 'Looks like the message about the cancellation didn't get to Mrs Hoggarth, Alfie.' It's probably not a bad thing; at least the fridge should be stocked with basics and the stove's already lit, he thought.

He decided to park directly in front of the cottage; it would be easier to unload the car, rather than having to lug everything from around the corner where the drifting would no doubt be horrendous. Zander braced himself as he opened the car door. Immediately, the cruel wind threw icy snow flakes at him. 'Jesus!' he said, buttoning up his coat and flicking up the collar. Hurriedly, he pulled his suitcase out from the back seat before he went to open the back door for Alf. In a flash, the Labrador leapt out and proceeded to snap at the snowflakes that swirled around them. He spun around in great excitement, bounding all over the virgin snow, before running his nose along it, finishing with a noisy sneeze. Despite the cold, Zander couldn't help but laugh. 'Come on, you nutter, let's get where it's warm.'

With his head bowed against the wind, he made his way up the path, which he was relieved to see had been gritted. Mrs. Hoggarth was nothing if not efficient when it came to looking after this place. Alf followed close beside him, unable to resist taking one last snap at the snow.

Zander hadn't had time to lift his case in before Alf leapt over the threshold and into the hall, his nose sniffing every-where. Zander closed the door, relieved at shutting out the cold night. Did Mrs. Hoggarth even have Christmas carols playing for the guests' arrival he wondered, as Michael Bublé's dulcet tones filled the cottage? He looked around in puzzlement, glancing at Alf who appeared intrigued by all the unfamiliar scents. 'What's up, Alfie?'

The sense that the house wasn't empty began to creep over him. Not only was festive music blaring through the cottage but a pair of boots and a soggy-looking pair of socks had been discarded on the floor. Surely Mrs Hoggarth wasn't still here? After giving the discarded footwear a thorough sniffing, Alf trotted into the living room. Zander followed, spotting a romance book that had been left on the coffee table in front of the wood-burner – which, judging by the flames, had been recently refuelled.

The sound of tuneless singing wafted down on the soothing scent of lavender. *What the hell's going on?* Alf finished his sniffing and shot up the stairs with Zander in hot pursuit. Before he reached the landing, Zander heard a commotion of splashing and a woman screaming at the top of her lungs.

'What the...' He hurried along to the bathroom to find Alf in the bath, his tail wagging so hard it was sending soap suds flying everywhere. But more importantly, standing up in the bath beside his dog was what he could only describe as a goddess. A completely naked goddess, and she was absolutely stunningly beautiful.

He stopped for a moment, feeling the punch of arousal in his groin, his mouth hanging open. Alf barked and jumped out, bringing Zander back to the present and sending a warm, soapy tidal wave sloshing everywhere. 'Alf, no!' Zander knew what was coming next, but before he had the chance to stop him, Alf started to shake his head from side to side, sending water flying around the bathroom. The goddess screamed again while Zander scrunched his eyes tightly shut; he'd just have to wait until the daft dog had finished.

'Alf! Sit!' Zander, his voice raised to be heard above the music, reined in his sudden bolt of attraction. Alf did as he was bid, his tail still wagging and looking up at his dad as if to say, 'Look, Dad, I found us a new friend.'

'What the ... oh, my God ... who are you?' The goddess hastily tried to cover herself with her hands but Zander couldn't help but notice the voluptuous curves of her body, the full breast squashed by her arm, its pink nipple peeking over.

He swallowed, marshalling his thoughts, then cleared his throat. 'Er, I'm Zander ... Zander Gillespie; I own Dale View Cottage. Who are you?' He could feel a smile tugging at his lips.

The goddess shot him an indignant look, then realising she was making a useless job of covering herself, sat back down in the bath. 'I'm Livvie, Livvie Weatherill. Did you say you were the owner?'

Zander nodded. 'Yep, the owner.'

He watched her mull this over. 'That's all very well, but why are you here?'

He couldn't help but stare at the fullness of the goddess's lower lip. 'I, er, I've come to stay here over Christmas.'

'Oh, so have I.'

'What? I think you must've got the dates wrong. I checked the website right before I set off and there'd been a last-minute cancellation, which meant the cottage would be empty, so I blocked it out and decided to pop here myself.'

'And I checked the website before I set off and saw that there'd been a cancellation and booked it myself. I've paid for it and everything – even though I got a discount.'

'Right...' Zander thought for a moment, still distracted by her full lips, struggling to push away the thought of how it would feel to kiss them. 'Well...' He scratched his head. Now he'd come to think of it, the website did seem to be slow when he was trying to block the dates out.

Alf whined and wagged his tail, flicking more bubbles everywhere.

'S'okay, buddy.' He ruffled Alf's ears. 'I think I'm beginning to see what's happened. I suspect we must've been on the website at exactly the same time and didn't see the updated information.'

'What, you mean ...?'

'Mmhm.' *The goddess has the cutest ski-jump nose.*

'Oh ... right ... I suppose that would make sense.'

'It would.'

For several long moments, the pair looked at one another in silence.

Zander was the first to speak. 'Actually, I should apologise about this guy.' He tugged at Alf's ear. 'He thinks that everyone's his friend; which, if you knew his backstory, you'd wonder why.' He looked down at Alf who was gazing up at him adoringly. The thudding tail wagging started up again.

'Oh, it's, er, it's okay.'

Silence hung in the air.

'Right ... well, I'll, er ... I'll leave you to get dry in peace, then if you come and join me downstairs, we can decide what's best to do. Come on, young man; I think you've caused enough trouble up here.' He took hold of Alf's collar and turned to go. 'Or, what I mean to say is, feel free to enjoy the rest of your soak, don't rush on my account, take your time, I'll just be downstairs.'

The goddess laughed, scrunching up her nose which Zander thought made her look insanely cute. 'Well, there's hardly any point me staying in the bath; there's more water on the floor than there is in here.'

He looked at the foamy puddles on the waxed floorboards and laughed. 'Erm, I suppose you have a point.'

9

LIVVIE

LIVVIE'S last thought before her relaxing soak in the bath was brought to an abrupt end, was how the warmth of the water was easing her aching muscles. Since lugging that case along from her flat, her shoulders had been complaining, and the soothing, lavender infusion hadn't taken long to work their magic. It was pure *bliss*. Well, it was actually her second to last thought; her *last* one had been how surprised she was that she wasn't feeling absolutely devastated about finding Donny with the slapper from next door. She hadn't had a chance to think any deeper on the matter before a great, black lump of fur had lunged into the bath with her, wagging its tail so hard, it was whipping the water right out of the bath. It looked pretty pleased with itself, too, in fact, if she wasn't mistaken, the hound looked like it was actually smiling.

'Warghhh! What the—' She watched the foam-covered hooligan leap out, dripping water everywhere. Before Livvie had time to process what was happening, a man appeared in the doorway, a faint look of amusement on his face as the dog started vigorously shaking itself, showering her – and everything else – with even more water.

'Arghh!' *Ohmigod, ohmigod, ohmigod, what the bloody hell is going on?* Her heart was racing and she suddenly realised she was standing, stark naked, in front of the stranger. Her face was already warm from the bath, but now Livvie could feel her cheeks sizzling. She made a desperate attempt to cover herself with her hands. *Oh, flipping heck, why does there have to be so much of me to hide?* She snatched a quick glance at the stranger, whose mouth was now hanging open. *Bloody cheek, surely I'm not that bad?* And, to make matters worse, he was incredibly good looking in a tall, dark and handsome, Henry Cavill kind of way.

ONCE ZANDER HAD CLOSED the door behind him, Livvie sat for a moment, her mind trying to process what had just happened. Surely, they can't both have been on the internet, looking at the cottage at exactly the same time; that would be way too much of a spooky coincidence. There must be another explanation, maybe a fault with the system; not that she knew much about computers. *Hang on! Rewind, you can worry about that in a minute; first you've got to get your head around the fact that you've just been standing completely naked, flashing your wobbly boobs, your massive arse and, worse, your lady garden in front of a complete stranger who just so happens to be absolutely drop dead gorgeous. And not just any lady garden; a lady garden that hasn't had any attention for longer than you care to mention – in the grooming sense that is; well, in the other sense, if you were being completely honest. And why does the fact that he's drop dead gorgeous make a difference anyway?* 'Oh, bloody hell.' Livvie groaned and clamped her hand to her forehead. 'Why do I always have to be such a disaster?'

The volume of the music suddenly lowered, making Livvie wonder what her unexpected housemate was up to downstairs. *No doubt, taking a stiff drink to recover from the shock of seeing all my wobbly bits. Come to think of it, I could do with one myself!*

She climbed out of the bath and reached for one of the fluffy towels, hiding her face in its soft warmth and wishing she had a magic wand so she could wave the last ten minutes away. 'Oh, bugger, how can I go downstairs and look him in the eye?' She pulled a face and started to briskly rub herself dry, catching sight of her wild bush of pubic hair. 'Oh, no.' Her face prickled with embarrassment. This was not good. 'There's enough there to put it in dreadlocks, or practice a bit of topiary.' Why hadn't she made an appointment to get it tidied up like she'd thought about when she passed the beautician's in the high street offering "precision waxing"? Because it sounded like bloody torture, that's why. *And why would it matter anyway? Once I've left here, I'm never going to see this man again, am I? Though the state of me has probably scarred him for life.*

Livvie's eyes moved to the faint silvery stretch marks that peppered her thighs, the odd dimple of cellulite. She sighed. 'Just when I thought it couldn't get any worse.' She folded the towel and hung it back on the rail. *I wouldn't blame him if he had to rush out and throw up in a hedge somewhere after seeing my doughy tree-trunks complete with these hideous stretch marks!* 'I'm such a beast; Donny's right.' She sighed, feeling her heart sink even further as she pulled on her pyjamas.

10

ZANDER

'You've behaved very badly, Alf,' said Zander as the pair made their way downstairs. Crossing the living room, he stopped briefly to turn down the volume of the music before they headed towards the kitchen. 'What on earth were you thinking, charging up the stairs and hurling yourself in the bath with a complete stranger? Where are your manners, Alf, that's what I want to know?'

Alf looked up at him, his tongue hanging from the side of his mouth and his tail wagging happily.

'And there's no need to look so pleased with yourself; you're in big trouble, young man.' But the smile that tugged at Zander's lips told a different story.

In the kitchen, Zander stood for a moment, his mind replaying the scene he'd just left in the bathroom. The goddess wasn't his usual type, but she was beautiful ... those huge round hazel eyes were mesmerising and, even though she'd been absolutely terrified to start with, there was a softness to them, a kindness that he could tell was genuine. As for her gentle, voluptuous curves ... wow, they were delicious. And her luscious, auburn hair, piled high on her head

... how he'd love to run his fingers through its silky waves, and don't get him started on that cute little ski-jump nose. Without warning, his heart rate picked up and he felt a warm flicker of something indefinable – happiness, hope? He didn't know, but it had lifted his sagging spirits. There was something so very appealing about this woman.

Alf gave a small whimper and wagged his tail, banging it against the leg of the table, shaking Zander out of his musings.

'Yep, you're right; time to get out of this wet coat and get you dried before you start to smell like wet cabbage, you little bugger.' He headed into the small utility room that housed the central heating boiler and hung his coat on one of the pegs next to the door. Flicking through the code of the padlock, he opened the small cupboard that was reserved for housekeeping and pulled out an old towel. 'Alf, here.' Zander knelt down and the Labrador shot across to him; he knew the drill and he loved it. 'I don't know why you look so pleased with yourself, your behaviour has been abominable. And you do know you're heading straight for the naughty step when we're done with this, don't you?'

Oblivious, Alf pushed his head into his dad, loving every moment of having his body massaged with the towel, swiping Zander's face with his tongue whenever the opportunity arose.

'And what have I told you about that? Your listening skills are shocking.' He ruffled Alf's head as he stood up; he'd heard Steff say something of the sort to Joel and Annabel and it had tickled him. Alf looked so happy, he couldn't help but smile. 'There, done. And try not to get yourself into any more mischief before the night's out, or we'll be having serious words.'

'Hi.'

Zander turned to see Livvie standing in the doorway, her face free of makeup, her complexion dewy from the bath and her stunning curls tamed into a thick plait that snaked over her left shoulder. A bolt of something hot and primal shot through him, penetrating right to his core; he sensed a connection he'd never experienced before and it knocked him off kilter for a moment. Alf went to lunge towards her, bringing Zander to his senses. He quickly grabbed Alf's collar, rooting him to the spot. He cleared his throat, suddenly conscious that he was staring. 'Hi.' He smiled. 'That was quick.'

'Yes, quicker than I was expecting, at least.' Her large hazel eyes twinkled.

'Almost didn't recognise you with your clothes on.' His eyes twinkled back.

Two dots of colour appeared on her cheeks 'Oh, don't. I'm so embarrassed.' She covered her face with her hands.

'Don't be; you've got nothing to be embarrassed about.' *Did that sound as corny out loud as it did in my head? Ughh! I am such a knob!*

Alf let out a long whine and pulled on his collar, giving his owner a welcome distraction. 'I don't think there's any need for that, do you?' Zander looked down at him.

'You can let him go; I'm not scared of dogs – well, not unless they fly into the bathroom out of nowhere and jump into the bath with me, then I'm pretty terrified – for a few seconds at least.' She gave him a smile that lit up her whole face; it made Zander's heart skip a beat.

'You might end up regretting it if I let Alf loose on you again; he loves making new friends, especially with women and children.'

He thought she looked unbelievably cute in her sage green brushed cotton pyjamas dotted with cream love-hearts. On her feet, he noticed, were a pair of fluffy slippers with what looked like rabbit ears.

She followed his gaze. 'They were a birthday present from my best friend, Bryony; we work together.' She waggled her feet in them.

'You and the rabbits or you and Bryony?'

'Sorry?'

'You said you worked together, and I wondered if you meant you worked with the rabbits or you worked with Bryony?' He gave an apologetic smile. 'Sorry, I'm known for my crappy jokes.' *Oh Jesus, did I really crack that absolutely pathetic gag? What am I doing? I'm acting totally out of character and I've no idea why. I need to wear an "L" for "loser" on my head, or a "T" for "tosser".*

'Oh.' She laughed. 'I work with Bryony who gave me the rabbits; they're very snug.'

'Ah. Good to know.' He fought the urge to come back with another "witty" comment.

A smile played over her lips. 'Mmhm.'

'Er ... coffee?' Zander wasn't usually lost for words. 'Something stronger? I have a bottle of wine, well, I have several bottles of wine, actually, and a couple of bottles of spirits.'

'Sounds like you were planning on having a party.'

'Something like that.' He wasn't going to tell her he'd been planning a party just for one – or two, if you included a wayward Labrador – that would make him sound like a sad loser; which he was, of course, but he didn't want her to know that.

'And are you planning on hanging on to Alf for the whole night?'

Alf's tail started wagging at the mention of his name.

Zander looked down at him. 'Not if he can promise to behave himself.'

Livvie made her way over to them, bending down to Alf, letting him sniff her hand before she started to smooth his ears. 'Oh, you're gorgeous, aren't you? And I hear you're a ladies' man, too. I'm sure there's no short supply of ladies chasing a handsome lad like you.'

'I take it you're talking to my dog?' Zander watched Alf – who was in raptures – slide down onto the floor and offer his belly up for a tickle.' *There I go again, Mr Wise Crack, talking bollocks.*

Livvie giggled. 'Er, yes; I'm not in the habit of talking to strange men like that.'

'Ah, so you're saying I'm strange?' *You just can't stop yourself, can you?*

Livvie straightened herself. 'Well, I haven't quite made my mind up about that yet; maybe I'll have a better idea after that coffee you promised me.' She cocked an eyebrow at him.

Zander's stomach flipped a somersault, taking him by surprise; were they flirting? They were definitely having a bit of banter, but she'd aroused some feeling in him that he'd never experienced before which was, at the moment, quite disconcerting. He felt unsure of the rules; uncertain how to tread in this unfamiliar territory. He didn't want to read the signs wrong and make a turkey of himself, well, any more of a turkey than he was making of himself right now.

'Wow.' How could a woman he'd only known for five minutes elicit such feelings in him?

'Wow?' she asked.

Bugger! Did I say that out loud?

'Oh, erm, well, what I mean is, we've found ourselves in a bit of a funny position and erm ... well, I've never known

Alf take to a stranger so quickly before.' He glanced down at Alf to see his paw on Livvie's leg, hinting for more tummy tickles.

'Really?' She moved her gaze to the Labrador. 'Well, the feeling's mutual, he's adorable.'

Zander's stomach somersaulted again. 'Right, what was I doing?'

'Coffee?'

'Ah, yes.' He made his way over to the coffee machine wondering how this rather odd situation was going to pan out and if his emotions would calm their bloody jets.

'THIS IS the cosiest room I've ever been in,' said Livvie, settling back on the sofa. On Zander's suggestion, they'd taken their coffee into the living room.

'I'm pleased you like it.' He threw a log onto the wood-burner, sending flames dancing up the chimney and the sweet smell of woodsmoke into the room.

'It's lovely; the whole house is, it's like something out of Country Living magazine.'

'High praise indeed, thank you.' He smiled at her as he sat in the chair beside her. Her delicate scent danced its way over to him and he inhaled deeply; it was delicious and made him want to nuzzle his face in her neck. *Down boy!*

'So, what do you think we should do about this ...' Livvie waved a finger between the two of them.

'Well, you've obviously paid for the use of the cottage for – how long did you say you'd booked it for?'

'Till the fourth of January.'

'Right.' He set his cup down on the coffee table and ran

his hand over his chin; it was exactly the same time he'd planned to stay for.

'Look, I'd really like to stay; I'll pay the full amount and—'

Zander put his palms up. 'I wouldn't hear of taking any more money off you; and I certainly don't want to spoil your break. But the roads will be treacherous and I'd rather not drive on them any more tonight, if that's okay; it's one thing tackling snow drifts during the day, but when it's pitch black, it's another story. It would mean me and Alf staying here for the night, unless you have any objections. I promise not to be a nuisance – though I can't make any guarantees as far as Alf's concerned; you've no doubt got the measure of him by now.' He looked at the Labrador who had his head in Livvie's lap, enjoying her rhythmic stroking of his ears; the pair already looked like firm friends. It took Zander by surprise just how much the image made his heart swell with happiness; there's no way Mel would have entertained even stroking poor old Alf, never mind looking as though she was enjoying doing it.

'Well, you certainly don't seem to be a mass murderer who's going to chop me up into little pieces and feed me to this lad.' Smiling, she nodded towards Alf.

'Good to hear you think that.'

'So that sounds absolutely fine to me, though I do feel bad chasing you out of your own home.'

'It's fine, honestly; it's a holiday cottage and you've booked and paid for it; by rights, I shouldn't be here. But, I promise, we'll be gone first thing in the morning, won't we, buddy?'

Alf ignored him.

'Oh, there's no need to rush off, on my account.'

Her words sent a wave of happiness over him.

'Thanks, I appreciate your understanding, the prospect of tackling the Beast from Wherever out there tonight isn't the most appealing.'

'I'm sure; I couldn't send this boy out there in that.' She smoothed Alf's glossy head.

Zander threw his head back and laughed heartily. 'I always knew you'd come in handy, Alf, old buddy, but you've saved me from a fate of freezing to death out on the moors tonight. I owe you an extra dog treat.'

On hearing the word "treat", Alf's eyes shot open.

'Oh, no, I didn't mean—' Livvie looked mortified.

'It's okay, I'm only teasing.' He held her gaze until Alf nudged his hand, hinting for the promised dog biscuit. 'And it looks as though I won't get any peace until I give this boy what he wants – not that he really deserves it after spoiling your peaceful bath. Actually, come to think of it, I'm rather peckish myself; I haven't eaten since lunchtime.' He pushed himself up from the chair.

'Same here, but funny you should say that, I've brought some supplies; I was supposed to be cooking a special meal tonight – long story – but things didn't turn out quite how I'd planned, so I brought it all here with me, rather than let it go to waste.'

Zander notice a shadow fleetingly darken her face. Was she running away from something, or someone? *That would make two of us.*

'Oh, okay,' he said. 'And there's no one joining you later in the week that you could save the ingredients for?'

'No, no one's joining me.' Livvie paused, staring into her coffee cup. 'In fact, no one knows I'm here, apart from you, of course.'

The sudden sadness in her eyes made him want to throw his arms around her and pull her close to him. She looked small and helpless, and he felt the need to protect her. Instead, he stuffed his hands into the pocket of his jeans and did his best not to give in to the urge.

'So now you've told me that, you probably don't want to hear that I am actually a mad axe murder and Alf is really the hound of Hades in disguise as a soft lump of a black Labrador, and is just waiting for the command to tear any living thing limb-from-limb.' He smiled, hoping to encourage hers to return.

'No.' She giggled. 'I'd really rather not hear that.'

'Right, well, seeing as neither of us is driving anywhere tonight, how about we crack open a bottle of wine?' Zander asked.

'Ooh, that sounds lovely.' Livvie got to her feet. 'And how do you fancy some tornado rossini with all the trimmings?'

'Tornado rossini? Wow; sounds fabulous, but are you sure you can be bothered?'

'I love cooking; I can always be bothered.'

'Well, that's good to hear, cos I love eating, and I can always be bothered to do that. Looks like we make the perfect team.' *What the ...? Where the bloody hell did that come from? Will you shut the hell up with your cheese!*

LIVVIE

Livvie watched Zander fill two glasses with wine. 'I take it you're okay with red? It'll go nicely with the steak, but if you'd prefer something else ...'

'Mmm, I love red.' In truth, she was more of a Prosecco drinker, but she didn't want to look ungrateful or fussy. Donny was the red fan, but he only ever bought cheap, harsh stuff.

'Here you go.' Zander passed her a glass and raised his own. 'Cheers.'

'Cheers,' she said, feeling a huge smile take over her face and noting how incredibly blue his eyes were; a striking contrast to his dark, almost black, hair. He was tall and towered over her diminutive five-foot-two by a good foot. Livvie's heart fluttered; she had a weakness for tall men.

'To new friends,' he said.

'To new friends.' They locked eyes as they clinked glasses. It triggered a swirl of something unfamiliar but exciting in her stomach.

She took a small sip of wine and was pleasantly

surprised by the burst of berry flavours that erupted in her mouth. 'Oh, wow. That's delicious!'

Zander smiled. 'It's my favourite; I'm glad you like it.'

'Oh, I do, it's lovely. The reds I've had before have always been a bit too dry for me and nowhere near as nice as this.' She took another sip and looked up to see him smiling down at her. Her cheeks flushed in response.

'By the way, I've just checked my phone and there's no signal,' said Zander, leaning against the Aga. 'It's never particularly great in this part of the moors, but I'm guessing the snow has wiped out what little there is; I don't suppose it'll be back on tonight. And there's no landline in the cottage, so I hope you don't need to contact anyone.'

'Oh, right, er, that's fine, there's no one I need to contact tonight.' The only person Livvie would consider getting in touch with was Bryony, but that could wait. Her friend would just assume the romantic evening with Donny was a roaring success and that she was too "busy" with him to think about her phone. Livvie didn't want her to think anything other than that at the minute; her friend had her own life to enjoy.

'And are you sure you don't mind preparing all this food?' asked Zander, casting his eyes over the shopping Livvie had retrieved from the fridge.

'Nope, not at all. I love cooking – and I can't wait to use the Aga – and it won't take long; especially if you help.' She flashed him a cheeky smile.

'Goes without saying.' He pushed up his sleeves. 'Just tell me what I need to do.'

A thought of what she'd like him to do, that had nothing whatsoever to do with prepping food flashed through her mind; Zander's lips on hers, before scorching their way down towards— *Stop that, you wanton woman!* Livvie could feel her cheeks blazing once more; she hoped he hadn't noticed.

'Right, well, you can make a start on those potatoes; I was originally going to make fondants but that'll take a bit too long, so I think I'll par-boil them then sauté them with some garlic and herbs.'

'Sounds good. So you want me to peel them then chop them into what size?'

'Chop them into cubes about so big.' She demonstrated the size with her fore-finger and her thumb. 'And while you're getting stuck into that, I'm just going to get changed; I don't want my PJs smelling of cooking when I go to bed.'

'Oh, okay.'

She looked up into his bright blue eyes and took another sip of wine. There was definitely something in the air tonight.

Upstairs in the bedroom, Livvie quickly peeled off her pyjamas and swapped them for a pair of plum coloured batik harem pants she'd made herself and a bottle green long-sleeved T-shirt. All the while, her mind running over what had happened since she'd arrived at the cottage. She'd wanted to get away from it all, from everyone, and have some time alone, but this situation with Zander had changed that; she didn't want to be alone, she wanted to spend time with him. She didn't know how it was possible with someone she'd only just met, but there was an undeniably strong connection between them and she sensed he could feel it, too.

She stopped for a moment, realising it had been a while since she'd thought about Donny. When she'd left Rickelthorpe, she thought she'd be spending the whole evening with her mind occupied by him and his misdemeanours, weeping buckets and feeling devastated. She wondered what he was doing with himself right now; he was no good at being alone and always needed to be entertained. He put her in mind of a spoilt little boy. What had he thought when he'd got back to the flat and found it empty? She shivered as she recalled her lucky escape earlier that evening when he'd almost caught her leaving. For a moment, hurt crept in as the image of him with that women pushed its way into her mind, causing tears to brim in her eyes. 'Tosser!' She snatched the tears away. She was going to enjoy being in Zander's company tonight and thoughts of her self-centred, cheating bastard ex-boyfriend weren't invited. 'Screw you, Donny!'

'You okay.' Zander looked up as she walked into the room.

'Yep, I'm fine thanks.' She picked up her wine and took a slug, watching him work on the potatoes. He was incredibly easy to be around.

'THAT WAS DELICIOUS.' Zander sat back in his chair at the kitchen table. 'You're a talented cook.'

'Thank you, you're not so bad yourself.'

'Thanks, but I was just the sous to your head chef. I do quite a bit at home, as a way of winding down; I do a mean roast dinner.' He picked up the bottle of wine. 'More?'

'Just a smidge.'

Through the course of the meal, they'd shared small details of their personal lives; what they did for a living, where they called home. They'd even touched on the subject of their respective families – though Livvie didn't go into too much detail about hers; there was no way she was going to share with him how low she was viewed by the people who should love her most and want the best for her, especially when his family sounded so supportive and loving.

'So, is it just you at home, or is there a Mrs Zander?' The wine had made her bold; ordinarily, she wouldn't ask such a direct question, but their circumstances were a little unusual and, she figured, the everyday rules didn't apply.

She noticed him pause and think for a moment, gnawing on his bottom lip.

'Look, you don't have to answer that; I shouldn't have asked, I was being nosy. Just ignore me.'

'It's fine,' he replied. 'You weren't being nosy; I've been wondering if there's a Mr Livvie.'

'Ughh!' She rolled her eyes. 'Where to start with that?'

'Ah. I'm guessing that's the reason for your last-minute booking of this place.'

She nodded. ''Fraid so. And you?'

'Mmhm. I wanted to get away from a ... let's just call it a "situation" back home, hence turning up here at such a late hour.'

'Want to talk about it?'

'Do you?'

Livvie swirled the wine around in her glass and shook her head. 'Not tonight. I'm having such a ... such a ... I'm having a really lovely time and I don't want to spoil it.' She looked across at Zander, all too aware of the electricity that crackled in the air around them, and from the look in his eyes, he could feel it, too.

He reached across the table and took her hand in his, rubbing his thumb across her fingers. 'Same here.'

The moment was shattered by a loud snort from Alf, who was lying flat on his back in his bed, gangly legs splayed in an ungainly manner. It was quickly followed by another, much louder one.

Livvie looked wide-eyed at Zander and burst out laughing. 'Was that from him?'

'It was; he's such a stylish hound. Honestly, I can't take him anywhere.'

Zander eased his hand away and a moment of silence fell between them. Keen to pull things back, Livvie asked, 'So, how did you come by such an adorable character as Alf?'

'It's a long story and the beginning, I'm afraid, isn't a very happy one.

'Seven years ago, I split up with the girl everyone expected me to marry.'

'Oh ... right.'

'Her name was Clara and she was sweet-natured, kind and beautiful; perfect, some would say.' Zander paused. 'Maybe too perfect.'

He took a slug of wine, conscious of Livvie's eyes on him.

'How did you meet?' she asked.

'Steff and John were having a summer party one Saturday afternoon. Clara was a work colleague of John's and he'd invited her along.'

'Do you think it was a set-up?'

'Oh, very much so. Of course, Steff and John denied it at the time but owned up and took all the credit when Clara and me got together; Clara had been completely in the dark, too.'

'Families.' Livvie gave a resigned smile

'Tell me about it.' He rolled his eyes. 'We'd been together for five years and lived together for three of them; she moved in with me in my house in Leeds. My family adored her and she slotted in from the moment she met them at the barbecue. So much so, we regularly used to join them on holidays; she'd even go shopping with my mother and my sister, make plans with them. It actually started to feel a bit weird that she spent more time with them than I did; like it was her family and I was the outsider.'

'I can imagine.'

'The last couple of years we were together, it was getting pretty obvious that Clara was keen to settle down and start a family. I couldn't help but feel that there'd been a subtle campaign building; like she'd joined ... not "forces", that's too strong a word ... it felt like she and my family had got their heads together and decided that it was time we got married; even Toby, who didn't usually get involved with stuff like that. '

'And you didn't want to?'

'No, and it kind of had the opposite effect really; it made me realise that I wasn't ready to settle down and get married – I was only twenty-nine, hadn't been out of medical school that long, and felt I was still finding my feet. I didn't know what all the rush was about. But it made me suddenly realise that Clara wasn't the person I wanted to spend the rest of my life with.' He sighed, running his fingers through his hair. 'That makes me sound like a real shit, doesn't it?'

'No, it makes you sound honest.'

'That's not what everyone else thought; least of all Clara's parents.'

'Oh dear.'

'It started with little comments dropped into the conversation here and there, at family get-togethers, meals out; pretty much any time we all met up, no one seemed to waste an opportunity. Drip, drip, drip; her family, my family, they were all doing it. I didn't realise at first, but then Clara started to leave magazines out at home, open on pages advertising wedding venues, or engagement rings, anything and everything wedding related. She even managed to find excuses to look in jewellers' shop windows on the pretext of getting me a new watch – which I didn't need.'

'Wow, that sounds fairly intense.'

'It was, and it began to feel pretty stifling.' Zander could feel his heart begin to race at the thought. I tried talking to my mother about it, but all she could say was that Clara and I were perfect together, that Clara adored me, and that I was being too pig-headed to accept it.'

He could see Livvie's mind processing what he'd just told her, her brow furrowed by a frown.

'Can I say something?' she asked.

'Feel free.'

'From the point of view of a total outsider, I kind of get the impression there was a thread of subtle manipulation running through the whole situation. I'm sure Clara didn't realise that she was actually doing it, but nobody likes to feel they're being manipulated.' Her face suddenly took on a worried expression. 'I hope you don't mind me saying all of that.'

Zander was struck by her astute take on the situation. 'Quite the contrary; that's exactly what I started to think, and my best mate Noah was the only other person who could see through it, too. It was so frustrating; I felt like my family just wouldn't listen, couldn't understand my point of view.'

'It must've been hard for them too. They probably just saw a sweet girl who was desperately in love with you, but marriage is a serious business and you've got to be true to yourself.'

Zander sighed. It was a relief to talk to someone who

really understood what he'd been going through without thinking he'd been a total bastard. And weirdly, it felt like a massive relief; as if a huge burden of guilt that had loitered at the back of his mind for all those years had suddenly been lifted. It had been hard for his parents to accept that he'd broken up with sweet, kind Clara or that she'd actually been capable of manipulation, no matter how subtle.

'One night over dinner, Clara was telling me how she'd been out for lunch with my mother and Steff at a newly renovated country pile that had started to hold wedding receptions. She was going on and on, saying how perfect it was, how that's where she'd choose for our wedding, saying how she'd got the perfect day planned. Then she suggested we pop in for afternoon tea over the weekend and something inside me just cracked. It felt like the pressure was building and building; it was too much, and I'd reached a point where I'd had enough. I tried to change the subject, but she just kept going on and on about it. In the end I, er ... er, I told her it was over.' Zander flinched as he recalled the look in Clara's eyes.

'Oh, right. I'm guessing she didn't take that news too well.'

He was relieved to see Livvie didn't look outraged or disgusted.

'That's an understatement. She's a sensitive soul, and I felt terrible because she sobbed and sobbed but I had no doubt in my mind that it was the right decision; it felt like a massive weight off my shoulders after I'd said it. I was dreading telling my family, but in a funny way, their campaign had helped me realise that, yes, I loved Clara, but not enough to want to make the commitment to marry her.'

'So what happened?'

'Would you believe she ran to my parents' house in tears?'

'Your parents' house?'

Zander nodded. 'Yep.'

And where did you go?'

'I went for a drive. A *long* drive.' He sighed.

'That doesn't seem very fair.' The look of concern on Livvie's face reached in and touched his heart. 'Clara went to your parents' house, meaning that you couldn't.'

'Yes; it would've been nice if I'd had the chance to speak to them first, but at the time, with everything that had been happening, it didn't seem so unusual. It didn't stop it from being frustrating though.'

'I'm not surprised.'

'Which brings me very nicely to answering your original question; how did I come by that wayward boy you describe as an "adorable character".' He smiled, affection etched all over his face, nodding towards Alf, who was still sprawled out in his bed.

Livvie giggled. 'I must admit, I'm very curious to know how splitting up with your girlfriend has anything to do with you getting Alf.'

Zander swallowed hard; it wasn't a memory he was keen to revisit if he could help it.

'Well, it was when I was on that drive after we'd just split up. I drove for ages and ended up pretty close to your neck of the woods actually. I pulled up by a green, it had a river running along the bottom, some massive oak trees edging it.'

'Down the long bank, opposite the kids' play area?'

'That's the one.'

'That's Scaggleby.'

'Yes, that sounds familiar. Anyway, I pulled up in the

parking area. Being dusk, it was quiet and there were no other cars around, so I decided to go and sit on the bench by the trees, hoping to clear my head and make sense of what had just happened.'

Livvie nodded. 'It's a pretty tranquil spot, I can see why you thought that.'

'Well, it wasn't tranquil for long. I'd been there about five minutes when this van pulled up and a man got out. He didn't see me, but when he walked past I could see he had a young black Labrador on a lead. I noticed the dog's demeanour didn't seem too happy – my parents have always had at least one Labrador at any given time and I'd grown to associate them with waggy tails and a happy disposition. Anyway, I couldn't shake the feeling that something wasn't right so I decided to follow them; it still makes my blood run cold today. As I was running to see what was happening, the blond man I'd seen walk by barged past me – I can still see him now, he had the most menacing look in his eyes I've ever seen, it actually chilled me to the bone. He charged over to his van and flew off down the road.' Zander shuddered at the memory. 'I still find it difficult to talk about, but let's just say I found the little lad in a bad way. I took him to a good friend of mine who's a vet. He rushed him to his surgery, kept him in for what seemed like ages.' Zander clenched his jaw and swallowed hard, trying to get a grip on the emotions that had resurfaced.

Livvie's hand flew to her mouth, her eyes brimming with tears. 'Oh, my God! No!'

'It was touch and go for him for a while, but I took time off work and went to see him every day; just sat beside him, stroking him and talking to him, willing him to pull through. I knew he'd have to come home with me, there was no way I could let him go to anyone else or, God forbid, a rescue centre. It took a bloody long time to earn his trust, but we got there, and we've been inseparable ever since.'

He looked up to see tears pouring down Livvie's cheeks and his heart lurched.

'What a bastard! How could anyone hurt him? He's just so lovable.' She rushed over to Alf who sensed her beside him and started wagging his tail. He put his head in her lap and she bent down, planting kisses on it. 'Oh, you gorgeous boy, how could anyone do those things to you.' She turned to Zander. 'I'm amazed he's so friendly or trusts humans at all after what he's been through, and he must know you saved him.'

'He's the most amazing little guy and I'd say he saved me because I felt pretty crap after splitting up with Clara. I felt like I'd let my parents down; I'd almost become a social pariah. And it didn't help that she was round at their house or Steff's house for months afterwards – even Toby and Jo's at times.'

'That must've been awkward.'

'Just a bit; I think they all thought I'd "come to my senses", as Clara's mother had put it, and we'd get back together.'

'Really?'

He nodded. 'But after I had a heart-to-heart with my parents, they understood why that was never going to happen. They ended up having to talk to Clara's parents which, didn't go down well; they accused me of leading her on, which I hadn't. It was a horrible time.'

'Sounds like it.' Livvie stroked Alf's head as he drifted off to sleep.

Zander left the table and came to sit next to her. Alf raised his head, his tail thudding against the warm flagstone floor.

'You know what – and you're probably going to think I'm

bonkers for saying this – but I always think everything happens for a reason.' Livvie looked at him earnestly. 'I think that everything caught up with you that night, and made you feel like you had to say something to Clara because you were meant to rescue Alf; you were meant to be in that place that night to save him. You were sent to him.'

Zander looked into her gentle hazel eyes. 'I like the sound of that. God knows what would've happened to him if he'd been left there all night. Well, I do know, but I don't want to think about it.' He rubbed Alf's proffered tummy.

'Me neither,' she said, joining in the tummy rub.

Alf groaned with happiness and stretched his legs out, basking in the attention.

'Alfred Gillespie, you are a dreadful old tart,' said Zander, laughing.

13

LIVVIE

'IT'S YOUR TURN NOW.' Zander went back to the kitchen table and topped up their wine.

Much to Alf's disappointment, Livvie stood up and joined him.

'What do you mean, it's my turn?' She noticed, though his hair was cropped close, his fringe was sticking up a little at the front in an endearing way. She resisted the urge to reach across and smooth it down.

'Well, I've just spilled my guts about the most serious relationship of my life – which, I hasten to add, is something I've never done with a woman – and now it's your turn to do the same.' He sat back in his chair, folding his arms across his chest. 'I know you said you didn't want to talk about it, but trust me, it feels better to share it with someone.'

'Oh ... right.' Visions of Donny raced across her mind, roughly pushing her happiness out of the way. She really didn't want to talk about him tonight, not when she'd been having such an unexpectedly wonderful time.

Zander picked up on her change of demeanour. 'Hey,

I'm sorry if I've said something out of turn; you don't have to share anything you don't want to.'

Livvie shook her head. 'It's okay, I can talk about it, but my story's not in the deep and distant past like yours. Mine is very much in the present.'

'Ah, that explains why you didn't look so keen to talk.'

Alf heaved himself off his squishy bed and came and sat beside Livvie, resting his head in her lap, looking up at her with his kind, brown eyes.

'He can sense something's bothering you. Honestly, let's just leave it.'

'No, it's fine.' She puffed out her cheeks and sighed, girding herself as she thought about the hurt that had sent her fleeing to the moors. 'Tonight, I was supposed to be enjoying a romantic meal with my boyfriend, Donny...'

'Okay, I'm guessing something fairly major happened to stop that and resulted in you arriving here.'

'You could say ...' Livvie filled Zander in on the details, from hearing the butt-dialled phone call, to booking the cottage.

'Shit, that's awful. This Donny sounds like a total slime-ball.'

'Oh, he's that alright; and I've been a bloody fool to put up with it for so long.' She gently pulled on Alf's ears as a flood of sadness overwhelmed her, and unstoppable tears poured down her cheeks.

In a moment, Zander was in the chair beside her, pulling her into a hug, stroking her hair. With her head pressed against the warmth of his chest, she could hear the strong, rhythmic beat of his heart through his shirt. She took a deep breath, inhaling the scent of his cologne; notes of citrus and sandalwood that tugged at her senses. *This feels so good*. The only time Livvie ever got a cuddle from Donny was as a prelude to sex; which was perfunctory and there was never an ounce of emotion in it. But this hug from Zander ... this felt so different; it spoke of comfort and warmth and was given with feeling. How odd, she thought, that it was this way round.

'He's the fool for not realising how lucky he was to have you.'

His words created a flicker of happiness in Livvie's heart. Did he really think that?

Their hug was broken up by Alf pushing his nose in between them. 'Hello, Alfie, scared you're missing out, are you?' Zander laughed, releasing Livvie.

I could've stayed there all night.

She wiped her eyes. 'I'm sorry I cried. I feel so stupid; I've only known you five minutes and here I am, sobbing my eyes out all over you.' She suddenly felt embarrassed, exposed.

'Hey, don't apologise; you already know stuff about me a lot of people I've been friends with for years don't. And I was pretty cut-up about Clara and me at the time, but it's been a while, so my tears have had chance to dry; yours are still very fresh.'

She gave a watery smile, his kindness was touching. 'It's good of you to be so understanding.'

'No problem,' he said, placing his hand on her shoulder, giving it a squeeze.

Just then, Alf trotted off into the utility room, stopping at the back door where he could be heard whining.

'Looks like someone needs a toilet break, which can, very handily, double up as a weather check.' Zander made his way over to him and flicked the outside light on. 'Don't build your hopes up for a walk, buddy, it's just a quick tiddle in the garden for you, young man.' He pulled the bolt back and opened the stable-style door. 'Woah!' Icy air leapt into the kitchen, swirling around Livvie's ankles.

'Ooh, blimey, that's freezing,' she said.

'Bloody hell, come and take a look at this.'

While they'd been ensconced in the cosiness of the cottage, snow had been falling heavily, drifting into banks against the drystone wall of the garden; it was at least five inches deep, more so in other parts. The wind was howling around the property while snow tumbled from the sky, swirling around, making it impossible to see across the moors.

'Wow! I'd heard the weather could change quickly out here, but I had no idea just how much. Do you think the roads will be okay?'

'Why, are you planning on driving somewhere?' Zander grinned at her, his blue eyes twinkling and doing funny things to her insides.

She giggled. 'No! I just wondered ... well, I was going to say ... erm, if the roads are too dangerous tomorrow, then maybe ... maybe you shouldn't try to go anywhere.' Livvie hoped he wouldn't think she was being pushy or forward or worse, clingy and needy. 'I wouldn't want you to, er ... I mean, you wouldn't want to risk having an accident.'

'Okay.' He paused for a moment. 'You mean you wouldn't mind me staying here for another night?'

The way he was looking at her set butterflies in her stomach fluttering about in a frenzy. 'No, I wouldn't mind.' *You're absolutely lovely and I've loved spending time with you tonight.* Her heart started pumping faster in her chest, she hoped the tractor with the plough wouldn't come along this way again before tomorrow. But a little voice of caution told her to calm her jets, reminding her that she'd only just met him, and in the most peculiar of circumstances at that. *Oh, shut your face!* Another voice pushed its way in. *It's about time you started to trust your gut feeling; and at this present moment in time it's telling you he's hot-to-bloody-trot and a decent bloke to boot!* It had a point; if she'd trusted her gut about Donny, she wouldn't have touched him with a barge pole.

Alf crashed into her thoughts as he bounded towards her and Zander. Covered in snow, he barged his way between them and straight through the door, where he shook himself dry in the warmth of the kitchen, sending icy droplets everywhere.

Livvie shrieked. 'Arghh! That's freezing!'

'Urghh! You little bugger! What have I told you about that?' Despite himself, Zander couldn't help but laugh at the happy expression on Alf's face.

Livvie put her hands on her hips, chuckling. 'That's the second time you've drenched me tonight, you rascal.'

Alf wagged his tail; to him, it was clearly a fabulous game.

'Looks like I'm going to have to dry you off again, you little sod.' Zander reached for the towel that he'd hung to dry on the wooden clothes airer in the utility room. 'Then I think we should move through to the living room, if that's okay with you, Livvie?'

'Sounds good.' She fiddled with the end of her plait, the way he said her name sending waves of something inde-scribable right through her. 'Though my clothes are a bit damp, so I think I'll go and put my PJs back on.'

'Good plan; I think I'll join you.'

Livvie looked startled.

'I mean, I think I'll got to my room and put my own PJs on.'

'Well, that's a relief.' She giggled but secretly, she quite liked the thought of him joining her in her bedroom. *Floozy!*

14

ZANDER

Basking in the unexpected glow of happiness Livvie's presence had created, Zander carried their drinks through to the living room; she was right behind, carrying a small plate of exquisite handmade chocolates that were left for the holidaying guests.

'These look amazing,' she said.

'And they taste as good as they look,' he said, setting the glasses down on the coffee table. 'They're from a chocolatiers' in a town not far from here called Middleton-le-Moors.'

'Oh, I think I've heard of that place, isn't it a well-to-do quaint little Georgian market town?'

'It is, and it's definitely worth a visit. If the roads are clear, I can take you there, if you like?' His eyes twinkled at her in the soft light. He hoped that didn't sound too pushy, but judging from the vibes he'd been getting from her, he thought she wouldn't find the idea totally repellent.

'I'd like that.' She smiled at him shyly.

Zander's heart flipped. She was having the most unbelievable effect on him, triggering feelings he didn't know existed and tapping into some primal, deeply-hidden part of him which was telling him, without any doubt, he needed to be with her. *Oh, Lord, I sound like I've lost my marbles, but I can't shake this feeling, and I know, I just absolutely know that she feels it, too.* He sneaked a glance at her. Her cheeks were slightly flushed and her eyes were shining; she was unbelievably beautiful. He was struggling to fight the overwhelming urge to pull her to him and kiss those full lips. He didn't know what she was doing to him but no other woman had ever touched him in this way. It all felt slightly crazy.

'I always thought that old houses were supposed to be draughty and cold, but it's so cosy and warm in here.' Livvie pulled him out of his reverie.

'Believe me, this place was cold and draughty when I first bought it. It was in a terrible state; leaking thatch, broken windows, gaps in the wall where bracken roots were growing through, outside toilet, you name it...'

Livvie looked around her. 'Really? It's hard to imagine it ever being like that.'

'It was shocking. I'm told it was owned by a reclusive old farmer who'd lived on his own for as long as anyone could remember. Anyway, judging by the wallpaper that was hung up using drawing pins, it hadn't been decorated since the fifties. The walls were covered with crumbling plasterboard and papered over – and all of this was boxed in.' He pointed to the oak partition that the settle by the hearth was fixed to.

'Why would anyone do that, it's so lovely?' She ran her fingers over the age-darkened wood. 'Or want to hide these lovely, uneven walls when they give the place so much character?'

'It beggars belief, doesn't it? But, I suppose, fashions change; it would've been to make the walls all straight and neat and contemporary. It meant I got it for a song; I'd inherited some money from my grandmother and was looking to invest it in a property. It seemed like perfect timing when this place came on the market. Anyway, once I'd had a proper look around and saw what needed doing, I joined SPAB so I could learn how to look after such an old property properly.'

'SPAB?'

'The Society for the Protection of Ancient Buildings.'

'That's a name-and-a-half.'

Zander laughed. 'They run homeowners' courses, teaching you how and why you should use lime in old buildings, rather than contemporary stuff like cement and concrete. Afterwards, I stripped the walls back and re-plastered them with traditional lime plaster, used limewash for the walls; helps the house breathe and function how it was intended, helps prevent damp.'

'Oh, I didn't know that. I love the finish it gives.' He watched her gaze move over to the prints he'd hung on the walls. 'And I love the paintings.' Livvie was admiring a watercolour of moorland scenery in all its summer glory, with soft, undulating swathes of heather, a fresh blue sky dotted with fluffy clouds. It was so vivid, you could almost smell the fresh air.

'That one's by a local artist called Gerald. He's quite a character by all accounts, and this is one of his tamer paintings.'

'Really?'

'I'm told that, until recently, he used to paint nude portraits of his wife.'

'Yikes! I'm not so sure they would've looked too good in here.'

'No, I'm not really into paintings of naked ladies in their eighties.'

'What?' Livvie's eyes were like saucers. 'Are you teasing me?'

Tickled by her expression, Zander threw his head back and laughed. 'I promise you I'm not. Honestly, the folk in the village are fabulous, but it's got more than its fair share of "characters", shall we say. I've never been anywhere like it, but it keeps pulling me back.'

Livvie looked up at him and smiled; he noticed her eye suddenly catching something that was hanging from the beam. Zander followed her gaze to the mistletoe he'd asked Mrs Hoggarth to hang in the house.

His heart started pumping faster as his eyes slipped from the mistletoe to Livvie's full lips. She was looking back at him, her pupils dilated, her lips slightly parted. He wanted more than anything in the world to kiss her and, if he was reading the signs right, she wanted him to. The atmosphere was heavy with something indefinable, electricity sparking around them. Neither of them spoke, but the eye contact they continued to hold was increasing its intensity by the second. Zander felt his breathing deepen as a surge of lust hit his crotch. Hesitantly he put his hands on the top of Livvie's arms and took a step closer. He noticed her breathing change too; she swallowed and parted her lips further, her eyes heavy with desire. Feeling bolder, he ran his finger down the curve of her cheek, feeling her skin soft and warm.

'Livvie,' he said, his voice smoky.

A crashing sound from the kitchen made Alf bark and in an instant, their special moment disintegrated into the air around them.

Livvie jumped and Zander took a step backwards. 'What was that?' she asked.

'I've no idea.' He strode over to the living room door,

pulling it open. Alf barged through, offering another cursory bark as he and Zander made their way to the kitchen.

All was as they'd left it except for a stainless steel pan lid, spinning on the floor. Alf ran over to it, bringing it to a halt and giving it a thorough sniffing.

'How on earth did that happen?' Livvie looked puzzled. 'There aren't any ghosts here are there?'

Zander laughed. 'Not that I'm aware of, though it does seem strange that the lid should just fall like that.'

At that moment, Livvie's mobile phone started to vibrate with an incoming call, pushing itself around the work top where she'd left it.

'Ah, I think we've found the phantom pan-lid pusher,' he said. 'And it looks like signal has been restored.' He handed Livvie her phone, feeling strangely disappointed that they were back in touch with the rest of the world.

'Thanks,' she said. He could see she was reluctant to check the name of the caller. 'Oh, why didn't I turn the bloody thing off before?'

'Are you worried it's going to be your boyfriend?' Zander gave her a sympathetic smile.

'*Ex*-boyfriend. And kind of ... yes. Or Bryony, worried because Donny's been hounding her about my whereabouts. I haven't told her anything yet; I'd intended to fill her in on all the details tomorrow. She's been on a romantic date with her boyfriend and I didn't want to spoil their night. Trust Donny not to give a damn though ...'

Zander nodded, noting the shadow of anxiety in her eyes.

'Listen, it can't hurt to check who it is. If it's the loser who treated you like shit, turn your phone off; if it's your friend, just fire off a quick reply telling her you're okay.'

He watched her expression change as she considered his suggestion. 'Yes, I like the sound of that.' She took a cautious glance at her phone and her face dropped. 'Oh, no!'

Zander instantly regretted his suggestion. 'The boyfriend, I mean ex-boyfriend?'

Livvie nodded. 'And Bryony; there's loads of missed calls and texts from both of them. I'm going to have to let her know I'm okay at the very least. I really didn't fancy this tonight; I just wanted to push him to the back of my mind. Oh, God, what am I going to do?'

'You still don't have to ring her, you know. Like I said before, just send her a text, explaining there are problems with signal because of the weather – which is true – let her know you're okay and that you'll call her tomorrow.'

Livvie nodded and Zander wished he could take the worry away from those beautiful hazel eyes.

'Yes, and I'll tell her not to let Donny know I've been in touch; the last thing I want is for him to start pumping her for information.'

Livvie tapped out a brief text and, with a sigh of relief, pressed send. 'There, done,' she said. 'And before I get any more messages, I'm going to turn my phone off.'

'Good plan.'

The pair headed back to the living room with Alf trotting behind, his tail wagging as usual. He flumped down on the rug in front of the stove, sleep claiming him in an instant.

Livvie kicked off her slippers and sat on the sofa, curling her feet underneath her while Zander took the chair. He reached forward and picked up his wine glass. 'It's been quite a day,' he said.

'It has.' Livvie yawned. 'And I'm feeling suddenly very tired.'

'That's probably because it's gone midnight and what you've been through has caught up with you.' Her yawn triggered one in him.

'From what you said earlier, I kind of get the feeling it's the same for you, too.'

He nodded and rolled his eyes. 'You could say. Anyway, you look absolutely shattered. I think you should get yourself to bed and get on the other side of a good sleep.' He quickly pushed away thoughts of holding her in his arms, feeling her skin against his, pressing his lips against hers ...

'I am, but I'll do the washing up first.' She went to stand up.

'The washing up can wait, I only intend to stack the dishwasher tonight; I'll set it away in the morning.'

'But, at least let me help—'

'Nope, no argument, I can manage and there's not that much. Go on, your bed is calling for you,' he said.

'Well, if you're sure.'

'Very sure.'

'Thank you.' She leaned across and kissed him on the cheek. 'And thank you for a lovely evening; I wasn't expecting to have such an enjoyable time when I set off from home.'

The softness of her lips against his cheek and the gentle fragrance of her perfume sent Zander's pulse racing and electricity buzzing up his spine. As she pulled back they briefly made eye contact; he knew she could feel it, too.

ZANDER LAY in bed knowing that on the other side of the wattle and daub wall lay Livvie. Sweet, beautiful Livvie. He could hear the cast iron bed creak occasionally with her movements, and he imagined her curled up beneath the duvet, the rich auburn waves of her hair splayed out across the white of the pillow. How he wished he was lying beside her. He threw his arm above his head, wondering how a woman he'd only just met could arouse such intense feelings in him, feelings he'd never had before. Certainly not with Mel. Mel! The woman – his girlfriend! – whom he'd barely thought of the whole evening. He very much doubted that he'd crossed her mind either. *Says a lot about our relationship*. He turned his thoughts back to Livvie and the feelings she'd awoken in him; did she feel the same connection? Judging by the sparks that had been flying, he very much thought so.

15

LIVVIE

'OH, ZANDER ... ZANDER, OH, YES ...' Livvie groaned in ecstasy. He was pressing hot, urgent kisses to her lips before dropping a trail of them down the length of her neck. She arched her back with pleasure. 'Oh, Zander ...'

'Morning, Livvie.' A voice broke through her thoughts. 'I've brought you some tea.'

There was that bloody voice again, spoiling their moment, she wished it would bugger off.

Slowly, realisation dawned on her as sleep slipped away and she gradually became aware of her surroundings, the events of yesterday flooding back. Hesitantly, she opened her eyes to have her fears confirmed: standing beside the bed was Zander, armed with a cup of tea and an amused smile. *Oh, bugger, bugger, bugger!* She scrunched her eyes tight shut as she felt her cheeks burn crimson; she'd been dreaming, and she had the horrible feeling she'd been saying his name out loud. *Arghh!* She swallowed down her embarrassment and did her best to act as if the last few minutes hadn't happened.

'Morning.' She could barely pluck up the courage to

make eye contact with him. 'Thank you.' She pushed herself up, conscious that most of her hair had escaped from its plait, no doubt giving her an unattractive wild-woman look.

'I wasn't sure if you took sugar, so I erred on the side of you not.'

'No, I don't take sugar.' She could still feel her face blazing.

'Good to know I got it right.' He handed her the steaming mug. 'And did you sleep well?'

Oh, those clear blue eyes were making mischief in her insides. He looked so handsome with the dark stubble that peppered his chin, and his hair sticking up in tufts. She nodded. 'Very well, thanks. I don't think I've ever slept in such a comfy bed, and as for this duvet ... it's so snug.'

'It's Hungarian goose-down, known for its very cosy properties.' He flashed another grin that made her heart flip.

'Ah.' She nodded shyly.

'Right, well, I was going to do myself a bacon butty; you're welcome to join me, if you like?'

'Ooh, I like the sound of that.'

'Great; give me ten minutes and everything should be ready.'

She watched him walk across the bedroom and disappear through the door. As soon as he'd gone, she clapped a hand over her eyes and cringed. 'Oh, my God! 'He heard me, oh no, he heard me! Ughh! How embarrassing!'

'Mmm. That smells so good.' Livvie headed into the kitchen where Zander, still in his pyjamas, was standing over a skillet of sizzling bacon. His shoulders looked strong and broad, sending a tingle through her and making her wonder what it would feel like to run her hand across them. *Push that thought right out of your mind; thinking that way has caused you enough embarrassment already this morning!*

'Hi.' Zander turned and greeted her with a wide smile. 'Take a pew, this'll just be two minutes.'

Though she'd eaten well the night before, Livvie's stomach rumbled at the mouth-watering aroma that filled the room. 'Okay. You're sure there's nothing I can do?'

'Nope, it's all in hand.'

Alf tore himself away from eyeing up the bacon and trotted over to her as she pulled out a chair at the table. 'Hi there, lovely boy.' She bent and rubbed his head. 'I bet this smell is driving you crazy.'

'Hah! Judging by the expressions on his face and how closely he watches my every move whenever I'm handling food, it's utter torture for him.'

Livvie laughed. 'Oh, poor Alf. I feel your pain; I love my food, too.'

'Have you seen outside, by the way?'

'Oh, no, not yet; I haven't opened the curtains in my bedroom. Why?'

'Take a look.' Zander nodded to the low, wide mullioned window that over-looked Great Stangdale moor.

Livvie peered out, the light making her eyes ache. 'Oh, wow!' The snow had stopped falling and a hard frost had left everything sparkling in the low winter sunshine. She scanned the vista of the dale, which was now a vast expanse of white, the only relief offered by little farmsteads dotted in the distance, a coniferous wood on the other side of the dale, and the stark, naked branches of the hawthorn hedges that delineated the fields. It was the stuff of Christmas cards.

'It's so beautiful; like a winter wonderland. I've never seen anything like it.'

'It's a bit different out here when it comes to winter weather; it's known to get a bit extreme.'

'Do you know if any more snow's forecast out here?' She looked up at the sky which had glimpses of blue peering through thick white clouds.

'It's supposed to be fine today; bright skies and sunshine they said. Pretty much the same tomorrow and then after that it's looking like more of what we had yesterday.'

'Oh, right.'

He placed the bacon in fluffy bread buns and carried the plates over to the table. 'Here you go, there's ketchup if you fancy, or do you prefer brown sauce?'

'Oh, ketchup all the way!' She turned away from the window and took a seat at the table.

'Me too.'

'So, do you think the snow plough's been out anymore through the night?' she asked.

'Well, I haven't heard anything along here, but I dare say it'll have been round the roads leading to the main ones. Having said that, unless the gritter's been out, the roads will be pretty treacherous with packed ice, especially out here where we're a bit higher up and more remote than the actual villages.'

Livvie nodded. 'I can imagine, especially with everywhere being so hilly. I wouldn't fancy driving down one; from the little I could see last night, I got the impression there were some pretty sheer drops out there.'

'There are; some of them plunge straight into the river, which will be full at this time of year.'

'Oh, blimey.' Livvie chewed on her bacon sandwich for a moment, secretly hoping that the plough and the gritter would leave them alone up here. She glanced up at Zander to see him looking at her.

'So are you sure you're still okay with me staying here for another night?' he asked.

Oh, bugger, he can read my thoughts! Livvie swallowed her mouthful and nodded. 'Of course. I can hardly push you out of your own house in such dangerous conditions.'

He laughed. 'Well, technically you could, but thanks.'

'S'okay. And anyway, how could I refuse when you make such awesome bacon butties?' She arched her eyebrows before taking another bite of her sandwich.

'Ah, I knew my bacon butty skills would come in handy one day.' His eyes twinkled back at her. 'Though, I was rather hoping you'd say it was my captivating personality and awesome conversational skills that meant you'd want me to hang around for a bit longer.'

'Well ... maybe there's that as well ... a little bit. And, of course, there's Alf.' Oh, blimey, if only he knew how much I'd love him to stay, she thought.

'Ah, good old Alf; he always wins the ladies over, don't you?'

Alf responded with a sound wag of his tail, his eyes moving from Zander's plate to Livvie's.

With the bacon sandwiches devoured and the dishwasher gurgling and glugging away, Livvie asked, 'Do you mind if I go and take a shower?' She sniffed her plait and pulled a face. 'My hair smells of last night's dinner.'

Zander chuckled. 'Be my guest. I'll be sure to keep Alf downstairs so there'll be no ambushes this time.'

'Thanks.' She laughed and ruffled Alf's ears. 'I won't be long.'

The shower kicked out deliciously hot jets of water. Livvie let it pour over her head and trickle down her face as she tried to make sense of the unusual set of circumstances she'd found herself in. This time yesterday, she'd been planning on getting her failing relationship with Donny back on track. But in the cold light of the morning, she wondered why the hell she'd even considered that. She dolloped shampoo into her hand and lathered it into her hair, scrubbing vigorously. It was so obvious that they were going nowhere; that Donny was just using her until something better came along. She hated to think it, but she only had herself to blame; she'd been warned by several people. He had a track record as long as her arm. But, pathetically, she'd let his cheeky-chappy banter talk her into first one date, then another and before she knew it they were living together. She'd always known Bryony hadn't been keen on him and had sensed she'd been careful with what she said for fear of spoiling their friendship but, foolishly, Livvie had allowed herself to be passively carried along on Donny's tidal wave of bullshit – there really was no better way of putting it. 'What a fool I've been!' Crossly, she stuck her head back under the warm water and rinsed the shampoo out of her hair and with it, any more thoughts of Donny.

Once showered, Livvie dug out a woollen tunic dress she'd made in shades of russet and a pair of contrasting bottle green and russet striped tights. She quickly dried her hair, twisting the sides and pinning them back, and applied a quick flick of mascara, then padded downstairs in her rabbit slippers.

While she'd been in the shower, Zander had lit the wood burner and flames danced merrily behind the glass. It was a comforting sight, she thought. The rich tones of Christmas carols being sung in Italian emanated from the sound system. Livvie loved this type of festive music and had played them at home, much to Donny's disgust.

She followed the sound of Zander's voice to the kitchen. He was sitting at the table, his mobile phone pressed to his ear. He waved when he spotted her but he was wearing a troubled expression and she didn't want to intrude, so she made her way back into the living room, quickly followed by Alf, who flopped down on the rug and started soaking up the warmth from the stove and the underfloor heating.

On the table was a book of photography – local images by all accounts. Livvie picked it up, plonked herself down on the sofa and started flicking through it, gasping at the stunning images. The villages of Lytell Stangdale, Danskelfe and Arkleby were achingly beautiful with their heavily thatched cottages and gardens brimming with a riot of summer blooms; they were even stunning when they were piled high with snow and frost was clinging onto the branches of the trees. They were in stark contrast to the bleak images of the stone markers and moorland crosses that stood, weary and isolated, bearing the brunt of whatever the North Yorkshire weather threw at them. There was a bird's eye view that showed just how steep the riggs were that loomed over the verdant valleys, scooped out in the last ice-age. But her favourite was a photograph of the moors swathed in rich purple heather; the image was so vivid, she could almost smell the blooms' sweet, honey fragrance. How wonderful it must be to grow up in a place like this, she thought.

Just then, Zander walked in. 'Sorry about that, it was just my big sister giving me an ear-bashing for not telling her of my change of plans.'

'Oh?'

'Ah, right, yes, I've just realised, I haven't told you, have I?' He rubbed his hand across the stubble of his chin.

'Told me what?'

'The reason I'm here and not in Carcassonne.'

'Carcassonne? Oh ... er, no.'

'I think this calls for a fresh cup of coffee; fancy one?'

'Please.' Livvie followed him through to the kitchen, sitting down at the table while Zander fixed a couple of coffees from the machine.

~

'Wow,' she said when he'd finished sharing what had happened with Mel. 'So we're both running away from our partners.'

'So it would seem.'

'And have you heard from Mel since she left?'

'Nope.' He shook his head.

'Oh, right.'

'And have you heard anything more from Donny?'

'I haven't dared turn my phone on this morning, though I'm sure there'll be more; he can be fairly persistent when he wants to be. And I really must ring Bryony; she'll be worried sick. Actually, if you don't mind, I think I'll go and do that now.'

Zander splayed his palms. 'That's absolutely fine with me. I'll just jump in the shower while you do that.'

Livvie could feel his eyes on her as she left the room. She made her way to her bedroom and picked up her phone, eyeing it nervously as she turned it on. As she expected, another flood of missed calls and texts landed, all but one of them from Donny. Her heart lurched up to her throat, anxiety making her stomach twist into a tight, uncomfortable knot. 'Here goes,' she said, taking a deep breath and tapping on the first of his texts.

'That wasn't too bad, I suppose,' she said, once she'd finished reading it. The tone of it was in his usual cocky style, trying to make a joke of what had happened, wondering when she'd be back. But after that, the messages got progressively more unpleasant, with him stating that he was annoyed that she'd left him without preparing his dinner and wondering what he was supposed to eat. 'Honestly, the nerve of the man!' It was so ridiculous, Livvie found it laughable. The final one had a sinister tone. "I'll find you." With a shiver, Livvie closed it.

After that text, she was reluctant to listen to his voicemails, wary of hearing his voice; it had a habit of getting right inside her head, drilling away at her and wearing her down until he got his own way. No, she'd call Bryony first; her friend's words were always good to hear.

Bryony picked up almost immediately.

'Liv, are you okay? Where the hell are you? I've been worried sick about you. Have you spoken to Donny yet?'

'Hi, Bry, I'm fine, honestly.'

'Thank God for that. So where are you?'

'After what happened with Donny and our neighbour, I just needed to get away from him and my family; I couldn't stand the prospect of spending Christmas with them and having to listen to what a failure I am.'

'No one could blame you for that, chick, but I wish you'd told me sooner, I was going out of my mind after Donny rang. He was quite unpleasant actually, accusing me of hiding you or knowing where you were.'

Livvie's heart squeezed for her friend. 'Oh, Bry, I'm so sorry, that's why I didn't get in touch, because I didn't want to spoil your special night with Josh, plus the weather's been affecting phone signal.'

'Hey, you've got no reason to apologise, it's that dickhead you were going out with that was causing the problems, as per usual – er, can I say that now you've dumped him?'

The last comment made Livvie giggle. 'Feel free.'

'Phew! Anyway, come on, fill me in on all the details.'

'Well, it's a long story.'

'I've got all morning.'

'Okay, here goes...'

Bryony listened quietly while Livvie brought her up to date with events of the previous evening. 'Hmm. This Zander sounds nice, and something tells me that you quite like him, would I be right?'

Livvie smiled to herself; her friend knew her well. 'I know it sounds bonkers, especially given the situation, but I really do, Bry. He's not only gorgeous, but there's just something about him that's making me feel stuff I've never felt before; it's really strong, and the weird thing is, I know he feels it too.'

'Woohoo! This sounds like a classic case of love at first sight to me.'

'And that's exactly how it feels – even though I feel a bit ridiculous saying it out loud.' Livvie could feel her cheeks beginning to glow. 'We nearly kissed last night.'

'No way? Sounds like you've got it bad; I've never known you like this before.' Bryony paused for a moment. 'And you're sure he's ... you know, okay? I mean, you don't think he's a raving serial killer who's going to put you in a stew or anything like that, do you?'

Livvie laughed. 'No, I've got a really good feeling in my gut about him, which is the complete opposite of what I had with Donny; then it was telling me to run in the opposite direction as quickly as I could. Sadly, I chose to ignore it, and look where it got me.'

'Right in the lap of Mr Gorgeous, by the sound of things.'

Bry gave a dirty laugh. 'Hey, I wonder what Donny would think if he found out he was the one responsible for you finding your soul mate?'

'Ooh, he'd hate that.' *Soul mate? Could Zander be her soul mate? Yes!* her gut was screaming at her but a little niggle that it was all a bit too soon kept prodding at the back of her mind, pulling her back down to earth.

'You always did say everything happens for a reason; this could very well prove you right,' said Bry.

That would be nice, Livvie thought. 'Do you really think so? He is lovely, and I'm enjoying his company and Alf is just absolutely gorgeous.' She twirled a curl of hair round her finger.

'Ah, you always were a pushover for a black Labrador; actually, you always were a pushover for anyone who was low enough to take advantage of you – Donny, King of the Knobs, and our battle-axe boss spring to mind.'

Livvie sighed. 'I need to listen to you more, then I wouldn't end up feeling rubbish as much as I do, or make so many crappy decisions.'

'Look, don't think about that now, just concentrate on having a bit of fun; and if that includes a little Christmas holiday romance and letting Mr Gorgeous have a quick rummage in your knickers, then go for it.' Another dirty laugh followed.

'Bry!'

'What? I'm just saying ... anyway, what do you want me to tell Donny if he gets in touch again; apart from "bugger off", that is?'

'Just tell him you don't know where I am, that you haven't heard from me, cos if he thinks you have, he'll hound you. I'll send him a brief text, telling him we're finished and that I'm having a break until the New Year and then we can give notice on the flat.'

She heard her friend sigh down the line. 'Listen, I'm one hundred percent in agreement with you about not telling him where you are, but if I tell him I haven't heard from you, he won't believe that for a second; he knows how close we are.'

Livvie thought for a moment, gnawing on her bottom lip. 'Yep, you're right. Just tell him that I sent you a text saying that I was fine and you weren't to worry, but that I wanted to get away from it all for a while and I didn't want anyone to know where I was.'

'Okay, cool. Hopefully, that should shut him up.'

'Fingers crossed.' Despite her words, Livvie had her doubts. When Donny wanted something, he was like a dog with a bone and wouldn't give up until he'd got it, whether it be information, money, even sex. 'Ughh!' Just the thought of him was beginning to make her skin crawl.

'You okay?'

'Yep, I'm fine. Listen, I'd better go, but I'll be in touch. Have a great weekend.'

'You, too; and don't forget what I said about giving Mr Gorgeous an invitation into your knickers. And text me later today, so I know you're safe – just in case, okay?'

'You're terrible! And, okay, I promise to text later today.'

'I know, and you love me for it. I'll look forward to hearing from you. See ya, chick.'

'See ya, Bry.'

16

ZANDER

ZANDER WATCHED Livvie disappear through the door on her way to the shower; she looked cute in her over-sized pyjamas and bed-hair. What he'd give to know what she was dreaming about when he took her tea in earlier, he thought, a smile playing over his lips as he rinsed the coffee cups. She'd definitely been saying his name – several times, at that – and what had those groans been about; he knew what they sounded like.

While Livvie was in the shower, he lit the wood-burner in the living room. Though there was under-floor heating throughout downstairs, Zander liked the cosiness created by the glow of a real fire in the inglenook. He put on his wellies and threw on his jacket then crunched his way over the snow to gather up more logs from the woodstore in the back garden, knocking snow off them while Alf bounded about like a hound possessed.

'Enjoying yourself there, Alfie boy?' He couldn't help but laugh at the Labrador's happy expression.

Alf bounded over to him, his jet black coat covered in

powdery snow, tiny clumps of ice clinging to his whiskers. Zander loved Alf's zest for life, especially after its less than happy start. He grinned at him and ruffled his head. 'And don't go getting any ideas about running inside and tearing round the house while you look like the Abominable Snowman, okay?' He scooped up a handful of snow and threw it. Alf raced after it, biting at the snow where it had landed.

Zander's ploy had worked, giving him time to close the utility room door before Alf could slip through it in search of Livvie. He was grabbing the dog towel just as Alf skidded in. 'Gotcha!' Zander threw the towel over him, giving him a quick drying off before carrying the basket of logs through to the living room.

When he'd finished, his fingers were still red from the cold, and the thought of wrapping them round a steaming mug of coffee suddenly became very appealing.

Just as he put a pod in the coffee machine, his mobile phone rang. It was Steff. Reluctantly, he decided he'd better take the call and get the inevitable ticking off out of the way.

He was still on the receiving end of what his sister referred to as a "loving ear-bashing" – if ever there was such a thing – when in walked Livvie, a vision in warm shades that perfectly matched her stunning auburn hair. He felt his mouth fall open as he took in her glowing, creamy skin that only served to emphasize her stunning hazel eyes and full, red lips. *The Goddess*, he thought as his insides turned to mush. *What was she doing to him?*

'Are you listening to me, Zandie?' Steff's voice brought him back to reality. 'You sound distracted; is there someone with you?'

He raised his hand in a wave to Livvie who, seeing he was busy, gestured that she'd go into the living room. He nodded and smiled. 'No, I mean, yes. I mean, yes, of course I'm listening to you.'

'Good,' Steff said, and continued to give him a gentle telling-off for not letting her know that he wouldn't be joining them in Carcassonne. She was being tactful by not referring to Mel and Zander was grateful for it.

As siblings went, Steff and Zander were close, and had an unspoken understanding that things would be talked about when the other was ready to share, pushing and cajoling were never put into play. He was close to Toby too, but his bond with Steff ran deeper.

'I just worry about you, Zandie, that's all. But as long as you know I'm here if you need me, need to talk or find yourself with the sudden irresistible urge to devour any of the delicious baking your niece and nephew seem very keen to partake in, then all you need to do is shout up.'

'Is that baking with or without the bogies?'

'Whichever you'd prefer. But joking aside, just holler if you need anything – and it still isn't too late to join us in Carcassonne. Poor little Cynthia will be bereft when she finds out lover boy Alfie isn't going to be here to give her Christmas cuddles.'

Zander was relieved the call had ended on a happy note; he'd go so far as to say that Steff sounded almost pleased that Mel had done a runner. When they returned from Carcassonne, he'd have a chat with her, get her take on things. Steff got on with everyone, but he had the feeling she struggled to gel with Melissa.

He made his way into the living room where Livvie was flicking through the book of local photographs. She looked stunning with her hair tumbling over her shoulders in thick, rich waves. She glanced up at him, her smile setting his heart racing in the way it only did for her.

SPEAKING to Livvie over coffee about his pathetic excuse of a relationship with Mel – or should that be, pouring his heart out over coffee, Zander mused – had made him realise just how easy she was to talk to. She didn't judge or criticise; she just listened.

Her comment that they were both running away from their partners had struck a chord, though it wasn't really Mel he was running away from, but rather, their situation. Having said that, he had a suspicion she'd be back sooner than she'd said, cutting her break short owing to a clash with someone or running out of money; that was usually the case with Mel. And he certainly didn't want to be around to deal with the fall out and have to listen to her ranting when that happened. If he was running away from anything, it was that.

Though Livvie had told him of her situation with Donny, Zander had a feeling she wasn't telling him everything. The effect the mere mention of his name had on her demeanour spoke volumes. What horrors was she trying to get away from, he wondered? He didn't like the thought of some obnoxious creep making her unhappy.

'Right, Alf, time for me to jump in the shower while Livvie's making her calls,' said Zander.

Alf briefly raised his head, then flopped it back down; there was no food on offer so he wasn't interested.

As he headed across the living room, Zander could hear Livvie chatting away in her bedroom. He didn't want to eavesdrop, but in old cottages, carpets and ancient floorboards with gaps here and there offered little in the way of sound-proofing. He took the stairs two at a time and crossed the landing to the bathroom. The tone of her voice and the occasional laugh suggested she was talking to her friend and he was relieved to hear that she seemed okay.

BY THE TIME he'd finished in the shower and got dressed, he noted that all was quiet in Livvie's bedroom, but something told him she was still in there. He resisted the temptation to knock and check how she was, and instead went downstairs where Alf was snoring in the kitchen.

'Right, Alf, I think it's time we went and had a little rummage around the shed.' Zander grabbed his keys from the worktop and headed towards the utility room and out through the back door. Alf woke up with a snort and trotted after him.

It didn't take long to find what he was looking for.

Four sledges were stacked neatly under the shed window; two blue, two red. When he'd made a list of what would be needed to furnish the cottage for holiday-makers, sledges featured pretty high on it. The sloping fields directly in front of Dale View Cottage would be perfect for sledging, he'd reasoned. And today, he thought, would be perfect for exactly that; provided Livvie was up for it, of course.

He didn't have long to wait to find out.

'What have you got there?' Livvie peered round the utility room door where he was leaning the sledges against the wall.

'I have two brand-spanking new sledges that are desperately in need of breaking in.' He beamed at her.

'Right.' She looked bemused.

'You can say no, I'll totally understand, but I wondered if you fancied joining Alf and me sledging in the field on the other side of the track?' He nodded towards the front of the cottage.

Livvie paused for a moment and he was relieved when her face broke into a wide smile. 'I'd love to! It's years since I've been sledging; I used to think it was great fun.'

'Brilliant,' he said, feeling his heart melting. 'Though, you might want to change into something you don't mind getting drenched. Oh, and have you brought some wellies?'

'Actually, I have; I thought I'd better if I was heading out into the countryside. Give me two ticks,' she said, hurrying off to get changed.

Zander couldn't believe how enthusiastic Livvie was at his suggestion; he was used to Mel refusing to do anything that meant she would look anything less than groomed to perfection. It was refreshing to see that Livvie embraced the idea with great gusto.

'I've just remembered, I don't have any gloves; I lost them a few days ago and haven't had time to look for them or buy new ones.' Livvie had returned to the kitchen dressed in a pair of thick navy trousers and a woollen Christmas jumper in bright red.

'Oh, okay. I'd give you mine but I think they'd be so big they'd fall off. Actually, I've got some glove liners that should do the job, they're very stretchy but they fit small, if you see what I mean?'

'Erm, I think so.'

Zander rifled about in the pockets of his padded jacket. 'Here you go, give them a try.'

'Perfect,' she said, pulling them on and wriggling her fingers.

～

'WOW, THIS SNOW IS SO DEEP,' said Livvie as they crunched their way over the track to the field, pulling their sledges behind them. Alf bounded about, only stopping for the occasional roll in the snow.

'It is, looks like a lot more was dumped after the road was ploughed.' Their breath hung in clouds in the chilly air; it was cold but Zander was relieved the icy, nipping wind of the previous night had dropped.

'And it's easy to see why the cottage is called Dale View.' Livvie shielded her eyes with her hand, the low winter sun bouncing off the brilliant white blanket of snow that covered the vast expanse of the moorland landscape. There had been a hard frost over-night and everywhere sparkled as if it had been liberally sprinkled with glitter. In the distance, plumes of smoke reached up to the sky from the chimney pots of the farmsteads that peppered the valley. In one of the fields there were tracks from a farm vehicle where a farmer had taken a bale of hay to the feeder for his flock of sheep. 'Oh, look, there's an owl!' She pointed to a place halfway down the field in front of them.

Zander looked to see a white bird gliding through the air, its heart-shaped face scanning all around before hovering for a moment then swooping down to the ground, its talons poised. A second later, it rose, clutching its quarry, and swept off to the cluster of trees that lined the river at the foot of the valley.

'It's a barn owl; they normally hunt through the night, but I've heard the population is thriving round here, so there's a greater demand on the food supply. I suspect that's why it's hunting in daylight hours.'

'It's stunning; I've never seen a real one.' Livvie seemed reluctant to tear her eyes away from it. 'And what's that creature?'

'Which one?'

'The one that's just run out from the trees. It's running across the field now; it's so graceful.'

'I see it, yeah, that's a roe deer; and look, there's another, smaller one behind it. I usually see them on a daily basis whenever I'm here.'

'Oh, they're so beautiful; how awesome to see them every day.'

They watched as the two creatures ran the full length of the field and leapt effortlessly over the hawthorn hedge, scattering a brace of pheasants who took off, their vivid feathers shining bright against the pure white snow.

'Wow! I didn't expect to be seeing barn owls or deer when I came here. I just expected to see sheep and cows.'

Zander loved her wide-eyed expression. 'Well, you won't see any cows; they're taken into the barns over winter.'

'Oh, I didn't know that,' she said, turning to him. 'And I can't believe you don't want to live here full-time; it's stunning.'

He laughed. 'Nice idea, but my practice is in Leeds and the commute would be too long, not to mention a night-mare in this weather.'

'I suppose it would be.' She was thoughtful for a moment.

Zander took advantage of Livvie's mind being elsewhere, his eyes drawn to her pretty features. Her cute little nose, with its sprinkling of freckles more noticeable in daylight. She met his gaze, the flecks of amber in her eyes even brighter than they were indoors. There was, without doubt, something utterly beguiling about her. His heart leapt as she smiled at him, pulling him out of his musings.

He cleared his throat. 'That's Withrin Hill Farm over there.' He pointed to a large farmstead that clung to the steep hillside. 'That's where Camm lives; the chap who ploughs the roads and brought you here. He's a good bloke and his partner Molly is hilarious. She definitely calls a spade a spade. They run a campsite up there with the help of her son Ben – he has a twin who's farming in New Zealand at the moment though there's a rumour he's coming back.'

'New Zealand?'

'Yep.' Zander nodded. 'Molly's brother farms out there, has done for years, and Tom's gone out to work with him.

'Oh, right.'

'If you look carefully, you can just see part of the campsite in the fields that stretch out and get flat at the side of the farmhouse. Apparently they've converted an old train carriage and gipsy caravan to camp in. It sounds amazing by all accounts.'

'So, is that what they call diversification?'

'It is.' He nodded. 'It's what keeps a lot of farms in business, and they're doing pretty well by all accounts.'

'That's good,' she said. 'It was really decent of Camm to guide me here. I think I'd be stuck in some hedge-back somewhere, covered in snow, if it wasn't for him.'

'Perish the thought.'

'And I like the sound of Molly; she sounds fun.'

'Yeah, she's great, and so are her group of friends.' Zander threw his sledge down. 'You'll have to meet them while you're here.'

'I'd like that.'

'And right along there is Danskelfe Castle.'

'A castle, wow.' Livvie's eyes followed his finger to where the grey turrets of the ancient building were peering out from a cluster of trees. 'Does anyone still live in it?'

'They do: the Hammondeley family, they own a lot of

the land around here as part of the Danskelfe estate. They're quite big employers from what I can gather, and according to Beth, they're branching out into big annual events.'

'It's in a lovely location, perched on the crag like that.'

'It is.' Zander found his eyes drawn to Livvie's mouth. *Oh, what I'd give to feel those plump, juicy lips on mine.* He shook his thoughts away. 'Right, race you to the bottom?' He needed to get his mind off the intensity of his attraction to her which was starting to make mischief in his underpants, and back on the matter in hand.

'You're on.'

It was a struggle to fit his long legs on his sledge and Zander felt like his knees were somewhere up round his ears but he didn't care; he was enjoying the crisp fresh air and spending time in Livvie's bubbly company. 'Right, come on, Alfie.' He patted the sledge and Alf jumped between his legs.

'Alf sledges?'

'He certainly does; he loves it, don't you, fella?' He ruffled Alf's head, earning himself a sloppy lick across his cheek. 'Ughh! What have we said about that?'

'He's so adorable,' Livvie said, giggling.

'He has his moments. Right, ready, steady, go!' Zander pushed the sledge forwards and the pair of them shot down the field. 'Woohoo!'

'Wait up!' Livvie followed close behind.

'Woah!' Zander and Alf ground to a halt, spinning round at the foot of the bank.

'Arghh!' Livvie shrieked as she flew over a large bump and went spinning around before tipping upside down and rolling down in a flurry of snow to where Zander had stopped.

'Beat you.' He grinned

Livvie was giggling hard, her laugh infectious. 'I don't know what happened.' She lay in the snow, her auburn hair strewn out around her. Alf shot over to her and started rolling in the snow. 'Alf! What are you doing, you crazy boy?'

Before they knew it, Alf had grabbed the rope of Livvie's sledge and started bounding up the hill. 'Hey, you rascal,' she called. 'Come back with that!'

'I'm afraid snow makes him even more mischievous.' Zander gave her a hand up and she dusted off the snow.

The pair watched Alf reach the top of the hill, where he hurled himself onto the sledge and started rolling all over it, kicking snow everywhere.

Livvie burst out laughing. 'Oh, he's hilarious!'

'He's certainly a character, that's for sure.' Happiness surged through Zander as he watched his hapless hound.

'It's just so heart-warming that he can enjoy himself like that after what happened to him.'

Zander sighed. 'It is; he's an amazing little fella. Though I don't fancy your chances of getting your sledge back now, I'm afraid. I can always get another one from the shed.'

'It's fine; I wouldn't dream of spoiling his fun, and please don't trouble yourself.' Livvie watched Alf race ahead. 'He's hilarious; I've never met a dog with so much personality.'

'Oh, he's got plenty of that alright.'

It was hard work walking up the bank in such deep snow and by the time they'd reached the top they were out of breath. Sweat prickled the back of Zander's neck. Alf ran around them, trailing Livvie's sledge behind him. She went to reach for it, but he ran off. 'Told you,' said Zander.

'Ah, he's so fast.' Livvie laughed, turning to him. 'But I don't mind taking it in turns – with you, that is; I don't fancy my chances of taking turns with Alf.'

Zander looked down at her, her eyes were shining and her cheeks were flushed; what he'd give to kiss her right now. 'Or we could share?'

Livvie thought about it for a moment. 'You mean we sit on the sledge together like you did with Alf?'

He nodded. 'Yep.'

'Okay, sounds good, though it could be tricky with your long legs; I'm a bit bigger than Alf.'

'I'm sure we'll manage.' There was no way he was going to give up on an opportunity to have his arms around Livvie. 'We'll get it on the flat bit, then if you sit on the front, I'll climb on behind you. If you dig your heels into the snow, it'll stop the sledge taking off before we're ready.'

'Aye, aye, captain.' Livvie gave a salute and did as she was instructed.

'Woah!' she said as Zander sat down behind her, pushing the front of the sledge upwards and her back into his chest.

He chuckled and put his arms around her, taking hold of the rope and stretching his legs out either side of her. 'Sorry, did I catapult you?'

'Just a bit.' She giggled.

'Ready? he asked.

'Ready.'

He pushed off and they went whizzing down the bank. Livvie hooted with laughter and he couldn't help but join in. They may have been acquainted for less than twenty-four hours, but having her pressed close to his chest, with his arms right around her, and her hair that smelt like a summer garden brushing against his chin felt so right; it was as if they'd known each other for a life-time.

They laughed the full way down, even more so as they

approached the bottom of the hill and the sledge spun round, before slowly grinding to a halt.

'That was awesome!' Livvie said. 'We went so fast compared to my pathetic effort on my own. I absolutely loved it!'

'Yeah, me too.' He grinned. 'I don't think I'll ever grow out of sledging.'

Zander wished they didn't have to get up; he was enjoying the feeling of having her in his arms and, if he was reading the signs right, she didn't seem to mind.

He was distracted from his thoughts by a bark from Alf that echoed round the valley. He looked up to see the Labrador tumbling down the bank with the sledge; he was heading right for them. Before they got chance to move, Alf had crashed into them, sending them flying across the snow.

'Warghh!' Livvie cried. She lay on the floor laughing so hard, tears were pouring down her face.

'Hey, steady on there, Alf. Who do you think you are, Eddie the Eagle?'

Alf leapt to his feet, his tail wagging, flicking snow every-where. Zander laughed, stroking Alf's head. 'You daft lad.'

'Oh, my cheeks are aching with laughing so much,' Livvie said. 'We so need to do that again.'

Zander looked at her, taking in her pretty face, glowing with happiness. 'Come on then,' he said, offering her his hand for a pull up. 'Good to see we haven't scared you off.'

'Not a chance. I'll race you to the top.'

'You're on.'

Livvie had set off before he'd had chance to grab the sledge. 'Hey, that's cheating.'

'It's not my fault you weren't ready when you should've been,' she called behind her.

With Alf running about beside him, it didn't take Zander

long to gain on her. He could hear her puffing and giggling as she tried to run. Before he knew it, she'd bent down and scooped up a handful of snow and thrown it at him, catching him on the chin. He felt tiny bits of icy snow disappearing under his scarf and down his neck.

'Arghh. That's bloody freezing!'

'That's snow for you,' she said with a grin, before haring off again.

He made a soft snow ball in his hands and hurled it at her, but it missed and was pounced on by Alf whose retrieving instincts were confused when it fell apart.

Zander couldn't remember the last time he'd had so much fun.

THEY CONTINUED SLEDGING for another hour; their final slide down the bankside ended in them flying over the bump Livvie had first encountered, parting them from the sledge and sending them tumbling down. They finished in a giggling heap with Livvie on top of Zander, his hands resting on the tops of her arms. The laughter stopped and their eyes locked. Electricity crackled in the air around them and Zander could feel the heat of something inexplicable burning in his gut. His eyes moved to her lips, the urge to press his own onto hers was too strong to resist and he put his hand around the back of her head, pulling her towards him. He could feel his heart pumping hard as lust raced around his body.

But the moment was ruined by Alf who ran towards them and shook icy clumps of Alpine snow all over them.

'Arghh! Alf!' Livvie squealed and rolled off Zander.

'Alf! Stop!' Zander groaned inwardly. *I love you to bits, but right at this moment I think you're an annoying little sod!*

'Ooh, my feet are absolutely freezing; they feel like blocks of ice,' said Livvie. Zander noticed her face was burning red.

'Yeah, mine too. I think it's time for a warm shower followed by a hot chocolate.'

'Now you're talking.' She grinned at him, dispersing any awkwardness.

They made their way back towards the house, neither mentioning what had just happened between them, but Zander was struggling to get the almost kiss out of his mind. *Oh, Lord, what am I doing? I'm still supposed to be in a relationship with Mel and all I can think about is Livvie.*

When they reached the cottage she stopped. 'You know what?'

'What?'

'This garden is just crying out for a snow man.' She looked up at him, her eyebrows arched in a challenge.

'You know what? I think you're right, but are you sure you're not too cold?'

'After heaving myself up that bank so many times? Nope. Well, my fingers and my feet are freezing, and I'm soaking wet, but if we start straight away, we can get one built before the cold really kicks in.'

'You're on.' Her enthusiasm was infectious; she felt bloody good to be around.

In no time they had the body made, rolling a ball of snow around the ground until it got to a size they were both happy with. The head followed quickly after, and soon Livvie was hunting around for branches for arms.

'I'll go and grab a carrot for the nose,' said Zander.

'I don't suppose you've got any coal for the eyes?' she asked.

'No, but I'll go and see what else I can find.'

In a flash, he was back armed with a slightly wonky carrot and a couple of fir cones. 'Will these do?' he asked.

'Oh, perfect!'

17

LIVVIE

'I CAN'T GET my wellies off.' Livvie said through chattering teeth. 'My hands are so cold I can't feel them and my socks are so soggy, they're making it impossible.'

'Here, I'll help.' Zander took hold of the foot of the boot and tugged, but it wouldn't budge and just resulted in her hopping after him which made her giggle.

'It might be better if I sit on the floor.'

'I think you're right.' Zander tried again, but this time ended up dragging her across the utility room with Alf following, thinking it was a game. The pair ended up in fits of laughter, tears of mirth pouring down their cheeks.

'Oh, no! They're never going to come off. I'm going to be stuck with wellies on for the rest of the day. I'm going to be known as the "Welly Woman" of Dale View Cottage.'

Zander laughed. 'Don't worry, you won't be.' With a bit of gentle coaxing, he managed to wiggle one boot off and then the other. 'There, see.'

'Oh, that's better,' she said, pulling off her drenched socks and displaying feet that were bright red with cold. 'Where shall I put these?' She dangled her socks at him.

'Just hang them up there for now.' He nodded towards the wooden airer.

'Okay.' She did as she was bid.

'Then why don't you go and get yourself warmed up in the shower or bath? I'll do hot chocolates after.'

'You've no idea how good that sounds. Mind you, two showers in one day, I've never been so clean.' She headed through the door. 'I won't be long.'

'Enjoy,' he called after her. 'There's no rush, just get yourself defrosted.'

Livvie made her way to the bathroom, fingers and toes tingling as the circulation slowly started to return.

She set the shower away then peeled off her wet clothes. 'Urghh!' She was drenched right down to her knickers and her skin felt goose-bumpy and cold. Soon, steam was swirling around the room as she piled her damp hair messily on top of her head then stepped under the spray of deliciously hot water. 'Oh, bliss.' She basked in its soothing warmth, letting the jets pummel the muscles in her back which were aching after tearing about on the moors.

Her mind started wandering over the events of the morning, one thought pushing its way to the forefront. *We nearly kissed – again.* Her conscience was getting to work. *And Zander's got a girlfriend – hasn't he?* She frowned, biting her lip. He'd told her that Mel had flitted off to London with other people, but he hadn't actually said they'd split up, so she guessed that they were still technically together. 'Oh, why does everything have to be so bloody complicated?' She grabbed the shower gel and squirted a hefty blob into her hand, the scent of winter berries rising in the steam. *And what would I have felt like afterwards if we had actually kissed? Guilty, that's what; it would make me no better than Donny. Ughh! Don't think about that loser! Oh, but to feel Zander's lips against mine would be ... sublime. I just know it would be the best kiss I've ever had.* Her heart started racing at the thought, setting her body off tingling for reasons other than the cold. There was nothing she wanted more at this moment than to feel his lips on hers, with the promise of something delicious to follow.

~

'THAT WAS QUICK.' Zander looked up from reading a local magazine at the kitchen table. Livvie was wearing her pre-sledging outfit of woollen tunic dress and stripy tights, her wet clothes bundled in her arms.

'It's the promise of a hot chocolate.' She grinned at him.

'Ah, I see.' He smiled back. 'Well, I can make you one now, or we can have one together after I've had a quick shower? It's up to you.'

'I don't mind waiting,' she said. He'd taken his wet clothes off and was just wearing a navy blue waffle dressing gown. Livvie tried not to look at the dusting of dark hair that was visible in the "v" at his chest, or at his muscular calf muscles that were on display, but it was difficult when her eyes felt like they were being drawn to him. 'I'll just go and put these on the airer with my socks.' She held up her soggy clothes and tried to push the idea of what it would feel like to slip her hands inside his dressing gown and smooth them over his skin right out of her mind.

'Right, and I'll go and throw myself in the shower.' He closed the magazine and stood up. 'Won't be long.'

'Okay.' It took all of her strength not to ask if he wanted her to join him. *You barely know him and he's got a girlfriend, you floozy!*

ZANDER WAS true to his word, and before long the pair were sipping hot chocolates at the kitchen table.

'Mmm, this is seriously good,' said Livvie. *And you smell seriously delicious, with your citrusy sandalwood cologne.* She tried to ignore the urge to press herself to him and nuzzle his neck.

'We aim to please.' Zander grinned, making her heart flip.

'Though, if you don't mind me saying, a handful of marshmallows would make it absolutely perfect.'

'Ah, point taken, that's what Steff would say, too.' He blew on his drink. 'I wonder if the village shop in Lytell Stangdale stocks them? I could always pop down and have a look. Speaking of which, I wondered if you fancied having a trip down there this evening? Maybe grab a bite to eat at the pub there – which is excellent, by the way – and with it being a Saturday night, I reckon most of the locals will be there; it'll give you the chance to put faces to the names I've been talking about.'

Livvie's face lit up. 'Ooh, that sounds great, but will the roads be okay to drive?' She was happy to see their almost kiss wasn't causing any awkwardness between them.

Zander nodded. 'While you were in the shower I heard the plough go by so I nipped out and checked the roads. They're not too bad, actually. I chucked a bit of grit about from the bin at the end of the lane which should've got to work nicely by now. And I'm happy to drive; my four wheel drive should manage it no problem – unless we get more snow, which isn't forecast until late tomorrow morning. I'll dig out what snow's around it, so we should be able to get out easy enough. Though, if you're absolutely sick of the sight of me and would prefer a night on your own, I'll completely understand.'

'Oh, don't think that! I've had great fun today and I'm definitely not sick of the sight of you.' *That's the very last thing I feel; I love spending time with you.* Butterflies started swirling in her stomach and she couldn't help but smile at the thought of an evening out with him. She ignored the little niggle at the back of her mind that whispered, "Mel".

'That's great.' He beamed at her. 'How about we have a bite of lunch in say, half an hour, then I don't know how you feel about board games? There are loads here if you fancy playing one?'

'Only if you promise me you have Cluedo; I used to love that game and it's ages since I played it.'

'I have Cluedo; it used to be a favourite of mine, too. Colonel Mustard, in the library with the candlestick.' The smile he gave her made Livvie's stomach turn somersaults.

18

LIVVIE

LIVVIE COULDN'T REMEMBER when she'd enjoyed an afternoon more. They'd played a couple of games of Cluedo, then moved on to Scrabble and finished off with a quick round of Snakes and Ladders.

They'd spent the remainder of the time until they were due to leave for the pub chatting about their respective childhoods. To Livvie, Zander's sounded idyllic, with his close relationship with Steff and Toby and his supportive, caring parents. His words had conjured up happy days filled with laughter and sunshine – with a generous smattering of Labradors. She'd felt embarrassed about her own less than loving background and had skimmed over how her father had left them when she was just six years old. At the time, it had been a huge shock and Livvie had been devastated, but looking back now, she could see that it had been inevitable. Ten years of putting up with her mother's sniping and bitterness was too much to expect of any man. Indeed, Livvie wondered that he'd stood it as long as he had. He'd remarried shortly after the divorce had come through, but sadly had only enjoyed a few years of happiness with his new wife before a massive heart attack took him at the age of forty-two. Livvie had secretly wondered if her mother's incessant nagging had brought about his early demise; something she could barely forgive her for.

Livvie bore a strong physical resemblance to her father, with her rich, auburn hair and hazel eyes. She'd also inherited his easy-going temperament and sense of fun, which had only served to irritate her mother and had become something Livvie had felt obliged to apologise for over the years. She'd confided in Bryony just how this had hurt her and felt a sense of relief when her friend had advised her not to take it personally; that they were the ones with the problem, not Livvie.

'It's not you she's angry with, chick, it's the fact that you remind her that someone chose to walk away from her; that someone chose another woman over her. It's like a slap in the face and I think it's the ultimate rejection she finds so difficult to accept, which is why she's projecting her bitterness on to you rather than accepting any responsibility for it, which isn't fair.'

'I'd never thought about it like that, Bry. She's just always criticised my appearance and I've always thought I must be ugly; I never thought to link it to Dad and how I must've reminded her of him – or rather, the memory of him leaving her.'

'You're anything but ugly, Liv!' Bry looked horrified at the thought. 'Don't ever think that; you always look gorgeous and you're always oblivious to how many heads you turn when we're out.'

'Don't be daft.' Livvie felt her cheeks burning.

'Seriously, you do, and it's about time you started to believe it.'

Livvie had thought about Bry's words many times since

that day – particularly so the explanation of her mother's actions. They'd offered a small glimmer of hope that her mother didn't dislike her as much as she'd always thought.

'HOW SMARTLY DO I need to dress for the pub?' asked Livvie. 'Is it a posh place?' She'd remembered the well-to-do feel of the village of Lytell Stangdale as she'd driven through it the previous evening, with its cluster of pretty thatched cottages and their dusting of snow.

'You look great as you are.' Zander ran an appraising eye over her. 'It's a quaint country pub, tastefully decorated, very welcoming and not at all stuffy. Does that help?'

'It does, thanks, but I still think I'll get changed; I haven't had the chance to go out like this for ages, so I'd like to make a bit of an effort. And I could do with running a brush through this wild mane.' She ran her fingers through her hair. 'What time do you think we should head out?'

'Is seven-ish okay?'

'Perfect; I'll be two ticks.' She pushed herself up from her comfy spot on the sofa and headed to her bedroom. For some reason, she felt she wanted to make an effort and she knew that reason had a name: Zander.

She rifled through the wardrobe and pulled out the knee-length shirt-dress she'd made just last week. It was in a rich emerald coloured needlecord with fine pin-tucks on the bodice; she teamed it with raspberry-red leggings. She selected a chunky necklace she'd found in a charity shop and a chunky bangle in contrasting colours. Her hair, she'd decided to leave loose for a change.

19

ZANDER

'OH, wow! I mean, er, you look nice.' *You look absolutely stunning!* Zander was aware that his mouth had fallen open, but he'd temporarily lost the ability to close it. Livvie's hair was cascading down her back and over her shoulders in thick, glossy waves and she'd added a slick of raspberry coloured gloss to her lips that only served to make them look even more desirable. With a struggle, he pushed down the urge to kiss her.

'Thank you,' she said, her cheeks flushing; she clearly wasn't used to taking compliments.

'Erm, so, are you ready?'

'Yep, I just need to put my boots on and grab my coat.'

'Okay.'

'Is Alf joining us?' she asked.

'I think Alf might be better off with a quiet night in.'

'Really? Isn't the pub a dog friendly place?'

'It is, but he can be a bit of a wanderer when it comes to food venues and on several occasions I've caught him doing his best commando crawl on his belly in the direction of the kitchen.'

'Ah.' She thought for a moment. 'But couldn't you keep him on the lead and fasten it to something?'

He looked at Alf who was flat out asleep in front of the stove. 'I suppose so. What do you think, Alfie boy; fancy a trip to the pub?'

Alf's ears twitched at the mention of his name and he jumped up, looking at Zander as if to say, "What was that, Dad?" Zander's heart squeezed for his loyal pet.

'Alright then, you can come; and you've got Livvie to thank for talking me into it. But, any behaviour of the greedy pig variety and you'll be whisked back up here before you can say "where's the kitchen". Got that, young man?'

Alf trotted over to him, his tail wagging so hard his whole body shook.

'Ahh, he's just so lovable, look at him.' Livvie laughed.

'He certainly knows how to charm the ladies.' Zander ruffled Alf's ears as they headed towards the kitchen.

Outside the temperature had plummeted. Frost sparkled on the crisp, frozen snow, illuminated by a pale yellow moon that shone down from a deep midnight sky surrounded by millions of glittering stars.

Livvie gazed heavenwards. 'Oh, look at that, I don't think I've ever seen such a clear night sky.'

Zander followed her eyes. 'Yeah, there's no light pollution out here, so you get to see the milky way in all its glory.' That she appreciated the same things he did sent a wave of warmth through him.

'It's so beautiful. I've never seen so many stars, there must be billions up there.'

'Well, at least the fact that it's clear means there'll be no snow while we're out, which is a good thing. It's still bloody freezing, though.' The cold was nipping at his nose and ears, and he pulled down his beanie hat as he made his way down the path. He opened the gate and Alf shot through, charging over to the sledging field. Zander whistled for him. 'Alf! We're done with sledging for today, fella, it's pub time now.' Alf bounded back, enthusiasm written all over his face.

The roads were icy in parts, with snow piled high at the sides where the plough had pushed it back. The drifting on the most exposed parts of the moor was worse than Zander had expected, but then again, the wind had been wild last night, he thought. The car skidded a couple of times and he noticed Livvie gripping onto her seat. 'Don't worry, we'll be fine,' he said, but he heard her breathe a sigh of relief when the sign for Lytell Stangdale peered out from the snow.

'Oh, it's so pretty here,' said Livvie taking in the quaint cottages with stunning wreaths fixed to their doors and Christmas trees twinkling in their windows, some houses had Christmas trees in their gardens, too. The overall effect was added to by the Victorian-style street lighting which illuminated the village in a soft glow, adding to the feeling of times-gone-by.

'Yes, chocolate-box pretty,' said Zander, driving slowly through the main street. He was surprised at the number of people milling around the village on such a chilly night; in odd clothing, too.

'Blimey, this place looks like it's stuck in an eighties time warp,' said Livvie as a man sporting an impressive mullet and a fluffy jumper in neon stripes hurried across the road. 'And she must be absolutely freezing.' They watched as a scantily dressed woman chased after him, unsteady in her heels thanks to the snow and ice.

Wearing a puzzled expression, Zander parked up opposite the pub, just near the village green where a huge

Christmas tree bedecked with hundreds of warm white lights stood proud. He noted more residents walking by dressed in clothes reminiscent of the eighties; he was sure when he'd visited previously, most of the men were dressed in simple jeans and shirts or T-shirts.

'Wow, time really has stood still here, hasn't it?' Livvie gazed after them, making Zander laugh.

'It certainly seems to have tonight, though I can't say I noticed it on my previous visits.'

They climbed out of the car to hear music pulsating from the village hall. Zander was tickled by Livvie's expression as she watched a man, who could have stepped straight out of the eighties, scurry along with a woman sporting a power suit with enormous shoulder pads and outrageously back-combed hair. Livvie looked at him askance. 'I've no idea,' he said laughing as he clipped the lead to Alf's collar before letting him out.

'I've never been anywhere like this,' said Livvie. 'It's like watching a repeat of those documentaries you see on the telly from years ago, where there's a spotlight on local communities in rural areas; they even seemed behind the times when they were originally aired.'

Zander laughed again. 'I know what you mean; but I promise you, it isn't usually like this.'

'It sounds like there's a party going on,' said Livvie as they made their way over to the Sunne. 'Do you think they're wearing their best clothes because of that?'

'I've no idea, but I agree, it does sound like there's some kind of party happening.'

Though the road was clear, there was still plenty of snow around the village, clinging to the skeletons of trees, settled on the hedges and at the roadside and pavements. Luckily, the path to the pub had been cleared and gritted, making it safe to walk on.

Zander opened the heavy oak door of the Sunne and was immediately enveloped by a surge of warmth, the mouth-watering smell of food mingling with undertones of woodsmoke from the open fire and the burble of amiable chatter. As he stood aside to let Livvie through, he felt the wave of happiness the familiarity of the place brought to him. 'Ladies first.' He looked down and smiled at her, feeling his heart squeeze.

'Oh, wow, what a yummy smell,' she said, stepping inside. 'No wonder it's torture for Alf here. I don't blame him for trying to sneak into the kitchen; I feel like doing the same myself.'

Zander chuckled. 'Bea the landlady is an amazing cook; her curries are to die for.' He closed the door on the frosty night.

'Now you're talking; I do love a good curry.'

'Yep, me too.'

'I hope there's one on the menu; I've got a real taste for one now,' she said, following Zander into the bar.

'I think it's a regular feature, so you should be in luck.'

Inside was brimming with more people dressed in what looked like eighties garb.

'Wowzers,' said Livvie.

'Wowzers indeed,' said Zander.

'And look at that tree,' she said.

Just to the right of the door, sat a perfectly asymmetrical Christmas tree, the glow of its warm white lights adding to the ambience of the room. Tastefully decorated in shades of silvery white and green, topped off with an angel in a shimmering gown and wings of pure white feathers, it could have been lifted straight from the pages of a glossy magazine.

'It's gorgeous,' she said.

Zander turned and smiled at her. 'It is.' He couldn't help but draw a comparison to Mel, who would, without doubt, have criticised it as being too small.

'Now then, Zander,' said a familiar voice. He turned to see Lycra Len – looking virtually unrecognisable out of his usual Lycra gear, the few straggly strands of hair he possessed now covered by a wiry looking cock-eyed mullet. Zander realised he was the chap they'd seen rushing to the pub earlier.

'Oh, hi, Len. I nearly didn't recogn—' Before he had chance to finish his sentence, Len was dragged off by the woman in the power suit towards someone she was clearly excited to see.

'Sorry, Zander; I'll catch you later,' Len called as he disappeared into a group of people.

'Okay.' Zander smiled and turned to Livvie. 'That was Lycra Len, so called because he's always out on his bike, whatever the weather, and he's always in Lycra.'

'Ah, except for tonight.'

'Yes, I'm not quite sure what's happened there and I have no idea who the woman is but there was a rumour he was getting back with his ex-wife.'

'Oh, right.'

They were halfway to the bar when a man with long, floppy black fringe and slick of lip gloss stopped in front of them.

'Ey up, Zander, mate, it's bloody good to see you!' Zander found himself being pulled into a bear hug by the man who proceeded to pat him on the back vigorously. Behind him, Zander spotted a man with a shock of gravity-defying orange hair, and ear-to-ear smile.

'And it's good to see you, too, Alf.' The stranger with the

floppy fringe bent down to fuss the Labrador whose tail wagging suggested the pair had been previously acquainted.

He must have clocked Zander's bemused expression. He threw his head back and laughed. 'It's me, Jimby Fairfax, and this here is Robbie, you know, the chap who did the plans for our cottage– though you might remember him better as Mr July from our charity calendar.'

'Now then, Zander.' Robbie nodded to him, his smile getting wider.

The penny dropped. 'Jimby, Robbie, I would never have guessed it was you two!' Zander chuckled. 'It's good to see you both.' He patted Jimby on the shoulder. 'And this is Livvie; Livvie, this is Jimby and Robbie; two of Lytell Stang-dale locals I've been telling you about.'

'Hiya, please tell me there's some sort of fancy dress party going on and you don't normally dress like this?'

'What do you mean?' asked Jimby, feigning a hurt expression. 'What's wrong with how we're dressed?'

Livvie's face dropped. 'Oh, er, I'm sorry, I didn't—'

'Take no notice; he's teasing.' Zander gave her a nudge. 'You'll soon get the measure of Jimby; he's the local mischief maker.'

'Tell me about it,' said a heavily pregnant woman whose attire and back-combed dark-aubergine hair suggested the eighties.

Jimby threw his arm around her and kissed her on the cheek. 'Ah, here's the woman I left home for; the gorgeous Mrs Fairfax. Vi, come and meet Zander's young lady Livvie; Livvie, this is my missus Violet and this,' he pointed to her bump, 'is Pippin, who's due to join us in a couple of months.'

'Hi,' said Vi. 'I should probably point out that Jimby's nicknamed the baby Pippin because I've had the biggest craving for apples while I've been pregnant; we're not really going to call it that.' She rolled her eyes affectionately.

'Oh, right,' said Livvie. 'It's a really cute nickname. And, I should probably point out that Zander and me aren't actually an item, there was a bit of a mix up and I'm just staying at the cottage with him.'

'Really? I'd never have guessed; you look kind of good together.' Jimby flashed a cheeky grin at Zander and waggled his eyebrows. 'Well, it's still good to meet you, Livvie.' He turned back to Zander. 'I had no idea you'd be coming here tonight or I would've warned you.'

'Warned me about what?' asked Zander.

'We're having a Christmas party in the village hall.' Jimby's eyes twinkled. 'To raise money for some new equipment for the school.'

'And Jimby thought it would be a great idea if it had an eighties theme,' said Vi. 'Hence the outfits; you know what he's like.'

'Well, at least everyone's fully clothed for this fundraiser,' said Zander. He noticed Livvie's eyes widen, and he laughed. He leaned into her and said, 'I'll explain later.'

'Good point,' said Vi. 'It would be a bit chilly to expect the men to get their bits out on a night like this.'

'Oh, right.' Livvie's eyes grew even wider.

'It's nowhere near as bad as it sounds,' said Zander.

'Thank goodness! But it's a relief to hear that you all don't normally dress like this,' said Livvie.

'Yeah, poor old Livvie here thought she'd stepped straight into an eighties time warp.'

'Well, most of us don't dress like this but I can't say the same for Maneater Matheson over there.' Vi nodded in the direction of a woman who was sixty if she was a day and doing a thorough job of invading the space of a man who would have looked at home in a New Romantic band. She was wearing a skimpy outfit made of what looked like a handful of chamois leathers sewn together that barely covered her modesty, while her over-processed yellow-blonde hair had been backcombed to within an inch of its life. 'I'm not sure who she's supposed to be.'

'Hmm' said Livvie. 'I bet she's freezing.'

'I'd watch that one this evening, Zander. I don't know what she's been drinking, but she's even more full-on than usual,' said Robbie.

'Thanks for the warning,' said Zander. 'Come to think of it, I can remember what she was like when we were having our photos taken for the calendar.' He turned towards Livvie. 'That's linked to why we were naked, but she was absolutely bloody terrifying; had her hands everywhere.'

'Ughh!' Jimby shuddered. 'Don't' remind me; I'm still traumatised by it.'

'Drama queen,' said Violet. 'Anyway, I thought you were supposed to be getting the drinks in.'

'I'm on my way and you're both welcome to come over and join us; we're at our usual table and can make room for a couple more.'

'Yes, come and meet the rest of the gang,' Violet said to Livvie.

'I'd love to.' Livvie looked up at Zander and smiled, making his heart beat faster and sending a wave of heat surging through his veins.

'Great.' Jimby beamed, rubbing his hands together. 'What can I get you to drink?'

'Well, I'm driving, so it's just a shandy for me, thanks,' said Zander.

'Oh, what a relief I won't be the only one sober tonight,' said Vi.

'Erm, I'm not sure what to have,' said Livvie.

'My sister Kitty loves the Prosecco here,' said Jimby. 'Her and Rob's wife Rosie are drinking it, so we've got a bottle of it over at our table; I can get you a glass if you fancy some of that? Or Molly's drinking Pinot Grigio which, judging by the way she's necking it, is pretty good.'

'Just as well she can't hear you saying that, Jimbo.' Robbie chuckled.

'Ooh, I love Prosecco; I think I'll have some of that, if you're sure it's okay?'

'It's absolutely fine. Come on, Robster, let's get the drinks in before everyone starts complaining they're dying of thirst.'

'Do you need a hand?' asked Zander.

'No, we're fine; you just go and get yourself parked with Livvie,' said Jimby.

'Zander, it's good to see you,' said another familiar voice. Zander turned to see a man wearing a large smile and a bright blond wig. 'It's me, Freddie from the village shop.'

'Oh, Freddie, I wouldn't have recognised you.'

Freddie laughed. 'I'm pleased you said that; I'm not so sure this wig's me, nor this boxy jacket, but me and Lucy have come as an eighties pop duo so we had to look the part, apparently.'

Lucy, wearing an equally bright wig, peered round him and waved. 'Hi there. We didn't know you'd be at the cottage this weekend.'

'Neither did I,' said Zander

'Oh?'

'It's a long story.' From the corner of his eye he noticed Vi arch her eyebrows and flick her eyes in Livvie's direction.

'Ah, okay.' Lucy gave her a knowing look.

'How long are you here for?' asked Freddie.

'I'm not sure exactly.' The question made Zander feel awkward since he and Livvie hadn't really discussed it. 'Anyway, can I introduce you to Livvie.'

'Hi, Livvie,' they chorused.

'This is Lucy and Freddie; they have the village shop here,' said Vi.

'Hi, there. I love that you've all made such an effort to get dressed up.'

'Thank you, though I'm not exactly comfortable in this dress; it's a bit on the short side, that's why I'm hiding behind Freddie.' She stepped aside to reveal an eye-wateringly short skirt that barely skimmed her knickers.

'Ooh,' said Livvie. 'At least you've got the legs to flaunt it.'

'I'm not so sure about that.' Lucy did her best to pull the hem down.

'That's not going to do it much good, Luce,' said Freddie. He laughed when she pulled a face at him. 'We'd better get back to Lucy's sister and her husband, but it's been nice to meet you, Livvie. Have a lovely night and hopefully we'll see you both around.'

As they followed Vi to the table Zander stole a glance at Livvie's pretty features; her eyes were shining and she looked happy and relaxed. He could imagine her fitting in really well round here...

20

LIVVIE

Vi LED the way across to where the friends were sitting round a table laughing and chatting. Livvie glanced around her, taking in the effortlessly stylish décor of the pub; its soft furnishings in rich, heavy tweeds, hand-forged wall lights and thick oak tables spoke of the countryside and comfort. And the overall effect was enhanced by the thick uneven walls, low-beamed ceilings and a welcoming atmosphere she'd never felt in a pub before.

'Here we are.' Vi stopped at a cosy corner by the old inglenook fireplace, where a roaring fire danced in a huge dog grate. 'Look who we found on their way to the bar and managed to talk them into joining us.'

They were greeted by a sea of friendly faces and a chorus of cheery hellos as well as much fussing of Alf, which put Livvie instantly at ease. 'Oh, wow!' she said as she spotted yet more people in eighties fancy dress.

'Now then, Zander,' said a man with a peroxide wig and a studded leather jacket. 'Good to see you; let me go and grab you a seat.' Zander watched as he disappeared into the crowd.

'Shuffle your bums up, you two; make some room,' said Vi to two women, who happily obliged. 'Right, you can park yourself there, Livvie, and here's Ollie with a chair for Zander. Just stick it on this side of the table opposite Livvie, Oll.'

Once Livvie and Zander were seated, Vi started on the introductions. 'Right then, you all know Zander, but everyone, this is Livvie; she's staying with him at Dale View Cottage – but they're not an item, apparently.' Vi cocked her eyebrow at her last comment which didn't go unnoticed by Livvie, who could feel her cheeks beginning to colour. She could also sense Zander looking at her and daren't look up to meet his gaze.

'So, Livvie, let me introduce you to Molly and Kitty – they're cousins, and Kitts is Jimby's little sister. The lady with the blonde curly wig over there is Rosie – she's married to Robbie with the orange wig and who you met with Jimby – and she also has the local beauty rooms which are absolutely awesome and I'd honestly recommend if you've got time while you're here.'

The three women said their hellos, exuding a warmth which touched Livvie's heart. Bryony would absolutely love it here, she thought.

Vi continued. 'And moving on to the blokes, the one with all the eyeliner over there is Camm.'

Camm nodded. 'Livvie and I have already met when I was out ploughing last night.' He gave her a friendly smile.

'Camm! I would never have recognised you! And thanks again for coming to my rescue last night; I think I'd still be stuck in a snowdrift somewhere if you hadn't.'

Camm chuckled. 'You're welcome. And can I just say, I don't make a habit of going out like this. But, anyway, it's good to see you got settled in okay.'

'I did, thanks. Last night seems like a lifetime ago now.'

'It does, I agree. At least we've had no more snow, though more is forecast for tomorrow.'

'And last, but not least, is Ollie, sporting the blond spike and leather jacket, otherwise known as an eighties rock legend for tonight's purposes – he's Kitty's husband,' said Vi. 'And with perfect timing, here's Jimby with the drinks.'

Once Alf had said hello and had a good sniff and tail wag at everyone, he went over to where the pub's resident rescue dogs Nomad and Scruff were curled up in front of the fire and flopped down with them. He was greeted by wagging tails and friendly sniffing.

'Ahh, that's so sweet,' said Livvie.

'They're good friends,' said Zander

'Bless him, it's lovely how he's just fitted in; it must be a special place.'

'It is.' She felt the warmth of Zander's gaze on her but resisted the urge the look up at him, conscious of other watchful eyes on them.

Conversation flowed freely and Livvie couldn't remember a time when she'd felt so welcome anywhere. Her face was aching with laughing so much – especially at Jimby and hearing about his escapades.

'I must say, I love your dress, Livvie,' said Kitty.

'Oh, thank you. It's nothing fancy; just something I rustled up on the sewing machine.'

'You made that yourself?' asked Molly.

'Yes.' Livvie nodded.

'Wow!' Molly turned to look at her cousin wearing an expression Livvie couldn't quite read. She was accustomed to her mum and her sister criticising her clothes – Donny, too – so her heart automatically steeled itself in preparation for others to do the same.

'It's a lovely cut and those pin-tucks are beautifully done,' said Vi, taking interest. 'If you don't mind me asking, where did you get your pattern from?'

'Erm, I do my own,' said Livvie. Happiness began to fill her heart; unless she was way off the mark, these ladies seemed genuine and not in any way mocking. A little glimmer of self-confidence gave her the push she needed to continue. 'I start by doing a rough scribble in my sketch book, then make a pattern out of tracing paper – or any paper I can get my hands on at the time actually; I've even been known to use newspaper if I'm desperate.' She took a sip of her Prosecco, which was slipping down rather well. 'I source my fabric from, well, anywhere really. The fabric for this dress came from a charity shop. I made my coat, too. It started life as a couple of blankets.' She pointed to the rasp-berry-red boiled wool coat that was folded up on the seat beside her.

'Double wow,' said Vi. Her eyes widened at Kitty.

Livvie sensed that unspoken messages were passing between the two women, though she didn't have a clue what they could be.

'Do you make a lot of your own things or is that your line of work?' asked Kitty.

'I make pretty much all of my own things, but it's got nothing to do with my job, that's selling wedding dresses – though the alterations are my responsibility. I studied art at college, with the hope of going on to do a degree in fashion design but it never happened.' Livvie didn't want to remember how her mother had sneered at her suggestion of going to university, or how she'd declared it a waste of time and money, refusing to offer any financial support. She shook that thought away as she saw Kitty and Vi exchange more loaded looks.

'Why?' she asked.

'Because you might just be heaven sent,' said Molly. She laughed at Livvie's baffled expression.

'I reckon Zander thinks that too, judging by the way he's looking at her, don't you, mate?' said Jimby, earning himself a nudge in the ribs from Violet. 'Ouch; I was only saying.'

'Well, don't,' said Vi. 'We were having a private conversation. Ignore him, Livvie.'

'Yep, shut your cakehole, Jimbo,' said Molly. She prodded him under the table with her foot.

'Ouch again, I'm only pointing out the obvious aren't I, Oll?' Jimby rubbed his leg where Molly's boot had made contact.

Ollie shook his head and laughed. 'Don't drag me into it, mate.'

Livvie did all she could to avoid making eye contact with Zander, hoping he couldn't sense her embarrassment. 'What do you mean – about the thing that Molly said?'

'Kitty and I have a business called Romantique, designing and making vintage-style underwear and burlesque costumes, but we've been getting more and more orders for wedding dresses, especially since we made Kitty's and mine,' said Vi. 'And we're struggling to keep up with demand.'

'It's because they were absolutely stunning,' said Rosie. 'And you should've seen the bridesmaid dresses.'

'They're being inundated with orders,' said Molly.

'Yeah, you'll be next Moll,' said Jimby. The cheeky glint had returned to his eyes.

'Bugger off, Fairfax!' Molly gave him a sturdier kick under the table which elicited a yelp from him. Livvie noticed Molly's cheeks burning red, while Camm remained quiet, rolling his eyes good-naturedly.

'Serves you right, Jimby.' Violet gave him a warning look.

'Romantique, what a gorgeous name for your business,' said Livvie; it was conjuring all sorts of wonderful images in her mind.

'The problem is, Vi's baby is due in February and I only work part-time owing to my family commitments – between us Ollie and me have four kids, and the youngest, Lottie, isn't at school yet,' said Kitty. 'Our eldest, Noushka, helps out when she can, but she commutes to university in York and we don't want to interfere with her studies.'

'Oh, right.' Livvie's mind was half wondering at the large age-gap between Kitty and Ollie's children and half wondering where this conversation was going.

'What they're trying to say, Livvie, is do you want a job at Romantique?' Molly gave her a wide grin.

'Oh, wow! I wasn't expecting that!' Livvie's heart skipped with excitement; was Molly joking? She looked across at Zander who was smiling broadly at her. What the women had just described was Livvie's dream job; she'd always wanted to design and make wedding dresses and had a sketch book full of ideas. But Lytell Stangdale was miles away from home ...

The conversation was brought to an end by a slender, well-groomed lady arriving at their table. 'Hello, darlings, how are we all?'

There was a chorus of hellos followed by Jimby saying, 'Bea, can I introduce you to the latest member of our gang? Bea, meet Livvie, she's staying with Zander at Dale View Cottage though they're not an item – allegedly.' His eyes twinkled mischievously. 'Livvie meet Bea – the landlady of the Sunne and creator of the most amazing food ever.'

'Hello there, it's lovely to meet you, my dear. And hi there, Zander, it's good to see you back here again so soon.'

'It's good to be back, Bea,' he said.

'Will you be joining us for the buffet fund-raiser – it's all part and parcel of the eighties evening and the latest event for raising village funds, though I expect you've already been filled in on that?'

'Yes, you must join us,' said Vi.

'Oh, you've got to,' said Kitty.

'Of course they are,' said Molly

'I just assumed you would be,' said Jimby.

'Do we need tickets?' asked Zander.

'Strictly speaking, yes, but we can make an exception for you two,' said Ollie.

'Wouldn't be the same without you,' said Robbie.

'Hear, hear,' said Rosie.

Zander laughed. 'What do you think, Liv?'

'Woah, it's "Liv" now is it?' Jimby waggled his eyebrows and received another dig in the ribs from, Vi. 'Bloody hell, missus, have you been sharpening your elbows?'

Vi gave him a warning glare, while Livvie wondered if it was possible for her cheeks to burn any brighter. 'I'd love to – if it's okay with you?'

'It's great with me.' He turned to Jimby and Ollie. 'But I insist on paying the price of the tickets.'

Livvie went to speak. 'But I want to pa—'

'My treat, no arguments.'

Livvie couldn't remember when she'd last felt so happy. What a friendly group of people; Bryony would like it here too, she thought. If only they were serious about her working for Romantique; and if only it were closer to Rickelthorpe. As for the comments about Zander, she supposed they were to be expected given their unusual circumstances; anyone would be forgiven for thinking they were an item. Wouldn't they?

It wasn't long before the men slipped into a conversation about cars, tractors and the most suitable tyres for snow. Molly looked at Livvie and feigned a yawn. 'I honestly think that's all they can talk about. Anyway, what's the story with you and the hot-to-trot-doc?'

'Moll, you can't go asking questions like that!' said Kitty. She turned to Livvie. 'Please excuse my cousin.'

'Honestly, what's she like?' Vi shook her head. 'Anyway, what is the story; we're all dying to know?'

'Oh, well, erm...' Livvie had resigned herself to having a permanently scarlet face that evening.

'Yes...?' Molly winked at her. 'There's no need to be shy with us, we share everything, don't we lasses?'

'Well, maybe not *everything*,' said Kitty. 'But most things...'

Livvie cleared her throat and launched into how she'd ended up staying at Dale View Cottage; ever-so-slightly aware that the Prosecco had loosened her tongue a little.

'Oh, you poor thing, going through all that just before Christmas.' Kitty rubbed Livvie's arm sympathetically.

'That Donny sounds like a right bastard,' said Molly, taking a drink of her wine. 'I'd have ripped his balls off.'

Livvie's eyes widened.

'She would, as well,' said Vi.

'Anyway, that's all very well, but don't you think fate's trying to tell the pair of you something here? I'm a great believer in fate, by the way,' said Molly.

'She is,' said Rosie. 'Molly and Camm are a classic example of it bringing people together who are meant to be, well, together.'

'Oh ... right.' Thoughts were stampeding through Livvie's mind. Could fate be the reason she and Zander had been thrown together at the cottage? There were certainly a few things that would suggest so.

'Look at it this way,' said Vi, 'don't you think it's odd that the pair of you were having trouble with your partners and ended up on the holiday cottage website at *exactly* the same time?'

'Well...' Livvie stole a glance at Zander. He was looking heart-stoppingly handsome with his strong jaw, punctuated by the dimple in his chin, his bright blue eyes that seemed extra dazzling tonight, and his mouth that permanently turned up at the corners and made you just want to kiss it. Oh, and don't get her onto those broad shoulders. 'I suppose it's understandable that Zander should have been looking at it; it's his cottage after all. And as for me, it was the first website that came up in the search, so maybe there could be something in it. But there's one major thing that kind of scuppers your theory; Zander is still with his girlfriend. Unlike Donny and me, they haven't split up.'

'Yet,' said Molly.

'Well, from the way he's been looking at you, I'd say it's only a matter of time.' Vi peered at her over the rim of her glass of apple juice.

Kitty scrunched up her nose. 'I'm afraid I have to agree.'

'Me, too,' said Rosie.

Just as Livvie's mind began to process what her new friends had been saying, Bea declared the buffet open and everyone joined the queue for food. She felt a hand squeeze the top of her arm and turned to see Zander looking down at her, smiling. 'You okay? he asked. 'You seem to be enjoying yourself, chatting with the girls.'

Her heart flipped as she looked up into those blue eyes she'd just been thinking about. 'I'm having a great time, thanks. They're lovely, so welcoming, I feel like I've known them for ages.'

'I thought you'd fit in well.'

His hand was still on her arm, triggering a flurry of butterflies in her stomach. An image of him folding his arms around her and pulling her close flashed through her mind. Could the girls be right about them, she wondered? Did fate really exist? She suddenly remembered Mel. There was no way she was going to even think about having a relationship – or dalliance even – with a man who already had a girl-friend; that would make her as bad as Donny and there was no way she wanted to be put in the same category as that loser.

'Hello, my dear, are you enjoying yourself?' Livvie's thoughts were interrupted by the plummy tones of a tall, skinny man wearing a frilly white blouse and a tea towel around his neck. His glasses were perched perilously on the end of his aquiline nose. 'I'm Jonty, by the way, landlord of the Sunne.'

'Oh, I'm pleased to meet you.' She beamed at him. 'I'm having a lovely time, thank you. I'm Livvie.'

'Pleased to meet you, Livvie.'

'Livvie's staying with me up at cottage,' said Zander. 'She's a friend.'

Livvie's heart plummeted at Zander firmly placing her in the "friend" category.

'Ah, right, I see.' Jonty looked from one to the other; he clearly didn't see at all.

'Great outfit, by the way. And apologies for us not dress-ing-up but our trip was a spur of the moment thing and so we had no idea about the eighties evening,' said Zander.

'Thank you, old chap, and no worries, you're here and that's the main thing. Wait till you see Bea in her outfit. As soon as she's done in the kitchen she'll be stepping into a rather glamorous costume; it's really quite something.'

Zander laughed. 'We'll keep our eyes peeled for her, won't we?'

Livvie nodded and did her best to make her smile reach her eyes. Despite her misgivings about Zander being in a relationship, it didn't ease the agony of being officially friend-zoned by him.

21

ZANDER

BEA'S FOOD was as delicious as Zander remembered, offering new twists on traditional buffet classics as well as throwing in a few unexpected bitesize delicacies.

Once they were all back at the table and tucking into their plates of food, Alf showed a sudden interest, leaving his cosy spot by the fire and heading over to the friends, his nose sniffing the air.

'These korma parcels won't do your insides any good, young man. And don't forget, I know you've already had your tea, so I think you can get back to your buddies who are far better trained than you are. Go on, scoot!' Zander pointed to where Nomad and Scruff were keeping a close eye on proceedings by the fire. 'Go on, go!' He pointed and Alf, reluctantly, followed the direction of his dad's finger, turning occasionally to make sure he hadn't changed his mind and was happy to share his meal with him.

Zander gave him a stern look and Alf continued on his way, before flumping on the floor and resting his head on Nomad's back.

'Oh, that face,' said Jimby.

'I know, it kills me to talk to him in that tone, but where food's concerned, I'm afraid it's necessary or he'd be up here helping himself.'

'I used to have a Labrador like that; Humphrey was the hungriest dog ever,' said Kitty.

'Make that greediest, Kitts,' Ollie said with a laugh.

'Hmm, I suppose you have a point, but he was gorgeous and had so much personality.' Kitty smiled fondly.

'He did, and the windiest backside from here to next week,' said Molly, making everyone laugh.

'Ahh, Alf is so special, I could take him home with me,' said Livvie.

Zander glanced across at her and something deep inside him stirred, fanning the flames that were burning ever brighter in the pit of his stomach; she was glowing, her eyes were sparkling and her full, plump lips were just calling out for him to kiss her. This was more than just some basic attraction, it was something far deeper, far more primal and the more he spent time with her, the stronger it was becoming. It was killing him not to do anything about it, and there had been a couple of near misses, but his conscience kept telling him he was still in a relationship with Mel – albeit dysfunctional and without depth on either side.

There was one thing Zander was sure of; he'd never felt this way with Clara and he certainly didn't feel this way with Mel.

'Is everyone ready for a bop?' asked Jimby. 'Or does anyone fancy another drink here?' The food had been cleared away and numbers were thinning as people headed to the village hall.

Zander still found it disconcerting to see his friend in fancy dress. 'A bop sounds good, but I've got Alf and I'm not so sure he'd agree, especially with the volume of the music. Though, if you want to go, Livvie, I don't mind waiting here for you.'

'Much as I'd love a boogie, I'm happy to stay here with you and Alf.' She smiled at him.

'Well, I'm ready to make some eighties shapes on the dance floor,' said Molly. 'I think you blokes have exhausted the topic of Landies, tractors, farm machinery, sheep, cows and other such boring bollocks; it's time we dragged you away from it.'

'Ah, we can always rely on good old Moll not to mince her words.' Camm smiled and downed the dregs of his pint.

'Sometimes it's necessary where you lot are concerned.'

Jimby scratched his head. 'You're very welcome to drop Alf off at our house, he gets on alright with our spaniels Jarvis and Jerry.'

'Or he's welcome to keep Ethel and Mabel company; Eth's secretly got the hots for him,' said Kitty. 'And Mabes is happy as long as she's having a cuddle; she's pretty calm for a working cocker.'

'Actually, Noushka's babysitting there so that might be the better option,' said Vi. 'There's just the dogs at our place, and they'll get over-excited when they see their buddy Alf, which has the potential to be the perfect recipe for mischief. They're like the canine version of Jimby. No offence.'

'None taken,' said the man in question feigning a hurt expression.

'It's true though, Jimbo.' Molly nudged him affectionately.

Zander thought for a moment; he knew just how easily Alf was led astray and he didn't want to risk him behaving badly in someone else's house. 'In that case, if you don't mind, Kitty, Ollie, then I'd love to take you up on your offer, thanks.'

'That's absolutely fine.' Ollie pulled on his coat. 'We might as well head over there now, get him settled in. Our two hounds are going to be over the moon when they see him.'

'Okay,' said Zander. He turned to Livvie. 'Won't be long.'

'THAT WAS PAINLESS,' said Zander. He and Ollie returned to the pub on a breath of crisp, fresh air. 'Alf settled straight away.'

'Yep, after Ethel's raptures calmed down, the pair snuggled up in front of the fire like an old married couple, with little Mabel squidged in the middle.' Ollie laughed. 'But, by heck, it's freezing out there; I know it's not far to the village hall, but you want wrapping up.'

'Right, come on you lot, there's no time to waste.' Jimby jumped up, rubbing his hands together. 'My feet are itching to dance.'

'Oh, Lord, help us,' said Vi, earning a giggle from the others.

As they were preparing to leave, a tall man with a gravity defying spiky black wig stopped, took Zander's hand and gave it an enthusiastic shake. 'Zander, bonny lad, it's good to see you.' The booming tones of Wearside Geordie gave the speaker's identity away.

'Gerald, it's good to see you, too; you're looking well.' Zander took in the slimline physic of the octogenarian who'd had a heart attack the previous summer.

'Aye, my missus is keeping me on the straight and narrow with me food, aren't you, Mary, pet?'

'Aye, I am that, Gerry.'

Zander struggled not to laugh at Mary who was sporting a jacket with a lethal pair of shoulder-pads.

'Flaming Nora, she could take off with those,' Molly said under her breath, making Vi snort.

'Mind where you're pointing them things, Mary, you'll have someone's eye out,' Jimby said, chuckling.

'Aye, they're what you could call generous, Big M,' said Camm.

'Well, you'd better watch out the pair of you, hadn't you?' Mary gave a gap-toothed grin.

'And who's this bonny lass here, then?' Gerald asked, eyeing Livvie up and down. He reached into the pocket of his skin-tight leopard-print leggings and pulled out a pair of false teeth, popping them into his mouth with a rattle.

Molly leaned in to Livvie. 'And there was me thinking he was pleased to see me.'

Livvie did her best to suppress a giggle.

'Ah, you can always tell when he spots a bonny lass; the teeth go straight in.' Mary put her hands on her generous hips and rolled her eyes.

It was Livvie's turn to snort and Zander pressed his lips together, trying not to snigger. 'This is Livvie,' he said. 'She's staying with me up at the cottage; or rather, I'm staying with her.'

'Don't ask; it's complicated.' Livvie released her giggle. 'Pleased to meet you.'

'Likewise, pet. I hope you have a lovely stay. Mind, once you've been here for a couple of days, you won't want to leave. Isn't that right, Gerry?'

'Aye, it is that, my angel of loveliness. Mary and me originally came here for a week in a holiday cottage, and that was it; we knew we had to live here, didn't we, pet?' He moved his ill-fitting false teeth around his mouth with his tongue, making them rattle.

'Aye, we did, and mark my words, you'll be just the same. In fact we're taking bets on how long it is before Zander moves here full time – only joking, pet-lamb.' She patted him sturdily on the arm.

Zander laughed, but he was beginning to understand what the couple meant; every time he visited Lytell Stangdale, the harder he found it to leave. Would Livvie feel the same way, he wondered?

OUTSIDE, the temperature had dipped dramatically and a thick frost had crept over everything in its path. Zander could see that Livvie was a little unsteady on her feet after her glasses of Prosecco. 'You can link my arm if you like, the trod looks a bit icy.'

'I think I will, or I'll end up going in a heap on my bottom – which I know is well-padded but I still don't fancy falling over and embarrassing myself.'

'What do you mean, your bottom's well-padded?' Zander frowned.

'Well, my family and Donny are always telling me I'm chunky and that I have a big bum.'

Zander could feel his anger slowly rising. 'There's absolutely nothing wrong with your bottom, it's perfect.' The words were out before he had a chance to stop them.

'Oh.' He was aware of Livvie looking up at him. 'No one's ever said that to me before. In fact no one's ever said any part of me's perfect before.'

He glanced down at her. Oh, Lord, those eyes, that full mouth, that beautiful face. He swallowed and pushed down the urge to kiss her. 'You shouldn't listen to Donny or your family; they're just trying to put you down and push their insecurities onto you. It's wrong.'

'Come on you love-birds.' Jimby was waiting at the door of the village hall to explain to Harry Cornforth why Zander and Livvie didn't have tickets.

'Yep, we'd better catch up,' said Zander. He thanked Jimby silently for sending him an excuse not to have to dig himself out of a great big hole of embarrassment.

Inside, the vast room was heaving with people; disco lights strobed around the space which smelt of warm bodies and floor wax. A lively eighties dance song was blasting out of the speakers and the friends wasted no time in hitting the dance floor and falling about with laughter.

Zander couldn't remember the last time he'd had so much fun or laughed so hard. Livvie had thrown herself wholeheartedly into the evening, sheer joy etched all over her face. He couldn't imagine Mel letting her hair down in such a way, not caring if she looked silly. In fact, he knew that Mel would have looked down her nose at an event like this, held in a little village hall. "Parochial" she would have sneeringly called it. Unlike Livvie; lovely Livvie, who was the polar opposite and was clearly loving it.

For the first time in a long time, Zander felt he could be himself, and it was utterly refreshing.

After dancing to a medley of eighties hits, Vi declared she needed a sit down and the friends were keen to keep her company.

They'd gathered some chairs together while the men went to the hatch in the wall to the kitchen which served as the bar.

Zander stood behind Livvie, sipping on a shandy, watching as she chatted away with her new friends, her face happy and animated, scrunching her nose when she giggled in the way that made his heart race.

'You sure you two aren't an item?' Jimby asked, raising his voice to be heard above the music.

Zander shook his head. 'I'm afraid not.'

'Ah, so you'd like to be?' Ollie joined them.

Zander looked at the two men and nodded. 'It's crazy, I've only known Livvie since yesterday but I feel like I've known her forever.' He rubbed his hand over his chin, hoping he didn't sound foolish. 'I don't know what it is, but she's triggered something deep in here, that I've never felt before.' He pressed his hand to his chest.

'I know that feeling.' Ollie glanced across at Kitty.

'Aye, me too, mate,' said Jimby. 'Sounds like you've met "the one".'

'Shit, I wish it was as easy as that,' said Zander. 'I'm still in a relationship – at least, I think I am – and Livvie's fresh out of one. I live in Leeds and she lives in Rickelthorpe which is a good eighty miles away from me, we've both got jobs to think about...'

'So where is she then, this girlfriend of yours? We've never met her and you've visited here loads of times; how come she never comes with you?' asked Jimby.

Zander released a noisy sigh; he knew what Jimby was driving at. 'It's a long story, but she's gone to London to party with friends for Christmas – won't be back until the New Year. And she's never come here because she says she doesn't like the countryside.'

The expression on their faces said it all, though they were too polite to articulate their thoughts.

'I know what you're thinking; when I say it out loud, I

realise it doesn't sound good.' Zander gave a half laugh. 'I'm suddenly beginning to realise how incompatible we are.'

'Unlike you and Livvie,' said Ollie.

Before Zander had chance to reply the next song boomed from the speakers. Livvie turned from her conversation with the girls. 'Ooh, I love this song,' she said, grabbing his hand and dragging him onto the dance floor.

'Woah!' He hurriedly passed his glass to Jimby, laughing at the happiness that shone from her as she threw herself into dancing. He leant towards her. 'Aren't you a little young to remember these songs? You don't even look like you're in your thirties yet.'

'I'm not, I'm twenty-eight, but my lovely dad used to play them all the time.'

'Oh, right.' His mind did a quick calculation: that would make her eight years younger than him; he found himself wondering if the age gap would put her off, but reasoned that she'd probably guessed how old he was when he told her about Alf and Clara.

THE FRIENDS DANCED the night away and before they knew it, the tempo changed, signalling the winding up of the party.

Zander felt momentarily awkward – slow songs meant smooching, didn't they? They could always sit them out if she didn't fancy it, he supposed, wondering what Livvie would prefer to do – secretly hoping she'd be up for it. He didn't have to wait long to find out.

Livvie suddenly threw her arms around him, resting her face on his chest, and, oh boy, did it feel good. He glanced around, catching a wink from Jimby and huge smiles from the rest of their friends. He wrapped his arms around her and held her close, inhaling her sweet perfume. It felt wonderful; she was the perfect fit. *Oh. My. Days. This is heaven.*

'Lovely.' Livvie's voice was so breathless, he barely heard what she said.

'Sorry?'

'You're lovely,' she said. 'This is lovely.'

His heart picked up pace; this was more than lovely, he thought. This was bloody amazing.

He swallowed. 'And I think you're lovely, too.'

She lifted her head from his chest, looking into his eyes. 'You do?'

'I do.' He nodded, pushing her thick curls back from her face. 'And I want more than anything in the world to kiss you right now.' His heart was pumping fast, the flames of lust burning brighter.

'And I want you to kiss me, too.'

Zander swept all thoughts of Mel from his mind and bent to kiss Livvie, anticipation of how her lips would feel against his building rapidly. But before they had chance to make contact, they suddenly found themselves covered in beer, their moment cruelly snatched away.

Livvie squealed and jumped back.

'What the—' Zander wiped the droplets of beer from his face.

'Oh, flaming heck, I'm so sorry,' said Jimby, looking sheepish. 'I was goosed by someone with a bloody shocking case of wandering hands.' He looked over his shoulder and shot Maneater Matheson an accusatory glare. 'When I tried to get out of reach, I tripped over Lycra Len's feet and ended up knocking his beer out of his hands; unfortunately it came sailing this way.'

'It certainly did,' said Rosie

'Are you sure you weren't too busy rubber-necking at Zander and Livvie?' Vi arched a quizzical eyebrow at her husband.

'I'm positive; well, maybe a bit, but that bloody woman's hands were getting into places that haven't seen daylight for years.'

'Oh, spare us please, Jimbo,' said Molly, pulling a face.

'I'm only explaining why I tripped. I should be getting sympathy, not a bollocking; I feel violated. If a bloke did that to a woman, there'd be hell on.'

'You do have a point actually,' said Molly. 'Do you want me to go and have a word with the old tart? I'd love to wipe that lecherous leer right off her wizened old fizzog.'

'No, just leave it; it's not worth spoiling a good night,' he said.

'What happened?' asked Lycra Len. 'One minute I had my pint in my hand, the next it was flying over here.'

'I'm afraid your drink was Jimbied,' said Vi.

'I was goosed.' Jimby nodded towards Maneater.

'You poor sod, rather you than me,' said Len.

'Here you go.' Kitty handed Livvie and Zander paper hand towels from the kitchen.

'Thanks, I didn't get too much on me; I think it was Zander who bore the brunt,' said Livvie, dabbing at her sleeve.

'It's not too bad, actually.' Zander pressed the paper towel against his shirt that was nowhere near as damp as his spirits after having his chance of kissing Livvie scuppered once more. He was seriously beginning to wonder if it wasn't meant to be; they'd been thwarted every time.

'I think that's our cue to leave,' said Robbie as the music came to an end and the lights came on.

'That was so much fun. I'm so pleased you suggested coming here tonight, Zander,' said Livvie, her eyes shining.

'Yeah, it was great.' He loved how she said his name. 'We timed our visit well.'

'By the way, I'm not sure how long you're both staying for, but you're welcome to join us for some of the other things that are going on,' said Kitty, pulling on her coat. 'Ollie and me are having our lot round for Christmas dinner. It's all very relaxed and you're more than welcome to join us; I've lost track of how many we're having so two more won't make a difference, will it, Oll?'

'Not at all, it'd be nice to see you there.' Ollie pushed his hands into his gloves. 'Listen, I'll just nip home and get Alf for you, save you both having to traipse over.'

'You sure?' asked Zander.

'Yep, I'll be back in a flash,' he said, heading across the bar.

'And Camm and me are having a bit of a family gathering on Monday afternoon; it'd be great if you could come to that,' said Molly. 'Ooh, bloody hell, Vi, look at the state of your ankles, they've puffed up like a right couple of puddings, you need to rest them, chick.'

'Yeah, they're feeling a bit splodgy,' said Vi.

'Oh, Vi, they look uncomfortable, you need to sit with your feet up tomorrow, get that brother of mine running around after you.'

'That brother of yours does that anyway.' Jimby winked at Kitty.

'Ah but, just a little more wouldn't hurt.' Vi gave him a theatrical wink in return.

'Too true.' Molly joined in the winking.

'And there's Christmas carols round the tree on the

green on Christmas Eve, which is always lovely,' said Rosie. 'Practically the whole village goes to that.'

'Wow, you do loads of stuff here,' said Livvie.

Zander noticed she looked a little unsteady on her feet.

'Tell me about it.' Molly wrapped her scarf around her neck. 'It's hard to keep up with things sometimes. You ready, Camm?'

'Sure am.' He made his way over to them. 'Time to tackle Withrin Hill.'

'YOU OKAY?' Zander asked Livvie when everyone had headed off home. They were standing beneath the soft glow of a street lamp while she tried to button her coat, all fingers and thumbs.

'I'm fine, just a bit cold.' Her teeth were chattering and she'd started to shiver.

'Would you like a hand with that?'

She shook her head, still struggling. 'No thanks, I can manage.'

He wasn't convinced; the buttons were all skew-whiff. 'Right, well, you look absolutely nithered, come on, let's get you to the car; we'll have things warmed up in no time.'

'Okeydokey, but I think I might need to hang on to you, everything's started to go a bit swimmy and the floor's moving.' She grabbed onto his arm, squeezing it tightly.

He couldn't help giving an amused grin. 'That's fine.'

22

LIVVIE

Livvie was woken by the dull thud of a headache; the sort that threatened to grow as soon as you stood up. Tentatively, she opened her eyes; the room was shrouded in darkness thanks to the thick curtains and she could only guess at the time. She lay there for a while, closing her eyes again, shutting out any distractions as her thoughts tried to arrange themselves into some kind of coherent order despite the subtle pounding in her brain.

The feeling that she'd had a great time the night before bloomed inside her and she could feel a smile pull at her lips. She recalled the cosy pub with its huge open fire, and she could remember having delicious food there, the flavours still vivid in her mind. She could clearly remember meeting Kitty, Molly, Rosie and their partners and how incredibly friendly they all were. And memories of dancing and laughing in the village hall lurked around, but over and above that, everything else was a smidge hazy.

She sighed and snuggled further into the duvet, enjoying the comforting rustle of the feathers; she'd have to invest in one of these back home, it was so much toastier than her cheap acrylic one, and besides, she most certainly didn't want to sleep under the one Donny had soiled with his indiscretions.

As she lay there contemplating the previous evening, Livvie gradually became aware of sounds of life from downstairs. *Zander!* Her heart skipped a beat and an image of him looking at her intently, his eyes full of passion, pushed its way blatantly to the forefront of her mind. It triggered a vague memory that began swirling round her head, gradually picking up momentum. They'd nearly kissed! Again! *What? No way!* Her eyes shot open and her heart started to thump against her chest as she remembered how close they'd come to touching lips and how desperately she'd wanted it. Anyone would think it was becoming a habit.

She didn't know how she was going to face him this morning. They'd found themselves in this situation before and they'd managed to brush it off easily. But something was telling her this latest "almost" kiss was a little bit different; there'd been a bit more meaning to it. Well, if she was being completely honest with herself, it had a whole bloody lot more meaning to it and that thought made her cheeks burn – yet again.

'Oh, what the bloody hell am I doing?' she said, scrunching her eyes tight shut.

Livvie toyed with the idea of staying in bed all day, avoiding Zander, postponing the excruciating awkwardness she anticipated, but the sudden memory of him bringing her a cup of tea yesterday morning scuppered that idea. 'Oh, well, best get this over and done with,' she said, pushing herself up and swinging her legs round. A groan escaped her lips as her head objected to the sudden movement. 'Ow!' She rubbed her forehead, looking down at the sage green fabric dotted with cream hearts. 'At least I managed to get my pyjamas on.' She rummaged for her slippers with her feet and took a moment while they wriggled their way into them in; she couldn't bear to bend down and risk the feeling of her brain hammering on the inside of her skull. *Been there, done that, don't want to do it again.*

The smell of frying bacon hit her nostrils as she made her way downstairs; she was relieved to find it made her stomach rumble in an agreeable way. Padding across the floor, she followed the sound of the radio and Zander singing quietly to himself.

'Morning.' She stepped into the kitchen and Alf, who'd been watching Zander intently, hurried over to her, wagging his tail as if he hadn't seen her for weeks. 'Hello, Alfie.'

Zander, who was tending a host of fried breakfast goodies in a pan turned and greeted her with a wide smile; even in her hungover state, she could see he looked genuinely happy to see her. 'Hi there, Sleeping Beauty, and how are we this fine morning?'

Livvie crumpled her face and ran her fingers through her knotted curls. 'My head's felt better, if I'm honest.' She tried to bend down to stroke Alf but it only served to make her head feel like there was a wrecking ball doing its worst inside it.

'Ah, that would be the demon drink.' He laughed. 'Prosecco and plenty of it, I seem to recall.'

'Oh, don't remind me.' She clapped her hand to her forehead at the memory of it slipping down rather well the night before.

'Never again, I'm guessing?'

'Too right, never again.' She pulled out a chair and flopped down at the table.

'How does a coffee sound?'

'Perfect.'

'I'll have one ready in two ticks.' He set the machine away and it glugged and hissed into life, pushing the delicious aroma of freshly ground coffee into the air.

She took a surreptitious glance at him; he was still in his pyjamas, the long-sleeves of the navy blue T-shirt pushed up revealing strong forearms covered in dark hair. Livvie felt a sudden irresistible urge to run her fingers over them; her heart surged at the thought. *Calm your jets, woman!*

'Oh, that smells so good.' She took the coffee he handed to her. 'Thanks.'

'You're welcome.' He smiled. 'And how are you fixed for a bacon butty; or I can do you a full Yorkshire fry-up if you're up to it?'

The thought of that was surprisingly appealing.

'THAT WAS DELICIOUS,' said Livvie, savouring the flavours that lingered in her mouth as she set her knife and fork down on the now empty plate.

Zander laughed. 'Well, it certainly didn't hit the sides.'

'Best cure for a hangover, I find.' She laughed too, relieved that her headache was inching away.

'Another coffee?'

'I quite fancy a tea if that's okay? If I have too much coffee, I end up feeling like I'm climbing the walls.'

'Not sure that would do your hangover much good.' He smiled at her. 'Tea it is.' He went to fill the kettle and set it on the Aga.

'Oh, look at poor old Alf, he's doing a very good "I'm starving" impression.' Livvie's eyes were drawn to the Labrador who had been patiently watching them devouring their breakfast from his bed. Drool had started to drip from either side of his mouth.

'Don't worry about him, he knows a sausage has been set aside with his name on it, and the wait is killing him, isn't it, Alf?'

The pair chuckled as Alf's face seemed to take on even more pleading expression. 'It's a reward for his exemplary behaviour in the pub and at Kitty and Ollie's, where I'm told his manners were impeccable.' Zander looked at him fondly.

'He's just the most gorgeous boy,' said Livvie. 'I'm really going to miss him.'

Her comment hung awkwardly in the air between them.

Zander coughed. 'Erm, yep, I'd best start packing my things up this morning. There's been no more snow; I had a look outside earlier and the roads aren't too bad at the moment. But there's more's on its way, so the sooner I get off the better.'

'Oh.' Livvie felt her heart plummet to her slippers. She wished she could snatch her stupid comment back. She liked being here at Dale View Cottage with Zander and Alf, enjoyed spending time with them. In fact, she couldn't remember the last time she'd been so happy and the thought of them not being here with her felt like a huge, black raincloud putting the dampers on a bright, sunny day.

'Why don't I make a quick list and nip down to the village shop before it shuts for the day; get you some provisions in case the snow gets too bad and you end up stuck here for a couple of days?' He brought two mugs of tea across to the table and set them down.

'You don't have to do that.' She glanced up at him, trying to read his expression. If she wasn't mistaken, he looked how she was feeling – or was it simply a case of wishful thinking on her part?

'I know but I want to; I don't like the thought of you tackling icy roads in your little car that doesn't have winter tyres on, or you being snowed in and hungry. Indulge me, I'd only worry otherwise.'

'Okay.' Livvie felt sadness settle on her shoulders. 'So, if you went back to Leeds, would you be going back to an empty house?'

'I expect so.'

'And all of your family are in Carcassonne?'

'They are, well apart from my cousin Beth who's skiing in Chamonix with her boyfriend Liam.'

'So would that mean you'd be having Christmas day on your own?'

'Well, my colleague, Noah, has invited me to his house for Christmas dinner, but kind as it is, I have no intention of taking him up on it; I wouldn't want to invade his time with his young family.'

A couple of beats fell before Livvie spoke. 'You don't have to go … you and Alf, you're welcome to stay here with me.' She looked up at him and their eyes locked.

'Oh,' he asked, his eyes searching hers. 'Right … are you sure? I mean do you really think you can put up with Alf and me – and our blokey bad habits – until the New Year?'

She giggled, feeling suddenly shy. 'I'm sure I can; I mean, it's your house and I'd feel kind of bad if you left and anyway, what I'm trying to say is, I'd really like you both to stay.' She watched Zander as he thought this over, a muscle twitching in his cheek, desperately willing him to accept her offer.

'Well, in that case, we'd love to, wouldn't we, fella?' He leaned towards Alf and gave him the thumbs up. 'I reckon

Livvie's only said it cos of you; you've won her over with that irresistible charisma of yours.' Zander may have been joking, but his broad smile told her his happiness matched her own.

Alf trotted over, hopeful that his dad's words were an indication that the sausage with his name on was about to appear in his food bowl. He wasn't disappointed.

A smile spread across Livvie's face as her sadness lifted and floated away. The thought of spending more time with Zander had made her spirits soar in a way she hadn't expected.

'So what do you remember about last night? Zander asked, peering over the rim of his mug of tea.

'Oh, well ...' Livvie felt her cheeks flush. 'I can remember being relieved that there was an eighties themed party going on and that the locals weren't really stuck in a tragic time warp.'

Zander chuckled. 'It was funny to see you trying to make sense of it; your face was a picture.'

'I can imagine.' She giggled. 'And I remember meeting your group of friends and them being really friendly.'

'They're your group of friends now; they've really taken to you. You slotted in really well just like I knew you would.'

'I like that thought.' His words sent a warm glow through her. 'And I can remember us all dancing and having the best time. Oh, and Jimby's dancing; it was hilarious.' She couldn't help but laugh. 'Though, I can kind of remember him going flying and sending Lycra Len's drink all over us.'

She took a sip of her tea. *And I can remember how wonderful it felt to have your arms around me, how it felt to press my face to your broad, strong chest and hearing your heart beating. It felt perfect and I never wanted that moment to end.*

They exchanged a look for several long moments. Was he feeling the same way as she was? She wished she knew.

Zander broke the silence. 'Ah, yes, good old Jimby. He's the most accident prone bloke I've ever met. I'm surprised he hasn't ended up with some serious injuries before now.' He looked at his watch. 'Actually, I think I'll still nip down to the shop to get some bits and bobs to tide us over before it shuts for the day, but when I get back, remind me to tell you about the photo shoot last summer; I still have a good laugh whenever I think about it.'

'Ooh, I'm intrigued; I can't wait to hear about it.' She watched Zander down the dregs of his tea.' Would you like me to come with you?'

'Not unless you really want to. I'll take Alf with me, give him a quick run around on the track along the moor. I won't be long; the shop closes soon so I'm just going to throw my clothes on and have a shower when I get back. I'm glad I de-iced the car earlier though, the frost was thicker than I expected and it took a while.'

'I guess that doesn't give me enough time to sort this birds' nest of mine out.' She pointed to her hair which she was dreading taking a brush through.

Zander laughed, getting to his feet. 'It'll just be a fleeting visit, but if the roads are fine we can both pop down tomorrow; it's a great little shop that stocks pretty much everything you can think of, deli stuff too, with a tea shop on the side – I'm told Lucy's famous for her chocolate-dipped flapjacks.'

'I'll look forward to that, it sounds great and I absolutely adore chocolate-dipped flapjacks.'

∾

FROM THE KITCHEN WINDOW, Livvie watched Zander's car pull away and head off steadily down the lane. The view of the moors was still stunning, covered in its thick eiderdown of sparkling white. Overhead, the sky was crisp and blue, with no hint of the blizzards they'd been warned of. She watched a blackbird pulling the blood-red berries from a holly tree in the garden; she hadn't really given it much thought before now, but the stunning bright fruit weren't there just to look pretty, they were obviously a useful winter food reserve for wildlife. The blackbird was soon joined by a robin who hopped along the snow-topped dry-stone-wall, tilting its head quizzically before pecking at the branches. In the distance, Livvie could see the resident barn owl, gliding over the field they'd been sledging in only yesterday. It flew to an ancient oak tree, alighting on one of its thick, frost-covered branches where it swivelled its head around in search of food and other predators.

'This is such a beautiful place.' She'd never felt so content, or so comfortable anywhere before. She knew if she said it out loud it would sound crazy, but Livvie felt as if her heart belonged here.

As she was gazing at the view, Bryony popped into her mind and the promise Livvie had made to text her again yesterday. 'Oops.' The day had turned out to be busier than Livvie had expected and texting her friend had completely slipped her mind. She'd do it now, before she had chance to forget again.

Livvie was in her bedroom, hunting for her phone, when there was a knock at the door. 'That was quick, I'll bet Zander's forgotten his house key,' she said as she hurried downstairs.

She opened the door, the smile dropping instantly from her face as her blood ran cold.

23

ZANDER

ZANDER'S WAKING THOUGHT, before he'd even had chance to open his eyes, was that Livvie had told him he was lovely. He played the moment over and over again; it made his heart swell inexorably and pushed a warm glow through him, right to his fingertips and toes. As did the memory of holding her in his arms as they'd swayed to the music. This feeling he had with her was overwhelming and he didn't know how to articulate it other than it just felt "right", like they were meant to be together. As plain and simple as it sounded, that was it. He sensed a powerful connection with her and a certain glimmer in her eyes told him she could feel it too. That they'd only known each other for a couple of days seemed irrelevant.

He threw his arms above his head and smiled as he relived the previous evening. Livvie had slotted in perfectly with his friends from the village; he knew she would, she was easy to talk to and friendly, just like them. He loved how she'd enthusiastically thrown herself into the dancing, her face a picture of unbridled happiness. Mel popped up in his mind, hurling cold water over his happy mood, she would never contemplate doing anything like that.

Mel, he sighed. What to do about her? Whenever he thought about her, he could feel his mood slump. How on earth had they managed to carry on as long as they had, with their stumbling, unhealthy relationship, limping on, not seeming to make either party particularly happy, he wondered. *A habit, that's what we've become; and a bad one at that.* They hadn't started off that way; Mel had been independent and full of life and enthusiasm when they'd first met. He didn't know what had happened to change her – or them – but the dynamics had shifted so gradually, he'd barely noticed. He should really text her and see if she was okay. Though he hadn't heard anything from her – he hadn't expected to – she'd done this sort of thing before, eventually turning up out of the blue after things hadn't quite gone her way. He'd send her a quick message when he got up, just a "checking in" sort that wouldn't really warrant a response, which was just as well, because he knew she'd have no intention of replying to it.

AFTER BREAKFAST, Zander climbed into his four wheel drive and made his way steadily along the icy twists and turns of the lane, the demisters on full blast; he was glad he'd had the foresight to warm the car up for a few minutes before he'd set off. The toastiness of the cottage belied how bitterly cold it was outside. As he focused his eyes on the road ahead, he found his mind wandering onto Livvie as it was wont to do since he'd first set eyes on her. She'd looked cute when she first came into the kitchen, her hair all mussed up, her large hazel eyes still heavy with sleep. And he couldn't help but smile as he remembered how she'd tucked into her breakfast with such enthusiasm; she had a hearty appetite; unlike Mel who seemed to survive on lettuce leaves, strong black coffee and even stronger cigarettes. His heart rate surged as he recalled how Livvie had shyly said she'd like him and Alf to stay. He knew she felt it, too; that gesture all but told him.

This break was turning out to be something really rather unexpected, he thought as a burst of happiness bloomed inside him pushing a wide grin across his face.

Before long, Zander stopped at a quiet track and let Alf have a quick run around, laughing as the Labrador leapt gazelle-like at the snowballs he threw for him before rolling around in unadulterated happiness, kicking his legs everywhere. He was panting heavily and covered in snow when Zander bundled him back into the car. 'Have fun there did you, fella?' he asked. Alf replied by swiping his tongue across Zander's face. 'Ughh! Dog breath! What have I told you about that?' Alf wagged his tail and Zander couldn't help but laugh, ruffling the Labrador's head. 'What are we going to do with you, eh?'

More noticeable in daylight hours, the hedges and drystone walls were still piled high with frozen-hard snow that sparkled quietly in the pale winter sun. The winding roads were made narrower than usual, thanks to the snow that had been banked up at the sides by the plough. Zander was thankful that they were, at least, still driveable, but it was easy to see how such conditions could be treacherous when added together. He made his way steadily along the lanes, mindful of oncoming vehicles in the middle of the road as well as wildlife with a death wish that had a disconcerting habit of appearing in front of him as if out of nowhere.

As he took the turn onto the road to Lytell Stangdale he

spotted a white van heading towards them. The driver, seemingly without any awareness of rural road etiquette, barged straight past a pull-in place, forcing Zander's car to skid into the snow, narrowly missing a wall. Owing to the narrowness of the lane, white-van-man was forced to slow down a little, mouthing what Zander could only assume was a torrent of foul-mouthed abuse and shooting him a glare that made his blood run cold. In that instant, something spiked in his senses; adrenalin kicked in and began pulsing round his body as a memory of something sinister hovered at the back of his mind, albeit frustratingly out of reach. He'd seen that face before, he was sure of it; the unnerving evil glint in the eyes made the hairs on the back of his neck bristle.

Unable to shake the feeling of unease, Zander nosed his way into the village and parked up near the shop. 'Right, Alf, you be a good lad, I won't be long,' he said, winding his window down a couple of inches. He was just about to climb out of the car when the ear-splitting squawks of a cockerel spliced through the peace, the snow seemingly intensifying its shrillness. Zander turned to see Hugh Danks – known locally as Hugh Heifer – on his daily walk with his prize-winning heifer Daisy. He was battling with Jimby's Leghorn cockerel Reg who seemed to have taken exception to Hugh's wellies that were making a loud slapping sound as he walked.

'Get out of it, you feathery little plonker!' Hugh kicked out at the bird while Daisy bellowed woefully. 'Go on, bugger off before I neck you!'

Zander stifled a laugh, his unnerving encounter with the road-rage driver temporarily forgotten.

Just then, a cyclist shot by, attracting Reg's attention. The bird flapped his wings and shot after the bike leaving Hugh shaking his fist at him and hurling a mouthful of expletives. 'And don't bother coming back, you little bastard!'

'You alright, Hugh?' Zander was making his way across the road to the retired farmer.

'Aye, fair-to-middlin', Dr Gillespie, no thanks to that bloody wayward bird of Jimby's. Got a thing about me and Daisy, it has. Summat needs doing about it.'

'It does seem a bit bad-tempered.'

'Bugger wants putting in a bloody pie if you ask me.'

Zander chuckled. 'Have a good day, Hugh, and I'll see you later.'

'Right you are, doc.' Hugh made his way down the road chuntering and grumbling.

The door-bell jangled cheerily as Zander stepped into the shop. 'Morning, Zander.' Lucy smiled from behind the counter. 'Did you and Livvie enjoy last night?'

'We did, thanks, we had a great time; we'd just headed down for a drink and a bite to eat in the pub and weren't expecting anything like the eighties evening.' Zander grabbed a wicker basket and started filling it with provisions. He picked up a rare-breed joint of beef from the fridge. 'This looks good.'

'Ooh, it's delicious; it's from a farm yon side of Middleton-le-Moors, has a lovely, rich flavour,' she said.

Zander nodded, slipping it into the basket followed by some fresh looking winter vegetables, earth still clinging to them.

'Now then, Zander.' Freddie popped his head round the door from the back. 'What are the roads like up at Dale View?'

'Not too bad; icy, and there's quite a bit of snow on the sides where the plough's been and where it's drifted, but they're passable in a four-wheel-drive.' Zander slid a bottle of red wine in alongside the joint of beef.

'Aye, there's more on the way, too. You'd best make sure you've got plenty of bread and milk in, in case you get snowed in.'

'Good plan,' said Zander.

The door-bell jangled again, heralding the arrival of Little Mary, her usual huge shopping bag that was almost as big as her hung over her arm. 'Well, hello there, young Zander, this is a nice surprise.' Her petite face was wreathed in smiles.

'Hello, Little M, it's good to see you, and if I may say, you're looking very lovely today.' Zander towered over the tiny old lady who didn't even scrape five feet.

Little Mary gave a coy giggle and patted her neat rows of curls that were usually pure white but today bore a distinctly pink hue. 'Thank you, I had my hair done yesterday, specially for Christmas. My hairdresser said this colour's all the rage at the moment so I thought, why not and treated myself. I daren't wear a hat, though, in case it squashes it, so my ears are absolutely nithered.'

'Ah, you fashionistas, eh?' Lucy smiled fondly at the old lady. 'Well, it looks very fetching on you.'

'It does indeed,' said Zander.

'Thank you.' Little Mary blushed to the roots of her newly coiffed hair. 'And I hear you've got a lovely young lady on your arm, Dr Gillespie.'

'News certainly travels fast round here.' Zander's eyes flicked over to Lucy who shrugged her shoulders and gave him a "don't ask me" look. 'The young lady you're referring to is called Livvie, who is indeed lovely, but she's not mine; it's complicated.'

'Oh,' said Little Mary looking from Zander to Lucy and Freddie.

'Looked like she was your young lady last night when you were having a cheeky little smooch at the village hall.' Freddie grinned, mischief twinkling in his eyes. 'The pair of you looked very cosy.'

'And I'm afraid I have to agree,' said Lucy.

Zander could feel heat rising up his neck and spreading across his face; he was relieved when the bell jangled again, and in walked Molly's mum Annie, wrapped up well against the cold.

'Morning, by it's raw out there. Even though the sun's shining, that wind's picking up and making it bloomin' cold.' She shivered, her nose red from the chilly air. 'Oh, hello, Zander, lovie, I'd heard you were staying here, and with a lovely young lady friend by all accounts.' She fished her shopping list out of her pocket. 'Are you staying long or is this just a fleeting visit?'

Zander ignored Lucy and Freddie's sniggering. 'Hi, Annie. I'm here until the New Year. How's Jack, by the way?'

'He's doing well, thanks. Dr Beth made him an appointment with the new consultant at Middleton Hospital who prescribed some different tablets for him, and they've really helped manage his Parkinson's symptoms; he's a lot steadier on his feet. Cheered him up no end, it has.'

'It's good to know he's being well cared for.' Zander placed his basket on the counter, hoping he'd be able to pay for his goods and make his escape before there was any further interrogation about Livvie.

'Yes, they're marvellous at Middleton Hospital; we're so lucky to have it, and Dr Beth at the surgery, too, she's fantastic. I'm not so keen on her colleague though, that Dr Goodliffe. His bedside manner's a bit abrupt; makes everyone feel like they're a nuisance. I don't mind saying, I was quite pleased to hear he's leaving.'

'You and everyone else,' said Freddie. 'Poor old Madge Danks went to him with a bad stomach ache and he sent her away saying it was trapped wind, turned out she had a burst appendix and ended up being blue-lighted to hospital.'

'Yes, our Molly told me about that,' said Annie, shaking her head.

'It's shocking.' Little Mary tutted. 'I always ask for Dr Beth, even if I have to wait a while for an appointment.'

'Yes, we do too,' said Annie. 'Anyway,' she nudged Zander with her elbow, 'enough about that grouchy old misery guts Dr Goodliffe, tell us all about this young lady of yours; our Molly says she's absolutely lovely and that you're very well suited.'

'That's what I'd heard.' Little Mary chuckled. 'And it would be so good to see you settled with a nice young wife.'

'Steady on there, Little M,' said Zander. 'I hate to disappoint you all, but there's nothing to tell, other than she's not my young lady and we're just friends, that's all.'

Freddie arched his eyebrows.

'It's the truth, you can ask her yourself.' Zander couldn't help but laugh. 'Anyway, I'm off before you all get totally carried away with yourselves and have me married off without me realising.'

'Ah, me think the gentleman doth protest too much,' said Freddie. 'That's twenty eight pounds seventy five thanks, Zander.'

'There you go.' Zander passed him two notes, smiling. 'Put the change in the Air Ambulance tub. And I'll see you all later.'

'Bye,' three amused voices chorused.

Outside, Zander fussed Little Mary's miniature dachshund Pete who was wrapped in a snug fleece-lined jacket; he was waiting patiently, his lead fastened to a hook on the wall. 'Hello there, little fella. I bet you struggle in this deep snow with those short, stubby legs.'

'Oh, by the way,' the shop door was flung open and Freddie peered round it, 'there was a bloke in here about five, ten minutes before you arrived; he's not a local, bit shifty looking to be honest. Anyway, he was asking about your place, said he was a plumber or something and you were expecting him. I forgot to mention it with us all teasing you about Livvie. Sorry.'

'Oh, right, thanks, Fred, no problem.' Zander's gut twisted, instinct telling him something wasn't right. His mind scrambled over Freddie's words; for some reason, they seemed to be slotting together with a conversation he'd been having with Livvie the previous day. It was then that it hit him; he knew exactly where he'd seen those piercing evil eyes before. 'Oh, shit, Livvie!' With his heart pounding, he hurried to his car, throwing the shopping on the backseat. 'Bastard!' he said, as he put the car into gear and drove off out of the village.

24

LIVVIE

'DONNY!' A chill spiked up Livvie's spine.

'Hello, Livvie, been hiding from me, have you?' The cruel sneer that distorted his face made goose bumps spring up all over her skin.

She swallowed, her heart pounding; she'd seen that look before and it didn't bode well. 'Wha ... what are you doing here?'

'Aren't you going to invite me in? I'm freezing my bollocks off out here, the least you could do is give me an explanation.' His eyes narrowed, taking on a cold, shark-like appearance.

'I don't want to talk to you, Donny, I've got nothing to say to you.' She went to close the door but, quick as a flash, he thrust his foot in it, wedging it open.

'Well, I want to talk to you.' He pushed the door roughly, forcing her back.

'Donny, you have no right to be here. This isn't my house.'

He ignored her and looked around the hallway, peering into the living room. 'Well, isn't this cosy? Holiday cottage, eh? I wonder which lucky git owns it; no doubt someone who hasn't done a day's work in his life, just had everything handed to him on a platter, not having to work their guts out like the rest of us.'

Livvie's mind was racing, wondering how he'd found her, how he knew this was a holiday cottage. Bry must have told him; she'd have been worried when Livvie hadn't texted her. She cursed herself for her oversight.

'And I gather you've been shacking up with some doctor bloke, is that right?' He returned his gaze to her, his eyes boring right into hers.

She flinched and looked away. 'It's his cottage; there was a mix up and we both ended up here.'

'Really? And you expect me to believe that, do you?'

Livvie felt suddenly galvanised by a surge of courage. 'Donny, you seem to forget that it was me who found you shagging our next-door-neighbour in our house, on the sofa I'd spent a small fortune on; and I know it had been going on since the woman moved in. And I know she wasn't the first, for that matter.'

He sniggered at her. 'You've only got yourself to blame; just look at the state of you, no man in their right mind would touch a fat cow like you with a effing barge-pole. You've let yourself go, you have.'

Livvie bit back tears. 'And you've come all this way to tell me that, have you?'

'No woman makes a fool of me, you should know that, Livvie. Jumping straight into bed with another man when we aren't even finished has made me very, very angry.'

'As far as I'm concerned we were finished the moment I caught you having sex with that other woman. And there's no way I'd ever get back with you.' Her heart was hammering hard in her chest, her breathing ragged. She clenched her hands to disguise that they were shaking; she was scared but there was no way she was going to let him see that.

He lunged across at her and grabbed her by the hair. 'I decide when we're finished. Me! Not you! Got it?' He shook her roughly.

Livvie was too stunned to answer. He was hurting her and she was struggling hard not to cry.

'Got it?' he yelled, shaking her once more, making her wince.

'Let her go,' said a voice behind him.

Donny froze. 'What the fu—'

'I said, let her go.' Zander moved towards them, towering over Donny's diminutive five feet six inches, wearing an expression that said it wouldn't be wise to argue with him.

Donny released his grip on Livvie's hair and she stepped back from him. He jutted his chin defiantly at Zander.

'I thought it was you; I'd never forget eyes as cruel and full of hate as yours.' Zander circled him.

'I don't know what the hell you're talking about, mate, but I've never seen you before in my life.'

Livvie looked on, rubbing her scalp where the hair had been ripped out, her heart racing, as the look on Zander's face made her think he was ready to break Donny in two.

'Oh, but you have; seven years ago to be precise, in Scaggleby, down the bank by the line of trees. You had a young Labrador with you, remember?'

'I haven't a clue who you are or what your problems is, mate, but you're talking absolute bollocks.'

'I can tell by your evil little face that you know exactly what I'm talking about. You remember that young Labrador and you remember exactly what you did to him, don't you?'

Donny shuffled from one foot to the other, suddenly

unable to make eye contact with Zander, a shifty expression on his face. 'You've got the wrong bloke, I've never had a dog.'

Repulsion surged through Livvie, making her feel sick; she was familiar enough with Donny's body language to know that he was telling a bare-faced lie.

'I haven't got the wrong bloke; I'd never forget the evil look you had in your eyes that night. I haven't seen anything like it until today when I drove past you. It was you, you evil bastard.'

'Piss off! You can't go around accusing innocent people of stuff like that. It's all in your head.'

Livvie broke her silence. 'I believe every word that Zander has just said; I can tell just by looking at you that he's right and you're lying. You're a hideous man, Donny and you ought to be ashamed of yourself.'

'Shut your face, you stupid cow! You don't know what you're talking about, the dog was a bloody nuisa—' Donny's face fell when he realised he'd landed himself right in it.

Livvie could feel herself getting breathless with emotion as she struggled with coming face-to-face with the monster who'd hurt Alf. The urge to slap him hard and wipe that arrogant expression off his face was building but before she had chance to act upon it Zander grabbed the collar of the smaller man's coat, pushing his face into Donny's so their noses were almost touching. 'Don't ever, ever, talk to Livvie like that again. She's perfect. And don't ever, ever lay another finger on her again. She's a beautiful, kind-hearted woman and she's way too good for you. And as for the Labrador you abused so shockingly, you twat, he survived and is currently sitting in my car – well out of your way – and unless you want me to call the police and tell them everything I know, I'd disappear if I were you, and keep well away from Livvie and this house. Got it?'

Still defiant, Donny didn't answer.

'Got it?' Zander yelled, pushing him hard against the wall.

Donny nodded. 'Got it.' He was scared – a classic bully – Livvie had never seen him look like this before; he'd always had the upper-hand in their relationship.

Zander let him go. 'Now clear off out of my house you trespassing piece of shit.'

'Don't worry, I'm off.' He turned as he reached the door. 'And you're welcome to that fat cow.' He nodded towards Livvie. 'She's all yours.'

Zander strode towards him and Donny disappeared down the path, slipping over on his way to the gate.

Zander followed him out, making sure he got back into his van and drove off, before he let Alf out of the four wheel drive.

A few moments later, Livvie heard the thud of a car door shutting and Zander talking to Alf; from what she could hear the Labrador seemed reluctant to walk up the path. She assumed it was because of Donny's scent, resurrecting old memories and fears. 'Oh, the poor boy,' she said, opening the door.

Alf was standing at the gate, his ears and tail down, looking anxious. Zander stroked his head. 'Come on, Alfie, this is your home, don't let him win.' He reached into his pocket and pulled out a dog biscuit. 'Look, this treat is yours if you follow me up the path, come on. Good lad.' He clicked his tongue, encouraging Alf to follow him. He opened the door and stepped inside, his hand outstretched, still holding the biscuit. 'What a good boy,' he said as Alf followed him into the house.

Once the biscuit had been eaten, Alf started sniffing around the floor, his hackles up, a low growl emanating from him.

'It's alright, Alf; he can't hurt you again,' said Livvie.

'You're right, he's gone,' said Zander, closing the door behind him. 'And I'm pretty certain he won't be troubling here again.'

On hearing Zander's words, Livvie started to shake uncontrollably as the tears she'd been holding back now poured in hot rivulets down her cheeks.

'I'm sorry,' she said, sobbing. 'It's my fault he came here. What if he'd hurt Alf again?' Before she knew it, she was wrapped in Zander's arms and with a deep breath, she let herself melt into him.

'Hey, don't cry, it's not your fault.'

'It is, I should've texted Bry last night; I promised her I would but I forgot.'

'And you think it was her who told Donny where you were?'

'I think he must've worn her down; he can be quite forceful.'

'I'd noticed.'

'She'll have been worried about me. I was supposed to text her last night to let her know I was still okay.'

'So she was doubly sure I wasn't a mad axeman?'

'Yes.' She nodded and Zander laughed. 'Me being thoughtless and not texting her, ended up sending Donny here.'

'You weren't thoughtless, we all forget to text people from time to time. I'm terrible for it – as my sister could happily testify. I'm just glad he didn't have chance to hurt you, but he's gone now so it's all good.'

Livvie lifted her head. 'But what he did to Alf ... it's

unforgivable; he shouldn't be allowed to get away with it or be near another animal.'

Alf trotted over on hearing his name. He sat beside Livvie's feet and rested his paw on her leg, whimpering softly.

Zander smoothed his hand over Alf's head. 'Don't worry, he won't be. I know I sent him off in the belief that I wouldn't report him, but after what he did to this little fella, there's no way I can let him get away with it. Once Christmas is over with, I'm going to have a word with PC Snaith – he's the local bobby here – and tell him everything I know; see if there's a chance of prosecution.'

'Good, he deserves to be locked up and have the key thrown away.'

'He does, but I don't think we should waste another moment thinking about him today.' Zander gave her shoulders a squeeze, his blue eyes peering into hers. 'And would you like the good news first or the fantastic news?'

'Oh, I, er ...' she wiped her eyes with her fingers. 'I think I'll start with the good news.' A tiny glimmer of happiness sneaked in.

'Okay, the *good* news is that I managed to pick up some marshmallows at the village shop.'

'That is very good news.'

'And the fantastic news is that I picked up the last couple of slices of Lucy's chocolate-dipped flapjacks. So what do you say to a hot chocolate with all the trimmings and one of those little beauties?' He grinned, rubbing his hands together.

Livvie sniffed and gave a watery smile. He was such a kind-hearted man – so different from Donny. 'The fantastic news sounds delicious; I'm definitely up for a hot chocolate and some flapjack.'

'Good! And don't worry, Alf, I picked up a treat for you, too, in the shape of some rather tasty-looking meaty dog biscuits – they actually look so good, I'm almost tempted myself.'

Livvie laughed. 'Do you mind if I just go and call Bryony first; put her mind at ease. I was just about to do it when Donny knocked at the door. I need to warn her about him, too.'

'Yes, of course, go for it.'

LIVVIE

LIVVIE FELT as if every ounce of energy had been drained out of her as she sat on the edge of her bed waiting for Bryony to answer her phone. When she'd finally got round to switching her mobile on, a slew of missed calls and texts had pinged through from her. Even more from Donny, with the voicemail messages getting increasingly irate. Poor Bry if she's had to face him, thought Livvie.

'Livvie, oh my God, I'm so relieved to hear from you, are you alright? I've been worried sick, I didn't know what to do or what to think. Donny came round and I'm really sorry but—'

'Honestly, Bry, I'm fine, I'm the one who should apologise to you for not getting in touch yesterday when I'd promised I would; you must've been going out of your mind.'

'I so was! I didn't know what to think, what with you being stuck in the middle of nowhere with some strange bloke you've only known for two minutes. And then when Donny came round, he seemed really concerned so I told him where you were staying. I regretted it as soon as he'd gone, so started ringing you again and, oh bloody hell, Josh and me were just about to set off and find you. Josh has heard some things about Donny and what he's capable of—'

'It's okay, Bry.' Her friend was gabbling as she always did when she was feeling anxious. 'He's been here ... this morning.' Livvie felt her throat tighten as tears threatened again. She took a deep breath and swallowed them down.

'Oh, jeez, Liv, I'm so sorry. How was he? Please tell me he didn't hurt you.'

Livvie went on to explain what had happened, her voice wavering at times, but Bryony's soothing words of encouragement helped her plough on.

'Well, I hope that slimy little bastard gets everything that's coming to him. And I'll tell you something else, hun, we never liked him, Josh and me. We always thought there was something dodgy about him and we were always worried about you. He was punching above his weight big time when he started going out with you, and he knew it, that's why he had to belittle you and chip away at your confidence the whole time. There, I've said it.' Bry released a heavy breath down the phone.

'Wow.' Livvie laughed. 'I had no idea you thought that about him.'

'Afraid so. I couldn't tell you though; it wasn't what you'd have wanted to hear at the time. And I love you too much to risk losing my best friend in the whole world ever.' Bry laughed too. 'So I can say it now: what the effing hell were you thinking, Liv? You and twat face had absolutely nothing in common. He's a slimy little sponging scumbag who was just free-loading his way through life, while you're gorgeous, kind, funny, clever and super-talented as well as a load of other things that I just don't have time to list or we'll be here all day.'

'So you're on the fence about Donny, then?' Livvie giggled, feeling brighter; Bry always had the knack of making her see the funny side of things.

'Hah! The little bastard's right off my Christmas card list. I can't tell you how it used to pain me to have to write his name on the one I sent to you.'

'Really? You hid it well.'

'It was bloody hard, I can tell you.'

After the pair had finished laughing, Livvie said, 'Anyway, that's enough about me, how are things with you?'

'Well, I have some news of the exciting variety...'

26

ZANDER

ZANDER WATCHED Livvie disappear through the door and make her way across the living room. She'd lost the usual bounce to her step and her shoulders were slumped; she'd had the stuffing knocked out of her. He hoped speaking to her friend would lift her spirits, and prayed that Donny hadn't done anything stupid there.

Zander rubbed the back of his neck, easing a knot of tension in his shoulders as adrenalin still pumped its way round his body, keeping him on the alert after their encounter with Donny. The fear on Livvie's face as Donny had grabbed hold of her hair jumped into his mind followed by an image of those cold, evil eyes, making his body tense again. Usually, when he was feeling this way – after an argument with Mel or a particularly difficult day at work – he'd go for a run, which is exactly what his instincts were telling him to do now. But there was no way he'd leave Livvie on her own; it was going to take her a while to feel settled again. Alf, too, for that matter. Zander felt the need to stay close to them.

He looked down at his faithful Labrador whose expression and body language he couldn't quite read. 'You alright, young man?' Alf gave his usual reply of a tail wag and a whimper but Zander could tell he'd been affected by Donny's presence.

Just then, Livvie's laughter floated downstairs and he breathed a sigh of relief; it was good to hear her sounding happy again. Things were obviously okay there.

'Come on, I think you deserve another treat, fella.' Zander headed into the kitchen with Alf hot on his heels.

After the treats were dished out, Zander sat on the floor beside Alf and wrapped his arms around him, stroking his velvety head. 'You're a brave lad, you know that, don't you?' Alf cuddled in closer. 'And you're safe now, nothing will ever hurt you again, I'll make sure of that.' Zander's eyes stung with tears. As a rule, memories of that night were pushed firmly to the back of his mind, well out of reach; he was loath to revisit them. He'd managed to tell Livvie about Alf's story from the edges of the memory, but seeing Donny today had brought it all flooding back in vivid detail, bringing with it the pain that still felt surprisingly raw.

'He knows.' Livvie's voice startled the pair of them. 'He knows how much you love him and that you'll keep him safe. That's why he's the way he is now; happy and upbeat with that amazing zest for life. He wouldn't be like that with anybody else; that's all down to you.'

Zander wiped his eyes and got to his feet. 'I, er, I didn't hear you come downstairs.'

'Hardly surprising when you've got this lad practically stuffed in one of your ears.' She smiled, rubbing Alf under the chin. 'Erm, I seem to recall there were rumours of a killer hot chocolate complete with all the trimmings.'

27

LIVVIE

'OH, WOW, THIS IS SERIOUSLY YUMMY.' Livvie wiped whipped cream from her hot chocolate off her top lip.

'Wait till you try the flapjack,' said Zander, passing her a plate bearing a plump, chocolatey slice.

Livvie cut a corner and popped it into her mouth, the buttery, treacly flavours flooding her taste-buds. 'Mmm, wow. Just when I thought things couldn't get any better.' She cut herself another piece.

'Told you it was good.' Zander smiled as he sat in the chair opposite. 'So how did the chat with your friend go? Was she relieved to hear you weren't holed up with a mad axe-man?'

Livvie finished her mouthful and nodded. 'Mmhm. She was very relieved to hear that but, as I guessed, Donny had been round, putting on a very convincing act of the concerned boyfriend by all accounts; that's why she told him where I was.'

'Ah. I bet she regretted it straight away.'

'She did, though I can't blame her.'

'And had she heard from your family? Don't they know where you are?'

Livvie snorted. 'My family don't know where I am because they don't care where I am. Bry knows that. Which reminds me, I must call them to tell them I'm not going to be there, for Christmas dinner at least. I'll do it later though, I'm enjoying this flapjack and hot chocolate way too much to spoil it.'

'They'll be disappointed you're not joining them?'

'Are you kidding? The only thing that they'll be disappointed about is not having anyone to rip apart for being a failure and our Cheryl will have no one to look down her nose at and feel all superior.' Livvie picked a pink marshmallow off the top of her hot chocolate. 'Not everyone's family is as close and loving as yours.' She popped the marshmallow into her mouth, chewing slowly.

'I'm sorry to hear that's how your family make you feel.'

The look he gave her made her heart flip; he was so bloody gorgeous. *Oh, those eyes...*

'If it's any consolation, I'm really happy to be spending Christmas with you and I promise not to make fun of you or look down my nose.'

His words made her cheeks burn and her insides turn to mush. 'Thank you. I'm happy to be spending it with you, too – and that gorgeous boy.' She looked across at Alf who had flopped in his bed, keeping his eyes open on the off-chance a stray marshmallow should find its way over to him.

'Ah, don't worry, I'm not fooling myself, I know it's Alfie boy who you're really pleased to be spending Christmas with,' Zander joked.

'Well, he is very special.'

'He is.' Zander glanced fondly over at him.

And so are you, Livvie thought. She was struggling to

make eye contact with him; the way he was looking at her was having a serious effect on her heart rate and making her stomach do some pretty reckless somersaults.

Zander cleared his throat. 'So what's Bryony been up to?' He was obviously conscious of the sparks that were flying between them.

'She had some news actually. She didn't want to share it at first, but I wheedled it out of her.' Livvie was glad of the change of subject.

'Oh?'

'Yes, I think I told you her boyfriend had booked a special night out for them?'

Zander nodded. 'You did.'

'Well, because of what had happened with Donny, she didn't want to tell me, but I finally dragged it out of her that Josh had proposed and she accepted.'

'Congratulations to Bryony and Josh.'

'Yeah, they go really well together. There's more.' She took a quick sip of her hot chocolate. 'Mmm, this is so good. Anyway, Josh has been offered this amazing job in London; it's his dream job apparently, so he's accepted, which mean's Bry'll be handing her notice in at Blushing Brides when we get back in the New Year and she'll be moving down with him as soon as she can.'

Zander sat back in his chair and folded his arms. 'Which is bittersweet for you.'

Livvie nodded and stirred her drink, swirling the marshmallows into the cream, her heart suddenly feeling the impact of Bry's news. 'Yeah, it is. Bry's the best friend I've ever had, and she's the only thing that's kept me working for the dreaded Mrs Harris.'

~

'Look at the time! It's nearly one o'clock in the afternoon and I'm still in my pyjamas.' Livvie had drained her hot chocolate, right down to the squidgy melted square of Dairy Milk Zander had popped in the bottom.

'That's okay, you're on your holidays; and you've had a bit of a peculiar morning.'

'True, but I should really go and get dressed. I think I'll put off having a shower and have a soak in the bath later tonight, if that's okay?'

'That's fine with me.' Zander shrugged. He peered out of the window. 'The sky's still nice and clear, how do you fancy getting a breath of fresh air with Alf and me? I've brought his frisbee and he looks like he quite fancies a game.'

Livvie gave Alf an appraising look and giggled. 'He does, doesn't he? And I absolutely love frisbee. Count me in.' She jumped up and went to the sink to rinse out her mug.

'I'll do that, you go and get yourself ready, we don't want those snow clouds moving in and taking us by surprise.'

'You sure? I don't mind rinsing my own cup.'

'Positive.'

Livvie wasn't used to a male doing stuff around the house. If Donny had a cup of tea, he'd leave it wherever he'd finished it, even if he headed to the kitchen straight after; it wouldn't cross his mind to take the mug with him and put it in the sink, never mind clean it. That was woman's work as far as he was concerned. *Bloody chauvinist!* He was the last thing she wanted on her mind just now.

She hurried to her bedroom and quickly changed into warm clothes. Running a brush through her wild mane had been as painful as she'd expected, especially the patch where Donny had pulled the hairs out by the roots. Jesus, that could've been so much worse, she thought as a shiver ran through her.

28

ZANDER

ZANDER FELT his heart squeeze as Livvie walked into the kitchen. She was wearing skinny jeans and a burnt orange jumper that emphasised her stunning eyes and her lustrous auburn hair which framed her face in glossy waves. His mind shot back to the moment he first laid eyes on her; it sent a twitch to his crotch. *The Goddess!*

He cleared his throat and reined his wayward thoughts in. 'That was quick.'

'It's the promise of a game of frisbee.' Her broad smile lit up her pretty face and Zander felt himself smiling back.

'Right, let's go for it while we can.'

As soon as Zander reached for his coat, Alf was on his feet, dancing his way to the door, his claws clicking on the flagstones.

Livvie laughed. 'Someone's keen.'

'Just a bit. Looks like he's put his horrible memories of you-know-who to the back of his mind.'

'Best place for them, or the local dump.'

'If only.'

THE AIR OUTSIDE was crisp and fresh while up above the low winter sun shone down, bouncing off the gleaming white landscape, the bright blue sky showing no hint of the blizzards the weathermen had forecast. Livvie noted her little car was still wrapped in its blanket of snow; it wasn't going anywhere in a hurry.

She shielded her eyes with her hand and took in the panorama of Great Stangdale. 'It's so beautiful out here, it's exactly the sort of place where I wish I'd grown up.' Her breath came out in a plume of condensation. 'Can you imagine having all this space as your playground?'

'Yeah, it's pretty amazing.'

'Did you grow up round here? Is that why you bought Dale View?' she asked, as they made their way along the lane and further into the moors.

Zander threw the frisbee and Alf tore after it, kicking up snow as he went. 'No, I grew up in the suburbs of Leeds, but we always visited this way whenever we got the chance, and my parents would rent a holiday cottage several times a year when Steff, Toby and me were younger; until they discovered the south of France and fell in love with Carcassonne and its glorious sunshine, then we'd head there. It was Beth getting a job out here that rekindled my love of the area. She kept inviting me to stay with her and her boyfriend Liam, said she knew I used to love it; she wasn't wrong.'

Alf came charging back, the frisbee clenched between his teeth. He dropped it at Zander's feet. Zander picked it up and he threw it again. 'There you go, fetch that.'

'So have you ever brought Mel here?'

Zander gave a half-laugh, an image of Mel's face at the suggestion looming in his mind. 'Trust me, if you knew Mel,

you'd know that the countryside and her don't mix; she told
me so in fact, just before I came here. She's got a key to the
cottage, but she's never used it.'

'Oh, right.'

They walked along in silence for a few moments.

'What does Mel do – for a job, I mean?'

'Not much; not these days, at least. But when I first met
her she was a very successful life-style blogger – or "vlogger", I should say. She was vivacious, driven and ambitious
to be the best in her field, always jetting off here there and
everywhere.'

'Excuse my ignorance, I mean, I know what blogging
and vlogging is, but I'm not really sure how you earn a living
from that.'

'I'm not exactly a hundred per cent sure about the
finer details; she didn't tell me exactly – I think she earned
money every time someone viewed her posts on YouTube
– but I do know that she was given things like free holidays, hotel stays, meals in fancy restaurants, clothes,
make-up perfume, shoes, on the condition she would blog
or vlog about them. You name it, she was sent it. And
because she'd got such a high profile, her endorsements
generated a lot of business for the brands she blogged
about.'

'Wow! That sounds amazing, I had no idea that's what
happened.' Livvie bent to pick up the frisbee Alf had
dropped at her feet and threw it for him. 'Go fetch, Alfie.'

'It was great for her, until things went sour.'

'Oh, what happened – if you don't mind me asking?'

Zander shook his head. 'I don't mind you asking. Things
started to go awry when Mel stopped blogging about the
things she'd been given. I should say, no one's obliged to
blog about the things they get sent for free, but it's kind of

hoped for, especially when it comes to the big stuff like pricey holidays to the Maldives and that sort of thing.'

'I think I can see where this is going.'

'Another vlogger arrived on the scene. She was doing the same sort of stuff as Mel but, from what I can gather, with a quirkier twist. Suddenly, Mel was no longer the golden girl whose lifestyle and image followers couldn't get enough of. Unfortunately, instead of it spurring her on to try harder, she just seemed to lose interest. It didn't help that she was involved in a number of arguments on social media; some of them got quite nasty by all accounts – once Mel starts having a go at someone she doesn't know when to stop – and she was accused of trolling. She tried to deny it all, of course, but it was there in black and white for all the world to see and she couldn't wriggle out of it.'

'So what happened?'

'She was dropped like a hot potato; her work dried up almost overnight.'

'Goodness, that must've been a shock for her.'

'It was, but she still didn't accept she'd done anything wrong; blamed everyone else, but she's the one left with no work and no money coming in to fund her extravagant lifestyle. She'll have gone to London to do a spot of networking, get her face seen, something she couldn't do at Carcassonne.'

'Have you heard from her since you got here?'

'Not a word. I've sent her a text, but I don't expect a reply – unless things aren't going her way. This latest escapade of hers has made me wonder if we're just going through the motions. If I'm completely honest, I don't know how we ended up together; we're not exactly compatible, but it just sort of happened, she moved in, bit by bit, without us ever having a discussion about it.'

'Opposites attract.'

'I suppose.' In truth, Zander had initially been attracted to Mel because she was tall, blonde and beautiful; his usual type. At the time, it suited him to ignore that she was a little too self-absorbed and cold. *Ughh! What a fool I've been.* He was conscious of his mood sinking as he thought about Mel. He didn't want it to rub off onto Livvie after the morning she'd had, and he wanted to enjoy his time with her; she felt good to be around.

Just then a rabbit tore out of the hedgerow, its bobtail disappearing through a gap in the drystone wall. It was hotly pursued by a stoat, resplendent in its winter coat of ermine – a stunning white all but for a lightning flash of chestnut-brown down the centre of its face.

'Wow, they were fast,' said Livvie, her eyes following their path.

'Yeah, I don't fancy the rabbit's chances; despite their diminutive size, stoats are pretty lethal hunters.'

'Oh, poor rabbit,' said Livvie.

'I doubt the farmers share your point of view.'

'Ah, I hadn't thought about that, though I still don't like the idea of an animal being hurt, Mother Nature or not.'

'Same here.' Despite his best efforts, Zander was still struggling to lift his mood.

Livvie seemed to be aware of it. 'Looking at that blue sky, I'd say the weather forecasters have got it slightly wrong. It may be absolutely freezing, but I can't see a hint of snow up there.'

Zander looked heavenwards. 'I see what you mean. I've noticed Lytell Stangdale seems to have its own unique microclimate and regularly thumbs its nose at what the weathermen say it's supposed to do.'

The low thrum of a tractor caught their attention. 'I

wonder who this is?' Livvie squinted along the track in the bright sunshine.

Zander followed her gaze; he recognised the tractor as belonging to John Danks, son of Hugh and Madge. It had a huge bale of hay fixed to a spike on the front of it. 'That's John Danks from Tinkel Top Farm.'

John's flock of sheep had clearly heard it too and hurried over to the gate in a cacophony of bleating. John came to a halt and hopped out, his cheeks ruddy from years of exposure to the harsh moorland winters. Alf ran over to him, wagging his tail.

'Ey up, lad, how're you doing?' He gave Alf a quick fussing. 'Now then, Zander, enjoying the fresh air?' He left the Labrador and hefted the bale off the tractor and rolled it towards the gate.

'Hi, John, yes, thought we'd get a walk in before the weather changed.'

'You do right. Mind, I think they've got it wrong about snow getting dumped here today.' He looked at Livvie and nodded. 'Now then.'

Zander could tell what was running through John's mind.

'Hi,' she replied. 'That's just what we were saying.'

'This is Livvie, by the way; she's staying at the cottage with me.'

'So I'd heard,' he said. 'Enjoying your visit?'

'Yes, thanks, it's a beautiful part of the world.'

'Aye, it is that. Right, well, I'd best get on. Enjoy your walk, and I might see you in the Sunne sometime.'

'No doubt,' said Zander. 'See you, John.'

'Bye, nice to meet you,' said Livvie.

'I'd hate to have a secret round here,' said Zander as they

watched John manoeuvre his tractor and rumble off back down the lane.

'I reckon that would be impossible,' said Livvie.

THE PAIR CONTINUED THEIR WALK, taking turns to throw the frisbee for Alf, chatting away about their respective jobs. Just as he was thinking about suggesting they should head back, Zander felt his phone vibrate in his pocket. He stopped and took it out, his heart sinking as he saw Mel's name on the screen.

'Everything okay?' asked Livvie.

He pressed his lips together, as a voice in his head screamed, "no". He was struggling to quash his disappointment. 'It's Mel; she's left London.'

'Oh.'

'She's in Leeds.'

He felt Livvie's gaze on him. 'And wants me to join me.'

'Okay, and is that what you want to do?' Livvie's eyes had suddenly lost their happy sparkle.

Zander released a heavy sigh in a huge puff of condensation. 'I don't know what the hell I want to do.'

But Zander knew exactly what he wanted to do; he just didn't know if he had the guts to do it.

29

ZANDER

OUTSIDE THE BACK DOOR, Zander kicked the snow from his wellies, heeling them off on the doormat. Since his text from Mel, he and Livvie had made their way back in relative silence, their only words directed at Alf who was oblivious to the slump in their moods.

'Coffee? Tea?' Zander asked, hanging his coat up.

'Tea would be lovely, but I'm happy to make it if you like?'

'Would you mind? I think I'm just going to go into the living room and call Mel, see what the score is.' Since the original text, he'd been bombarded with more from her, as well as four or five calls he'd decided not to pick-up while he was with Livvie.

'Of course, that's fine.' He sensed her watching him as he walked away.

With a heavy heart, he flopped into the armchair and called Mel's number. It was picked up almost immediately. 'Zander! Where are you? I've been trying to get hold of you. Anyone would think you've been ignoring me.'

'Hi, Mel, what's the problem? And I haven't been

ignoring you by the way, it just wasn't a good time to take your calls.' He couldn't hide the lack-lustre tone to his voice and he didn't care

'Oh, right. Well, the problem is that my London trip was not at all what I was promised.' She paused, seemingly expecting a response from Zander. When none came she continued. 'What's the matter with you? You could at least sound pleased to hear from me.'

Zander sighed. 'It's just a bit unexpected, that's all, after what you said and how you left.' Was her voice always that annoying, he wondered?

'Oh, you're not still sulking about that are you?'

He rolled his eyes. 'I'm not sulking. As I said, hearing from you is just unexpected.'

'I thought you'd be happy for me to grasp an opportunity like that; who knows where it could lead?'

'And where did it lead, Mel?' He pulled at a loose thread on the hem of his shirt.

'It made me realise how much I missed you and it led me back home, so I thought I'd join you in Carcassonne.'

Oh, shit! 'I'm not in Carcassonne; I didn't fancy going after you pulled out. I'm at the cottage in Great Stangdale.'

A loaded silence hung in the air. Zander could hear Livvie talking to Alf, her words of praise and kindness floating through to the living room.

'Who's that? Is that a woman's voice I can hear? You're not alone, are you?'

Oh, double shit. He took a deep breath and launched into a brief explanation of the situation – excluding the parts that he knew would cause her to fly off the handle.

'And she's still there, this Lizzie?' There was no disguising the hostility in her voice.

'It's Livvie, and yes she's still here; she paid for the cottage. By rights, I'm the one who shouldn't be here.'

'Then why are you?'

This was draining. 'Because of what I just explained. It's all perfectly above board, Mel.' Oh, Lord, he knew that wasn't strictly true if his mind and heart were anything to go by.

'How would you like it if I went on holiday with other men?' Her voice was beginning to feel like it was stabbing into the side of his head.

'You did exactly that when you took off for London.'

'That was different!'

Before Zander could reply the call was cut. 'Jeez.' He sank into the sofa, his mind reeling from the bashing it had just received.

30

LIVVIE

LIVVIE FILLED the kettle and sat it on the Aga hotplate, then went to get Alf's towel so she could dry him off.

'You're a funny lad,' she said as he wriggled around in happiness as she rubbed the towel over him. He delivered a sloppy lick across her face. 'Ugh! I think your dad's told you about that, hasn't he?'

Alf replied with a wag of his tail.

With the kettle boiled, she poured the water onto the tea bags in the pot and set it on the table until Zander had finished his call. Her stomach clenched at the thought of Mel's text and how it had thrown a wet towel over the afternoon. Their walk had been lovely, crisp and fresh and Alf's enthusiasm as he'd bounded backwards and forwards had warmed her heart. At one point she'd even felt Zander's hand brush against hers as if he was going to take it in his. That was seconds before his phone had vibrated in his pocket, stealing her happiness away.

She didn't want to eavesdrop, but he'd left the living room door open and she couldn't help but hear the odd snatch of a word. By all accounts, he didn't sound too happy.

She busied herself, checking in the cupboards to see what ingredients they had that could be put to use for dinner that evening. Was he staying for that? She didn't know, but there were plenty of things in to make wholesome meals for several days.

She checked the time. 'Ah, that explains why you're giving me that look, Alf. Would you like your dinner?'

Alf's ears shot up and he ran to the utility room where his food was kept. Livvie laughed. 'Hungry, eh, after all that fresh air and running around?'

As Alf was getting stuck into his food, Zander walked back into the kitchen; his face, she noted, looked weary.

'Everything okay?'

He threw his phone down. 'Depends on your definition of okay, but put it this way, Mel thought I was in Carcassonne and had an idea that she'd be joining me there after her failed trip to London.'

'Oh dear.'

'Oh dear indeed.'

'So what are you going to do? Are you heading back home?' Livvie's heart started hammering in her chest, the thought of him leaving making her voice catch in her throat.

'Well, Mel didn't sound too happy – she heard your voice in the background and cut the call.'

'Oh, no, I'm so sorry; I tried to be quiet but I didn't want you to think I was eaves dropping or anything.' She pressed her hand to her mouth, feeling terribly guilty.

'Don't apologise. Anyway, in answer to your question, I'm certainly not going back today. I bought some very tasty-looking chorizo and butter beans from the village shop and I quite fancied making a Spanish stew for dinner tonight. Does that sound okay to you?'

'It sounds delicious. I love chorizo.' Livvie felt relief

gently push sadness out of the way. The thought of spending another day with Zander made her inexorably happy.

'DID YOU JUST HEAR SOMETHING?' asked Zander as Alf's ears shot up.

'I think it's outside; the wind's picked up, it'll just be that.'

'Yeah, you're probably right. He picked up the bottle of red wine. 'Fancy some more?'

'Mmm, please, it's delicious, as is this stew.' Livvie held her glass as Zander poured. 'Not too much though; I don't want to get tiddly again.' Her face was already feeling flushed.

'Ah, the infamous night when you drank the pub dry of Prosecco.' Zander's mouth twitched with the hint of a smile.

'I did not! Though I have to admit, I did have more than I usually do.'

'Ah, so is that why you told me I was lo—'

'Told you what, Zander?' said an angry voice.

Livvie's heart started and she turned to see a tall, well-groomed ice-maiden standing in the doorway, her face set hard as stone.

'Mel! What are you doing here?' Zander's smile vanished along with the happy glint in his eye.

'Shouldn't you be addressing that question to Lizzie?'

'It's Livvie, and I've already explained the situation to you.'

Despite the tension in the air, Livvie noticed that Alf made no attempt to greet Mel; instead he went to Livvie, resting his head on her lap while she smoothed his ears.

The sound of a horn beeping in the cold night air cut through the silence.

'The taxi needs paying; I had to get one from that funny little place, can't remember the name, anyway, you'll have to go and settle it, I don't have any cash on me.' Mel stalked into the kitchen, snatching Zander's glass out of his hand. 'And my case is there, too.'

Livvie noticed him roll his eyes as he reached for his wallet. 'That would be about right,' he said.

Mel watched Zander leave the house before she turned to Livvie. 'So, what's your game, lady?' She took a slug of wine.

The question took Livvie aback. 'I don't have a game. Zander said he'd explained everything to you.' She wasn't going to back down, no matter how intimidating this ice-queen was.

'And you expect me to believe that?' Mel sneered, leaning against the worktop, swirling the wine around the glass.

'Yes, I booked this cottage online through the holiday cottage agency – there'd been a last-minute cancellation so I grabbed it and—'

'Cut it out, Mel. Livvie doesn't have to explain herself to you. I've told you how it is and it's been good of her to let me stay rather than be in Leeds on my own.'

'Well, I'm back now, so you won't be on your own; we can head off first thing.'

'Actually, I've been invited to a party at one of the local farms, and I'd really like to go to it. You're welcome to come too,' he said.

Livvie's heart sank like a lump of lead. Why did he have to do that? She'd been looking forward to going, to seeing her new friends again, but there's no way she could go as a

spare part with Zander and Mel. In less than five minutes
everything had changed.

'I think I'll go and run a bath and have an early night; it's
been a bit of a day.' Livvie looked across at Zander, hoping
she'd managed to disguise her disappointment.

'Hey, you don't have to rush off; it's only just after nine.'

'If Lizzie's feeling tired, just let her go.' Mel turned, scru-
tinising Livvie's face. 'Come to think of it, you do have a bit
of a haggard look to your eyes; an early night will do you
good.' She gave a viper-like smile.

Livvie pushed herself up and reached for her plate. 'If
you insist on having an early night, I insist on seeing to the
dishes,' said Zander. He had a look in his eyes that she
couldn't quite read.

'Okay, thank you.' She wanted to get out of the room as
quickly as possible. 'See you in the morning.'

She was conscious of Zander's eyes on her as she
retreated. 'Sleep well, Livvie,' he said, while Mel just pinned
her with an icy glare.

'That was well out of order,' Livvie heard Zander say as
she headed through to the living room.

'What?'

'You know exactly what. There was no need to make
bitchy comments.'

'Oh, get over yourself, I was only saying what the rest of
us can see, that's all.'

As hot water thundered into the bath, filling the room with
lavender-scented steam, Livvie sat in the wicker chair and
let the hot, salty tears flow. She knew she had no right to feel
the way she did. Zander was with somebody else, she knew

that; she'd always known that. But this feeling she'd had from the moment they'd locked eyes – and she knew he felt it, too –made their circumstances seem so unjust. Her gut feeling was telling her loud and clear that they were meant to be together, but the situation they were in was telling them they didn't stand a chance. And, anyway, why would Zander pick someone like her when he had the perfect, stunningly beautiful Mel, she thought. Anyone could see there was no comparison.

'I wish I'd never come here.' She sobbed into the towel. 'And now my eyes are going to look even more haggard.'

As she climbed into the steaming water, she was glad that the noise from the pipes and the water tank filling meant that any sounds from downstairs were drowned out. The last thing she needed was to hear Zander and the ice-queen laughing and joking. As she let the soothing warmth penetrate her skin a thought made her heart freeze: if Mel was staying the night would she and Zander be sharing a bed? Her spirits dipped even further as she answered her own question – of course they would.

Livvie heaved herself out of the bath and dried herself off; she wanted to get back to her room before she encountered either of them on the landing.

31

ZANDER

WELL THIS WAS a bolt out of the blue – and not a particularly welcome one at that – thought Zander as he regarded Mel who was now occupying the seat Livvie had just vacated. He was sad she'd felt she had to scurry off, but he could understand why she did. Mel wasn't a woman's woman by any stretch of the imagination; she could be bitchy and intimidating.

'So, what made you come here after all this time of never being tempted to visit before?' he asked.

'Because I was missing you, Zandie.' She reached across the table and put her hand over his. Her smile was insincere, her motive transparent.

'Really?'

'Of course I did. And did you miss me?'

'So what happened to tear you away from London?' Zander freed his hand, batting her question away; he didn't want to have to lie to her.

'I don't want to talk about it, but it wasn't what I was expecting.' Mel's mouth set in a hard line.

Zander could only imagine what that meant. He

looked across at her, attempting to assess his feelings for her. She was attractive, with her sculpted cheekbones, platinum blonde hair and model-like figure. But there was a coldness to her and a hard look in her eye that was becoming less and less appealing. As for her selfishness, well that was really beginning to grate. There was no getting away from it, their relationship had reached its expiration date.

While Mel rambled on, Zander's mind wandered. How had he not noticed these things before? Was it because he'd simply chosen not to and was content to continue with their relationship that was purely based on no deeper a connection than physical attraction? Or was it the easy option and better than being on his own?

Or was it because of his feelings for Livvie?

The answer to that was screaming at him, loud and clear.

THEY'D TALKED for another hour, or rather, Zander had listened while Mel talked about herself and bitched and moaned about Anna, and what a terrible friend she'd turned out to be.

He rubbed his brow, he didn't know how much more of it he could listen to. 'I think I'm going to call it a day,' he said.

'Same here.' She ran her tongue seductively over her top lip which triggered an immediate reaction in Zander's jeans.

He cursed inwardly as she ran her foot up his leg, seeking out his crotch, massaging it gently. He stood up. 'I don't think so, Mel.'

'What do you mean? You used to love me doing that,

especially in restaurants; it used to drive you crazy I seem to recall.' She smirked, forcing him to look away.

'Come on, Alf, time you paid a visit to the garden.' He opened the back door and the Labrador rushed out. Zander followed him, glad of the cool air and the moments away from the intensity of the kitchen and Mel.

'Right, I've locked up and I'm heading up to bed,' he said.

'Okay, I won't be a moment; I just need a quick ciggie.'

'Can you do that outside?' An image of his house at Leeds sprang into his mind, the oozing makeshift ashtrays, the foul lingering smell of stale cigarettes.

'Fussy man.' Mel reached inside her handbag and pulled out a box of Marlboros and a lighter.

With a heavy heart, Zander climbed the stairs. It felt weird to know that he'd be sharing a bed with Mel when Livvie was in the next room; almost like a betrayal. What he'd give to suggest to that Mel that she sleep in one of the beds in the snug, but there was no way he could do that; the fall-out would be unbearable.

Upstairs, he was pulling off his jeans when Mel came into the room. She closed the door and slinked her way across the carpet, undoing her hair that fell like a gleaming halo in the soft light. Reluctantly, his eyes were drawn to her as she slowly undressed and stood before him naked, her body smooth and lean. Zander's mind shot back to his first glimpse of Livvie, catching her in all her delicious, voluptuous nakedness, her body just as nature intended. He gasped, feeling suddenly aroused at the memory; she was breath-taking. She was the opposite to Mel who was so waxed and polished, Zander was surprised she didn't squeak when she walked.

Pulled from his thoughts, and before he realised what

Mel was up to, she'd pushed him back on the bed and strad-
dled him.

With a groan, he closed his eyes and the face he saw was
Livvie's.

~

'SOMEONE NEEDED THAT.' Mel rolled off him, smirking. 'I
knew you'd be pleased to see me.'

Zander didn't reply; he simply leaned across and flicked
off the bedside light.

What the hell was I thinking? He covered his eyes with the
back of his arm. *I'm a bloody idiot! A weak bloody idiot! Sex
with Mel was the last thing I wanted. Shit! Shit! Shit! Why didn't
I just tell her I wasn't interested?* Because he was always interested and she knew that.

He lay awake for half the night trying to get his head
around what he'd just done. The only explanation he could
come up with was that his attraction for Livvie had meant
that his testosterone levels were buzzing around his body on
high alert with nowhere to go. It wasn't Mel he'd wanted sex
with, it was Livvie – he knew that much – but he'd needed to
channel his urge somewhere, pathetic weak male that he
was. And he was pretty sure Mel knew what she was doing
by offering herself on a platter. God, he felt cheap.

32

LIVVIE

LIVVIE HAD HOPED to have dozed off before Zander and Mel came to bed so she wouldn't have to hear evidence of their togetherness. But her mind, it seemed, had other ideas and she'd lain awake, going over the time she'd spent with Zander and what he'd said to Donny about her being perfect and beautiful – did he really say that, she wondered, or had she imagined it? And if he had said it, did he really mean it?

She sighed and rolled over, hearing Zander muttering something as he walked along the landing past her bedroom door. How she wished she could turn the clock back to last night before Mel had arrived.

A few minutes later, Mel hurried by humming, making no attempt to be quiet, clicking their bedroom door shut.

Before long, the rhythmic squeaking of the cast-iron bed started up, accompanied by much theatrical groaning and moaning from Mel. Livvie squeezed her eyes tight shut. 'God, this is awful,' she said as she pulled the duvet over her head, but there was no escaping their sounds of love-making. Livvie felt her throat tighten and tears sting her eyes. She felt utterly confused and utterly sad. There was no other option, she'd have to leave first thing.

THE FOLLOWING MORNING, Livvie rose just as daylight was peering through the clouds. She poked her nose through the curtains to see there'd been a gentle dusting of snow overnight; she hoped it wasn't enough to stop her car from tackling the lane.

Hurriedly, and with her heart hammering against her ribcage, she threw her clothes in her case, got dressed, scribbled a brief note to Zander saying she was heading off, and tiptoed downstairs. It saddened her to think she wouldn't get chance to go to Molly and Camm's house party or to say goodbye to her new friends, but after last night, Livvie felt she had no alternative.

She made her way to the kitchen where Alf jumped up from his bed and trotted over to her. 'Morning, Alf.' She bent and pressed her head against his, fighting back tears. 'It's been lovely getting to know you, you're a one of a kind, special boy.' Her heart felt heavy as she swiped her tears away. A floorboard creaked upstairs making Alf's ears twitch. 'Bugger!' Quickly, Livvie pulled on her coat, wound her scarf around her neck and propped the note against the radio. 'Take care of your dad for me,' she said. She unlocked the door and slipped silently out of the house.

The freezing air took Livvie's breath away as it nipped at her exposed skin; she was glad that she'd hung on to Zander's glove liners. The weather had worsened in the short time since she'd first looked out; the wind had picked up and pin-head sized flakes of snow had started to swirl around her. The ground was frozen hard and she crunched her way round to the side of the house where her little car was still buried under a mound of snow. She groaned inwardly; it was going to take a considerable effort to clear it.

Fifteen minutes later, and with fingers numb from the cold, the windscreen and the rear window were snow free, as was the path to the lane. She'd never worked so fast in her life, desperately trying to be quiet, all the while unable to shake the feeling that she was being watched. Luckily, the snow had come off in huge chunks, just leaving a film of frost beneath. She'd started the engine to speed up the process and melt the ice, hoping that the wind would help disguise the noise. It seemed to do the trick, and before she knew it, she was making her way cautiously along the icy lane as tears flowed freely down her cheeks.

The roads looked very different in daylight and Livvie wasn't completely sure of which way to go, having driven round in circles in the dark on the night she'd arrived here. She settled on heading to Lytell Stangdale and taking it from there; there were bound to be some signposts for other places and roads that sounded familiar, not that she knew where she was going.

It soon became apparent that there was no way of leaving the area without having to tackle a hill of some description, whether climbing or ascending, and Livvie's heart jumped into her mouth when she came to a junction and face-to-face with an ice-covered lane. According to the sign, downwards led to Lytell Stangdale, while upwards took you further up onto Great Stangdale Rigg. There was no way she was going to tackle that and risk getting herself stuck in a six-foot snow drift!

Fear dried her tears as she negotiated the right turn and steadily nosed her way down the bank. A couple of glides over thick patches of ice where springs ran across the road had set her heart racing, making her breathing shallow, but she'd managed to right herself, gaining traction on the side of the road where long grass and cow parsley skeletons peered stoically from the snow – Camm's voice advising her to drive into the skid and leave her brakes alone ringing in her ears.

Just as she'd righted herself from the last heart-in-the-mouth moment, she felt her car slide into another skid, picking up speed at an alarming rate as it glided down the increasingly steep hill, sliding first one way, then the other. Livvie wrestled with the steering wheel, panic gripping her insides, her mind going blank as to what she should do. Before she knew it she was heading towards a sheer drop down a ravine that led to a river. 'Oh, shit, shit, shit!' The car was completely out of her control as it slipped over the edge, bumping and bouncing over the uneven surface. She gripped onto the steering wheel, squeezed her eyes tight shut and tried to scream.

33
ZANDER

Zander woke with a feeling of regret deep in his gut as the events of the previous evening lined themselves up and paraded along the forefront of his mind. *What demon from hell told me it was a good idea to have sex with Mel? Why didn't I tell her we were finished like I'd intended to do?* He sighed and threw back the duvet, the room still shrouded in darkness thanks to the thick curtains. *Because you were thinking with your balls and not your head – or your heart, for that matter – you stupid arse!*

'Where are you going?' Mel yawned and curled her fingers round his wrist.

'To make a coffee.' He wriggled free of her grip, her touch sending a spike of annoyance through him.

'Really? Wouldn't you rather spend a little longer in bed? I could make it worth your while.' She ran her long nails up and down his back. It made him shiver but not in the enjoyable way she hoped.

Zander pushed his fingers into his hair. 'I need to let Alf out.'

'Ughh!' She flopped back on her pillow. 'That bloody dog; you put him before everything, no doubt even Lizzie.'

Mel really knew how to set his hackles up. It was her default mode and he was sure she took pleasure from it. 'It's Livvie. And Alf's used to routine – like most dogs. He'll be waiting for me.'

'In that case, you'll be pleased to know, I let him out earlier.'

'You did?' This was a first, Mel was rarely out of bed before eleven if she didn't have to be.

'Yes. I thought I'd treat you to a lie-in, amongst other things.' Her hand reached out, curling around the taut muscles of his abdomen.

He brushed it away. 'Don't, Mel; I'm not in the mood.' His mind raced over the reasons she could have for behaving so out of character.

She huffed. 'And just what are you in the mood for, Zander? A cosy chat with frumpy little Lizzie?'

'It's Livvie, as you know full well. And she's not frumpy, she's bohemian, which I think is rather nice.'

'Huh. Really? Is that what you call it? Well, I'm afraid I have to tell you that "bohemian" little whatever she's called has left.'

'What?' Zander felt the air being whipped from his lungs. He turned to Mel, despising the look of glee in her ice-cold eyes. 'When? How do you know?'

'Because I happened to see her leave.'

'How long ago?'

Mel shrugged. 'I'd say about half an hour ago, maybe more, maybe less; I wasn't really concentrating on the time.'

'And you didn't think to mention it?'

'Why would I? You were sleeping like a baby.' She sat up and draped herself around his neck, pressing her nakedness into his back. 'And I wanted to wake you in a special way, if you know what I mean?' She nibbled his earlobe.

Zander could feel anger searing its way up inside him. He shrugged Mel off and stood up. 'I can assure you, that's the last thing I want right now. And I can tell you exactly why you didn't wake me, Mel: you didn't want Livvie here and you knew I'd try to stop her from leaving. And I'll tell you something else, she left because of you, because you made her feel unwelcome, because you were being a bitch. That's why.' He pulled on his pyjama bottoms.

'I think that's a bit extreme, don't you? She left because she knew she was in the way. Come on, Zander, it's hardly normal for a total stranger to wedge themselves between a couple, is it? It's just plain weird.' Mel pouted. 'And that's how she felt, so she did the right thing.'

'Oh, really, and how do you know?'

'Because she left a note.'

He pushed his arms through his T-shirt and paused. 'She what?'

'She left a note.'

'Where is it? What did she say?'

It didn't go unnoticed that Mel couldn't make eye-contact with him. 'Just that she didn't want to get in the way and that she hoped we had a lovely Christmas.'

'Where is it? I want to read it for myself.' Did she really say that, he wondered?

'I haven't got it anymore.'

'What? Why?'

He watched Mel taking her time to think of an answer. 'Because ... Alf chewed it.'

'Alf chewed it?'

'Mmhm.' She still refused to look at him.

'That's bollocks and you know it. Alf doesn't chew.'

'Well, he chewed your precious Lizzie's note.'

Zander stormed downstairs and into the kitchen where he was greeted by a waggy-tailed Alf who ran straight to the door to be let out. Mel was clearly lying about seeing to that earlier. 'Morning, buddy. Don't suppose you've seen a note anywhere, have you?'

Alf just whimpered and scratched at the door until he was let out.

Zander slid his feet into his wellies and followed Alf as he trotted along the snow cleared path that led right around the house, to the empty space where Livvie's little car had been.

He couldn't remember the last time he'd felt so sad as he watched the Labrador sniff up Livvie's scent. 'She's gone, fella.' He stood a while, his heart heavy, not caring about nor noticing the cruel, cold, wind that was whirling around him, nor the snowflakes that were soaking through the thin cotton of his clothing. All he could think about was Livvie, out on the moors in her car that wasn't equipped for the conditions a North Yorkshire Moors winter could throw at you. He'd heard plenty of stories of unsuspecting drivers who'd set off and ended up getting stranded in deep snow-drifts; or worse, coming off the road. He turned his gaze to the lane where snow had started to cover the hard frost that had taken everything in its grip through the night. His heart flipped as he noticed her just-visible tyre tracks, an idea sparking in his mind. He needed to go out, follow her tracks while they were still there. He'd call Camm, too, ask if he'd seen her, or if he'd ploughed the roads yet. Zander's mood felt suddenly brighter as he clicked his tongue for Alf. 'Come on, lad, let's go find Livvie; bring her home.'

As he made his way back to the house, one thing became glaringly obvious: it was over between him and Mel and she'd have to go. Today. He'd take her back to the station himself, just as soon as he'd found Livvie.

Inside, he stormed upstairs and burst into the bedroom where Mel was stretched out naked in a deliberately provocative pose. 'Get your stuff together.' He started picking up her discarded clothes from the floor and throwing them into her open suitcase.

'What? Why? What are you doing?'

'Putting your stuff in your case to speed things up.'

'Zander! Why are you acting like this? You're being crazy!'

'I've been crazy letting this pathetic excuse for a relationship carry on for as long as it has. And what are these, eh?' He snatched up a packet of condoms from a corner of her case. 'It's been a long time since we've used these, hasn't it? I'd say pretty much since you went on the pill a good eighteen months ago.'

Mel's face blanched. 'They're not mine ... they're, they're ... they're Anna's ... she ... she wanted me to look after them for her.'

Zander shook his head. 'And you expect me to believe that, do you?'

'It's true.' She leapt out of bed and went to put her arms around his neck.

He grabbed her wrists and stepped back; he was done with her manipulation. 'Just pack your stuff; I'll drive you to the station at Middleton. You can go back to Leeds and pack up your stuff there, but I want you out of my house tomorrow. We're finished, Mel; we have been for a long time. You know it as well as I do.'

Her face twisted bitterly. 'And is this all because of that tubby little ginger plain thing? You're dumping me for something like that? You bloody fool.' She sneered, leaning towards him. 'Let me tell you this, you won't get a second chance with me.'

'Just get your stuff together.' Zander grabbed his clothes from the previous evening and went to get dressed in the bedroom that Livvie had recently vacated.

He massaged his temples with his fingers, hoping his anger towards Mel would subside; he didn't like feeling this way. His eyes scanned the room that still bore a hint of Livvie's sweet perfume; it triggered a yearning in his belly. Something silver glinted on the dressing table. He went across and picked it up; it was an earring in the shape of a star – one of Livvie's. He rolled it around in his fingers before pressing it to his lips; at least he had something to remember her by if he didn't catch up with her today.

'I CAN'T BELIEVE you really mean it.' Mel chased Zander down the stairs.

With her suitcase in his hand, he strode across the living room and out of the front door.

'Trust me, I really mean it.' He threw her case on the back seat of his car while Alf watched intently from his position in the boot.

She stopped in the doorway, her hands clenched into tight fists. 'Zander, no!' She screamed at the top of her lungs, stamping her feet. 'I'm not leaving!'

'I think you'll find you are.' He took her arm and guided her down the path, opening the passenger door of the four wheel drive. 'Get in, Mel.'

'No! You can't make me.'

'Just get in the car, Mel.'

'Please, Zandie, don't do this.' She pouted like a spoilt

child, desperately trying to squeeze out crocodile tears. 'I have nowhere to go, I've got no job, no—'

'And whose fault is that? You'll have to stay at a friend's or go back to London.'

'I can't ... my friends are all useless and selfish.'

'Not my problem.'

'You sound like you don't care.' Her voice had taken on a whiny tone that grated.

'I don't. Just get in the car.'

Mel finally did as she was bid and they set off in silence, her arms folded tight across her chest and her mouth clenched in a hard line.

Before they'd left, he'd called Withrin Hill Farm; Molly had picked up and he'd explained briefly what had happened. She'd told him that Camm had set off half an hour earlier to plough the roads, with Ben following up and spreading grit from the bins on the roadside. 'We want to make sure the roads to our place are nice and clear for everyone coming here this afternoon,' she'd said. 'But I'll see if I can get hold of him, tell him to keep an eye out for Livvie. Try not to worry, Zander, I'm sure she'll be fine and we'll see you both this afternoon.'

Judging by the tracks in the road, Livvie's car had been the only one out on the lane around Dale View which was a relief; he hoped she hadn't got far. As he drove on, Zander kept his eyes glued to them, the wipers flicking back and forth, swiping the snow off the windscreen. His mind wandered onto the prospect that he may never see Livvie again. He had no way of contacting her. He hadn't thought to take her mobile number, or her address, but he'd had no need; he hadn't expected last night to turn out the way it had with Mel arriving on the doorstep and pushing Livvie out. All he knew was that he had to get in touch with her

somehow. His hopes brightened as he suddenly remembered she'd told him where she worked. *What was the name
of the shop again, "something Bridal" or "something Brides"?
"Blushing Brides", that was it!* He could call there and get her
number from the owner or Livvie's friend, Bryony, provided
she'd share it, of course. A second later, his hopes slumped
once more when he recalled Livvie had told him the shop
was closed until the New Year. *Bugger! Would the website he
used to advertise the cottage have details of her address?* He
hoped so.

Familiar with driving in the snow, Zander allowed
plenty of time to slow down as he approached the junction
for Lytell Stangdale; he was relieved to see there was still
just one faint set of tracks. He reasoned that most drivers
who tackled this lane would be locals in vehicles equipped
with sturdy, chunky tyres, like four-wheel-drives or tractors;
this set in front of him were still narrow – they could only
belong to Livvie's car, he was certain. Or, at the very least,
hopeful. As he looked left, Zander stole a glance at Mel
who'd been tight-lipped since they'd set off. Her face was
pinched into a spoilt, angry scowl; he'd seen that plenty of
times before and he'd be glad to see the back of it.

He'd chosen not to say anything as it would only lead to
further confrontation, but he knew she'd lied about Alf
chewing the note; he'd seen it torn up into little pieces and
pushed into the bin. She was spiteful and sly and he'd had
enough of turning a blind eye to it.

As the four wheel drive made its way down the steep
slope of the hill, its tyres moving quietly over the snow,
Zander spotted Camm's tractor creeping its way up towards
them. He exhaled a noisy sigh of relief, but the feeling was
quickly snatched away from him when he saw Livvie's tyre
tacks swerving all over the road and leading to the edge of

the sheer drop on the left. 'Jesus, Livvie!' He cranked his car into a lower gear and gently eased his foot on the brake. In a moment, and despite a few hair-raising skids over the frozen flow of the spring water that had Mel gripping onto her seat, the car came to a halt on the roadside.

Mel remained where she was, silent and stony faced as Zander jumped out, rushing round to the rear where he opened the door for Alf. 'Come on, lad, let's see if we can find her.' Alf leapt out and bounded off, following the zig-zagging tracks, stopping briefly when he reached a patch of freshly crushed snow where the tyre marks had come to an abrupt end. He sniffed around for a moment then hared off, disappearing down the bank side. With his heart thumping, Zander ran down the road after him, slipping and sliding, towards where the tyre tracks stopped. Just as he reached the spot, Camm pulled up in front of him and swung down from the tractor. 'Zander, I've had a message from Molly to keep my eyes peeled for Livvie, but I'm afraid I haven't seen any sign of her.' His gaze fell on the disappearing trail and Zander's distraught features. 'Oh, hell. You think that could be her?'

Zander nodded, breathing heavily. 'I'm sure of it; I've followed the tracks all the way from the cottage.'

'Right, let's get down there.'

Just then, Alf started barking.

'I wonder if he's found her?' Hope flickered in Zander's heart. He cupped his hands around his mouth and called as loud as he could, 'Livvie! Livvie!' If she could hear him, he wanted her to know they were on their way for her.

The two men scrambled down the steep bankside, snow soaking their clothing and finding its way inside their wellies, though neither of them noticed. Zander had never know his heart pound as furiously as it was right now, desperately willing Livvie to be alright.

'There's her car.' He pointed to the little silver banger that had come to a halt on its roof. Alf was sniffing round it frantically, whimpering, his tail wagging in interest. He gave another bark. Zander felt panic twist in his stomach, but did all he could to stay calm, telling himself that losing it wasn't going to help Livvie.

'I see it,' said Camm. 'But it's hard to tell from here if she's managed to get out.'

'Camm! Zander!' A male voice came from behind them. They looked up to see Ben hurtling down towards them. 'Mum told me you were looking for Livvie,' he said when he reached them. 'I've come to help. Is it her? Is she okay?'

'We haven't found her yet, but that's her car and I reckon she's still in it as I can't see any footprints,' said Zander. He strode towards the vehicle, his legs pushing hard through the knee-high snow.

'Thank God,' he said when they reached it, a wave of relief washing over him. 'Livvie, are you okay.' He bent down, clearing snow away with his hands, and peered through the window. 'Livvie!' His heart squeezed when he saw a pair of frightened, tear-stained eyes looking back at him.

'Zander,' she said, her bottom lip quivering.

'She's here!' he said, a discernible shake in his voice as he began scraping the snow away from the door as fast as he could. 'It's okay, Livvie, we'll have you out of there in no time.'

34

LIVVIE

THE CAR HAD VEERED ALARMINGLY BACK and forth across the road before plummeting down the bank side. Terror had taken a firm grip of Livvie as it swerved sideways then flipped onto its roof and slowly rolled over and over until it ground to a halt in a large wedge of drifted snow. All the while, her heart was galloping, fear squeezing every last breath out of her lungs. She tried to scream, but no sound came out.

When eventually the car had come to a stop, she remained motionless for several long moments, shock rendering her unable to move. She was hanging upside down, suspended awkwardly by the seatbelt that was digging into her neck. She was feeling dizzy which in turn made her feel sick, and her pulse was thrumming in her ears. She was slowly becoming aware that her right arm was hurting where it had slammed against the door, as were her legs that had made hard contact with the steering wheel. Her head didn't feel great either. She reached up and touched her face; thankful to find she wasn't bleeding.

What had happened slowly started to sink in and Livvie's eyes filled with tears. Panic had scrambled her brain and she couldn't even begin to think how she was going to get out. From what she could see, the car was well and truly embedded in deep snow which was blocking the door. She tried to unbuckle her seatbelt, but it wouldn't budge, so she tried to slacken it, hoping she could wriggled her way out, but it just gripped her all the tighter. 'Arghh!' she cried in frustration.

It wasn't long before the bitter cold started to seep in, making her shiver uncontrollably. She felt indescribably sad and frightened.

She swiped the tears away from her eyes and was struggling with her seat belt once more, when the sound of a dog barking drifted down from the road. *Alf?* Hope suddenly flickered to life. Could it be him or was it just wishful thinking, Livvie wondered. Alf had a distinctive bark, and another round of it made her sure it was him.

She wiped a circle in the condensation on the window with the side of her hand and peered out. It was him! It was really him! He was there, sniffing round the car, whimpering, his tail wagging harder than she'd ever seen it wag before. *Oh, Alfie, you clever boy!* Suddenly, someone was calling her name. 'Zander!' Her voice came out in a croak, a fresh wave of tears tightening her throat. *He'd come looking for her. He'd actually come looking for her.* In a moment, she saw his handsome face peering through the glass, his eyes a mix of relief and concern.

'Livvie, thank God! Are you okay?'

She nodded, tears spilling back into her eyes and running off her forehead.

'Do you think you've broken anything?'

She shook her head. 'No.'

'Good.' He looked relieved. 'We'll have you out in no time.'

The kindness in his voice made her heart twist.

Alf was beside himself with excitement; whining and trying to push his way to her. Suddenly, a black, wet nose was squished against the window and she couldn't help but laugh. *Oh, Alf.*

Zander was soon joined by Camm and a young man she didn't recognise and, in a moment, all three were working like crazy to clear the snow away from the car. Livvie sniffed and wiped her nose with the back of her hand. She had another go at undoing her seatbelt but it was difficult to see what she was doing and it remained resolutely stubborn.

'Hang on, Livvie, leave your belt until I've got the door open, then I can help you; we might have to cut you out of it,' said Zander.

'Oh, okay.' She hadn't thought of that.

In a moment the door was pulled open and he had his arms around her. Camm opened the front passenger door and reached in. 'Got her, Zander?'

'Yep, got her.'

'Right, let's get this done.' Camm had a brief wrestle with the belt before they heard a loud click, and Livvie felt herself drop into Zander's arms; she winced as her shoulder objected sending a shooting pain right across her upper back.

Zander carefully eased her out and helped her to he feet. 'You okay to stand?'

She nodded, resting against the car; still feeling dizzy, she closed her eyes to quell the wave of nausea that rose in her gut. While she steadied herself she was aware of the two men's voices expressing relief that the airbag hadn't gone off in her car. 'Would've made it harder to get Livvie out, no doubt about it,' she heard Camm say.

'Just as well she didn't carry on head-first,' Zander replied. Livvie scrunched her eyes tightly shut; as horrible as it had been, in that moment she felt thankful that her car had swerved sideways and rolled slowly.

Though Alf was excited to see her, he sensed she felt unwell and sat quietly beside her, his paw resting on her leg.

'I'll let you have a moment before I go into doctor mode and give in to the urge to check you over. You look pale, I suspect you're in shock, maybe bumped your head and I dare say you feel like you've been on a rollercoaster after that tumble.' He looked up towards the road. 'You travelled quite a way.'

'Didn't she just?' said Camm, his hands on his hips.

AFTER A BRIEF CHECK OVER, Zander declared Livvie fit to start making her way up the bank assisted by him and Camm. With her arms wrapped around their shoulders they pulled their way up to the road side. The snow was deep and the incline steeper than it had looked on the way down, and all were panting heavily by the time they'd reached the top.

Livvie's neck and shoulder were hurting but she didn't like to complain since everyone had gone to so much trouble for her. The climb had been hard and she was sweating in her jumper and heavy coat, but it did nothing to detract from the icy wind, laden with tiny dots of snow, that sliced cruelly at their faces. What she would give to climb into a hot bubble bath right now.

Zander turned to Camm and Ben once they'd staggered

to the top. 'Thanks for your help the pair of you. I don't know how we would've managed without it.'

'No problem,' said Camm. 'We're just glad Livvie's okay.'

'Who's that, by the way?' Ben nodded towards Zander's car.

'It's my ex, Melissa. It's because of her all this has happened.' He glowered towards the woman in question.

'Oh, right.' Camm looked in the car's direction.

'I was taking her back to the station at Middleton and keeping my eyes peeled for Livvie en-route when we saw the tracks going over the side here; it wouldn't have crossed her mind to help.'

'So are you taking Livvie to the station with you?' asked Ben.

'I don't see what else I can do.' Zander frowned, rubbing the stubble of his chin. 'Will you be okay with that?' He turned to Livvie.

Livvie nodded, though the prospect of trailing over to who-knows-where in the same vehicle as the very reason she was leaving held little appeal.

'One of us could drop your ex off, so you could take Livvie straight home,' said Camm.

Home, he said home. The thought that they considered Dale View her home sent an unexpected warm glow through Livvie.

Zander thought for a moment. 'Would you really not mind doing that?'

'Not at all,' said Camm.

'If it's all right with you, Camm, I'd rather let you have the Landie so you can do the Middleton run, while I take over ploughing.' Ben eyeballed Zander's car with caution, nodding towards it. 'The passenger over there looks a bit scary to be honest.' He handed Camm the keys to the Landie.

Zander laughed. 'Trust me, she can be.'

'Thanks for the warning; I'll make sure she behaves herself. And don't forget, if you're up to it, you're welcome to join us this afternoon. It's all very low-key and chilled.' Camm smiled at Livvie. 'No crazy dancing necessary.'

'And Mum's made masses of game stew with absolutely ginormous dumplings; honestly, it's awesome, not to be missed.'

'Sounds good,' said Zander, scooping Livvie up off her feet and making her heart leap. 'But for now, I think we'd better head home. I'll be in touch, and thanks for this, you two; I owe you one.'

'No worries.' Camm turned to Ben and squeezed his shoulder. 'You take it steady; your mother'll have my guts for garters if anything happens to you.'

'I'll be fine, I've driven this thing loads of times.' With that, Ben climbed into the tractor and rumbled off.

Once they'd reached his car, Zander set Livvie down and opened the front passenger door. He was greeted by an icy glare from Mel.

'Why have you opened my door? It's absolutely freezing.'

'Camm's taking you to the station so I can get Livvie back to the cottage.' He reached into the back and lifted out her case, throwing it into the back of the Landie that had just pulled up beside him.

Livvie watched in silence as Mel looked across at the mud-spattered Landie, her lip curling in disgust. 'You expect me to get into that?'

'It's either that or walk.'

Livvie hardly dared to look at Mel whose eyes she could feel burning into her.

'Right, I've moved your case across.' Zander shot her an expectant look, his face, Livvie noted, was uncharacteristically hostile. When Mel didn't move, he nodded impatiently for her to get a move on. 'Come on, Mel.'

Mel seemed reluctant to take the hint. 'But can't *she* go in that thing?'

'Right, that's it.' Zander took hold of her arm.

'Hey, get off me! I'll get out myself!' Mel got out, looking daggers at Livvie as she made her way to the Land Rover. She climbed in and slammed the door.

'Good riddance,' said Zander as the Landie turned round and headed off down the lane.

35

LIVVIE

THE WARMTH of the car was a welcome relief after the sting-ingly cold air outside and Livvie sank into the heated seat, allowing it to sooth her aches and pains. They travelled along the snowy lanes in silence, Livvie's mind going over the last half hour. Had Zander really sent Mel packing? She didn't want to be unkind, but she hoped so. She stole a glance at him from the corner of her eye, taking in his strong jaw peppered with dark stubble, his straight, noble nose and the thick, dark eyelashes that framed his blue eyes.

'You alright?' he asked, turning to her, taking her by surprise.

'Mmhm.' She nodded. 'My shoulder aches a bit.' That wasn't strictly true, it was bloody throbbing. 'And I've got a bit of a headache, but other than that, I'm fine. Glad to be out of my car and in yours.' She gave a small laugh. Had she really been in a car that had skidded off the road and rolled over and over before landing on its roof with her inside? Sitting here beside Zander, it seemed somehow impossible, surreal even. That's the sort of thing that happens on the telly, in some far-fetched drama, she thought, not to boring, ordinary people like her.

In no time they were back at Dale View Cottage, where Zander had sat her down and carried out various checks, asking her questions, looking into her ears, her eyes, checking her bruises.

'Good,' he said, smiling. 'The fact that you didn't lose consciousness is a bonus and I can't see anything that gives me concern. Though from your answers, I'd say you're suffering from a mild concussion, and a bit of shock, which might make you feel quite tired over the next few days, so you should really take it easy; it's important that you listen to your body. You've got a few bruises there that should get pretty colourful by tomorrow, but other than that, I think you'll be fine.'

Livvie smiled, relieved at his prognosis; the last thing she wanted to do was sit in A&E over at Middleton Hospital. 'Thank you.' She'd tried to ignore the embarrassment of him lifting her jumper up at the back; after all, he'd seen it all before, she told herself! Though, it still felt a little weird to feel his hands on her, the intimacy of skin touching skin.

'How does a cup of tea sound to help wash your parac-etamol down?'

'Sounds good.' She watched him go through the process of making tea, her mind reaching back to the previous evening when she'd heard him and Mel through the walls. Mel's unbridled enthusiasm had been toe-curlingly embar-rassing at the time. *Had he really done that? Had he really had sex with Mel after what he'd told her?* She didn't know what to make of the situation, what to think about the mixed messages that had been flying around over the last few days.

'Come on, let's have these in the living room.' His smile

made her stomach flip as he nodded towards the door, two mugs in one hand, a plate of biscuits in the other.

'Okay.' Livvie followed, Alf close behind.

'And after you've had your tea, why don't I run you a bath to help those aches and pains?'

'Sounds lovely, but I can do that myself. I don't expect you to run around after me.' She winced as she eased herself down onto the sofa.

'It's no trouble; I can't help but feel responsible for what happened to you.' A shadow crossed his face; it tugged at Livvie's heart.

'It wasn't your fault; I just thought it was best if I wasn't around so you could get things sorted with Mel. And it was probably my crappy driving that meant I ended up coming off the road.' She gave a shallow laugh, trying to make light of the situation.

'Well, it certainly helped me get sorted with Mel, but I still wish it hadn't been at the expense of you having an accident like that.'

'Hey, no harm done – well, except to my poor little car. I don't know—' Livvie's words were cut off by a loud rumble from her stomach. 'Ooh, excuse me!' She giggled, pressing her hand against it.

Zander's eyebrows shot up. 'You sound ravenous after your escapades, here, you must try one of Lucy's home-baked cookies from the village shop. Shortbread with Belgian chocolate chips, they're delicious I'm reliably informed.'

'In that case, how can I refuse?' She took a biscuit from the plate and nibbled at it, thoughts tumbling around her mind as she watched the flames dancing behind the glass of the wood-burner.

The pair enjoyed a few moments of silent contemplation

in the soothing atmosphere of the cottage. Alf was curled up on the rug, his ears cocked in readiness for the sound of a crumb hitting the carpet.

'What happened with Mel, if you don't mind me asking?' Livvie picked up her tea, peering over the rim of the mug. As soon as the words had left her mouth she regretted the question, cursing herself inwardly. 'Actually, it's none of my business, please just forget I asked that.'

'I don't mind telling you; I actually feel it is your business after what's happened ... after what's been happening.' He puffed out his cheeks, releasing the air in a noisy sigh. 'It's a number of things really, but I didn't like the way she spoke to you last night, or how she did her best to make you feel uncomfortable. She wouldn't normally trouble herself to come out here, she hates the countryside. The only reason she was here was because she felt jealous, threatened by you.'

'Me? But she'd never met me.'

'Well, er ... she obviously sensed something.'

Livvie felt the heat of a blush warm her cheeks as happiness gave her heart a little squeeze. *Mel sensed something? Was this him acknowledging he felt the same electricity between them as she did? And was it so strong that Mel could pick up on it?* Livvie suddenly recalled how their friends from the village had teased about how they looked like they were an item, but they'd both laughed it off or ignored it. This, however, was the first time Zander had hinted at his feelings for her. Yes, they'd almost kissed a couple of times, but they'd never addressed it; they'd acted as if it hadn't happened.

Zander continued. 'And it really struck me how Alf never goes near her, but he adores you even though he hasn't known you for long; I always think dogs are good judges of character.' He paused for a moment, a muscle twitching in his cheek. 'And, if I'm completely honest, I knew our relationship had run its course. Mel did, too, but she was desperate to cling onto it because it made life easy for her.'

'Oh, right, well, regarding Alf, the feeling's mutual; I think he's awesome.' Alf's ears flickered at the mention of his name.

'Then, there's the matter of my feelings for you.' Zander turned to face her. 'I've never felt anything like this before, Livvie, it's just about knocked me off my feet.'

Livvie felt her blushes intensify. She took a sip of her tea, seeking refuge behind her mug. Butterflies took off in a flurry in her stomach, looping the loop, while her heart started to pound. She swallowed. Oh, Lord above, this was so confusing. 'But last night ... I heard ... I heard you and Mel ...' She didn't want to say she'd heard him and Mel getting down and dirty, but she was struggling to work out how he could so easily switch from that to declaring such strong feelings for her.

Zander clamped a hand to his forehead. 'Arghh! I know, I'm such a prat. I regretted it as soon as ... well, you know. I can't believe I was so weak, but she was there and ... If it's any consolation, I wasn't thinking of Mel—'

'Please don't go there.' Livvie held her free hand up. She didn't want to hear what she thought he was going to say; it would sound unbearably crass and she didn't want to think of him like that.

'No, you're right.' He looked suitably chastened. 'But I do deeply regret it.'

Livvie sighed, her mind was all over the place and she really didn't know how to answer him. Zander was a free agent now; free to kiss her without it making her feel like she was doing the dirty on another woman. But, although he knew his relationship with Mel was over, he'd still gone and had sex with her and that really bugged Livvie. Consequently, kissing him was the last thing she felt like doing. She just wanted to sit here, in this beautiful, cosy room, sip her tea and eat delicious biscuits, without having a complicated conversation that would only add to her headache. She closed her eyes and rested her head against the back of the sofa, the twinge in her shoulder reminding her of the morning's earlier events. *Why are things never straightforward?*

AFTER SOAKING in the bath until her skin was wrinkled and prune-like, Livvie changed into her pyjamas and headed downstairs. Zander was in the kitchen, sitting at the table, eyes focused intently on his phone. He looked up when she walked in. 'Hi,' he said, his face lighting up.

'Hi.' She smiled and bent to stroke Alf's head.

'How was the bath?'

'Good, thanks.'

'You look better.'

She pulled out the chair opposite him. 'I feel it; though I'm still trying to process what happened. And then I keep remembering about my car being stuck down that bank side.'

'Well, I hate to say it, but I suspect that's a write-off.'

'Really?' Livvie didn't want to think about the ensuing problems that would cause.

'But don't worry, Camm's been on, said he'd popped in to the garage at Middleton-le-Moors and arranged for someone to come out and tow it away when the weather improves. Said they'd check it over for you, too.'

'That's good of him.' That was one thing less to worry about; she wasn't even going to think about a replacement or how she'd get back home at the moment.

'Yeah, he's a good bloke. He said Molly had asked him to remind us of their get-together this afternoon – if you're up to it.'

The thought of seeing her new friends again sent a warm glow through Livvie. 'I'd like that, if it's okay with you?'

'It's great with me; they're a good fun crowd – though, if I remember rightly, I don't need to tell you that. If you take it easy – no booze with concussion, I'm afraid – you'll be fine and we can come home when you're ready. I actually think it'll do you the world of good after the last couple of days.'

Livvie couldn't argue with that, noting that the happy sparkle had returned to his eyes.

ZANDER

WHILE LIVVIE WAS in the bath Zander's mind began replaying scenes from the last twenty-four hours. The sense of relief at getting her out of her car and into the four wheel drive was still overwhelming; he'd felt physically sick when he'd seen the tyre tracks disappearing over the edge of the road and finding her car on its roof. There was no denying, his feelings for her ran deep.

If that's the case, then why did you go and shag Mel last night, you utter knob? Though the accusing voice of his guilty conscience made him cringe, he still couldn't come up with an answer to that, other than his testosterone levels were in over-drive, running riot round his body, thanks to his intense attraction to Livvie, and he needed to do something with them. It was a split-second decision when he'd opted to take Mel up on her offer of a sanctuary for them. One he bitterly regretted.

'Arghh!' he said. Alf looked at him as if he'd lost the plot. 'I've cocked-up big time, buddy.'

Alf harrumphed and snuggled back down; there were no biscuits on offer and he wasn't interested.

THE ROADS to Withrin Hill Farm were clear thanks to Camm and Ben's vigilant ploughing and gritting efforts, and the snow that had threatened earlier had come to nothing. But the bitter wind was still whirling around, blowing dense, angry-looking clouds further along the moors, keeping the snow off them for now.

'It's easy to see why this is called Withrin Hill,' said Livvie as the wind pushed and shoved the car as they made their way up the lane to Molly and Camm's.

'Yep, it's very aptly named. We'll keep an eye on things and if it looks like snow's imminent, we can head home. I should imagine the last thing you'll need today is getting stuck in more snow or having a long walk back,' Zander said as they pulled into the neat farm yard where a handful of Landies and four-wheel drives were lined up.

'Too true. Oh wow, what a beautiful house, so different from the cottages in the village,' said Livvie.

Zander looked up at the rambling Georgian farmhouse that stood steadfastly against the howling winds of the capricious moorland weather. 'Yes, it's old but not as old as the ones in the village. I believe it's been in Molly's family for generations, which is typical of the farms around here; either that or they're tenanted out by the Danskelfe Estate.'

Before Livvie had chance to answer, the door to the house flew open and Molly called to them. 'Great to see you, get yourselves in here where it's warm.'

'Hi dere,' said three-year-old Emmie, peering round her mother's skirt, waving a chubby hand at them.

'Oh, my goodness, she's so cute,' said Livvie.

'How're you feeling after your escapade this morning,

chick?' Molly pulled Livvie into a hug. 'Sounded bloody awful.'

'Buddy awful,' said Emmie.

'Mother, that's another pound in the swear box,' said Ben. He caught Zander's eye and chuckled.

'It's fair to say, it won't go down as the best way I've spent a morning.'

The pair followed Molly and Emmie down the hall to the large kitchen with warm yellow-ochre walls, where an ancient cream Aga threw out a gentle warmth. There was a huge casserole dish simmering on one of its hotplates, kicking out a mouth-watering aroma that made Zander's stomach rumble. Beside it, Molly's mum Annie was busy beating a huge bowl of mashed potato, while her dad Jack was helping himself to a little tot of damson gin. A nineties playlist was belting out hits from the iPod speakers and the room was full of friendly faces who called out their delight at seeing Zander and Livvie. Noushka, Ollie's daughter, was dancing with her half-sister, eleven-year-old Lily and her best friend Abbie, twirling them around with her fingers, while their brother Lucas was surreptitiously trying to stick something on his Uncle Jimby's back. Somehow, amidst the chatter and banter, Lottie, Kitty and Ollie's angelic-looking toddler, was fast asleep in her pushchair, thick, dark lashes resting on plump, rosy cheeks. It made Zander smile; he remembered Steff sitting her two beside the washing machine when they were babies, swearing that it helped them sleep.

His eyes settled on the large kitchen table, it had been extended by the addition of another two smaller ones of a slightly different height at either end; huge festive table-cloths had been flung over them disguising the fact. A variety of mismatched wooden chairs were set around it before bright white plates with Christmas crackers laid across them. In the centre of the table sat a squat miniature Christmas tree, decorated with glittering baubles and sparkly shapes that were clearly little Emmie's handiwork. A wave of happiness washed over him. He thrived on this kind of family get-together, full of warmth, noise, chaos and love; he couldn't help but smile as he thought how much like Steff's home it was, and how like the one they'd grown up in. But, from what she'd shared with him, so unlike the one Livvie had experienced. He turned to see her hazel eyes shining as she took it all in.

'Oy! Get your grubby mitts off that brownie, Jimbo!' Molly gave the back of Jimby's hand a slap just as he was about to help himself to a corner of a traybake.

'Ouch, that hurt! I was only making sure it was edible in my capacity as quality control executive.'

'Huh, a likely story. And what's that you've got stuck on your back?' She peeled off the sticker Lucas had just fixed on, handing it to her cousin.

He read it with frown. 'Eh? "I've just farted". Lucas, you little bugger! I wondered what you were up to.' Lucas ran off sniggering and Jimby grinned, catching sight of Zander. 'Now then, me aud mucker.' He strode across the room, bottle of beer in one hand, clapping Zander on the shoulder with the other. 'Good to see you made it, the pair of you – and Alf, too. He glanced across to where Alf was getting acquainted with Molly's Labrador, Mabel. 'Camm and Ben've been telling us all about what happened this morning.' He turned to Livvie. 'Must've been a right shocker for you. Are you okay?'

'It was scary at the time, but I'm fine now. I think I've learnt my lesson about driving in snow with the wrong type of tyres.'

'Aye, makes a big difference out here.'

'Can I get you a drink?' asked a pretty girl with a glossy curtain of long, dark hair.

'Oh, hi there, Kristy – this is Livvie, by the way; Livvie, this is Kristy, she's Ben's girlfriend,' said Zander.

'Hi Livvie, good to meet you. I heard about your accident and I'm so pleased you're okay.' The young girl beamed at Livvie and leaned in conspiratorially. 'Ben and me have made some punch; it's really fruity but it's lethal.'

'Ah, I'm afraid I'm driving and Livvie's got a mild concussion, so much as I think it sounds delicious, unfortunately neither of us can have it; doctor's orders, I'm afraid.' Zander laughed when he saw their disappointed expressions. 'Maybe next time.'

'Don't worry, you're not the only ones on juice or water.' Vi waddled over, a wide smile on her face, her aubergine-tinted hair glossier than ever, a glass of apple juice held aloft.

'Hello, there, Vi, you're looking well,' said Zander.

'Ah, I'm counting down to the day I can have a cheeky little gin and tonic.' She turned to Livvie. 'Remind me to have a word with you about Romantique before you head off, but first, I must pop to the loo; all this apple juice ...' Vi pulled a face as she rushed off.

'Oh, will do.'

Zander wondered what that meant. He'd heard them jokingly offer Livvie a job the other night. Were they serious? If so, would Livvie be tempted to stay here in Lytell Stangdale?

That thought set his mind whirring.

～

BEFORE LONG, the men had grouped together, engrossed in their usual favourite topics of tractors, Landies and four-wheel drives. 'So, Zander, when are you going to come and take over from bloody useless Dr Goodliffe?' asked Jack.

'It's a nice idea, but not very practical for me living in Leeds I'm afraid.'

'Ah, but you could always move here full time,' said Robbie.

'Means you'd be closer to Livvie.' Jimby winked at him.

'Aye, everyone already thinks the sun shines out of your arse which puts you way ahead of Dr Goodliffe,' said Camm.

'And you get on well with Dr Beth,' said Ollie. 'In fact, I think you'd make a great team at the surgery.'

'I agree,' said Jimby.

'Same here,' added Robbie.

'It's worth thinking about,' said Jimby. Zander noted his expression was serious for once.

His mind wandered for a moment; Beth had jokingly suggested he join her in the partnership at the surgery but he'd never really given it serious thought, being happy where he was, working with Noah. This was definitely food for thought.

Conversation eventually turned to Mel. 'Dear God, she's a frosty one,' said Camm. 'She barely spoke two words to me all the way to Middleton. Her face was set like granite.'

'Lucky you,' said Zander. 'She'd been screeching at me earlier; my ears are still ringing.'

'So, me aud mucker, now she's out of the picture, that leaves things nice and clear with you and Livvie.' Jimby waggled his eyebrows mischievously.

Zander sighed. 'Hardly.'

'Hey, even I can see that you've got the hots for each

other; it reminds me of Kitty and me, skirting around each other for ages,' said Ollie.

'Uhh, tell me about it.' Jimby rolled his eyes. 'Please don't take as long as Oll before he got his arse into gear – seventeen years, wasn't it, mate?'

'Aye, something like that – worth it in the end, though.'

'If you want my opinion, it was pretty clear the other night at the village hall that Livvie likes you.' Robbie nudged Zander's shoulder. 'More than likes you.'

'Hmm. That was then, something's happened, or should I say, I've done something bloody stupid that I think makes her feel differently about me now.'

'Come on, tell all, let's see if we can help,' said Jimby.

Zander dragged his hand down his face. 'I know it sounds stupid – soppy even – but I've honestly never felt anything like this about a woman before. From the moment I set eyes on her, I got this powerful feeling in my gut that she was "the one". There, I've said it, you can have a good old howl at me now.' He felt his face burn with embarrassment but, somehow, he didn't care; it felt good to get it out in the open.

Ollie patted him on the back. 'Hey, mate, you're talking to the right blokes here, Jimby and me know exactly where you're coming from.'

'Too right,' said Jimby, winking at Vi across the room.

'Yes, but you won't believe what I did last night.' Zander cringed at the memory.

'Surely nothing can be that bad,' said Ollie.

'I slept with Mel.' Zander looked around; their shocked expressions told him exactly what they were thinking.

Silence hung in the air for several long seconds. Jimby was the first to speak. 'Well, in the cold light of today, it might feel like you've pissed on your chips, but with a little bit of distance, I've got a good feeling that things will be fine.'

'Same here,' said Ollie. 'Livvie's had a bit of a time of it from what you've said, what with her ex, your ex, and the car accident, but it's clear that she has feelings for you; and there's something about you two together that just seems right, but being a useless bloke, I can't put my fingers on the right words or the right way to describe it.'

'Oll's right,' said Camm. 'Just give her a bit of time, things have a habit of working out. Trust me, I know all about that.'

The other men nodded in agreement. 'You two are meant to be together, even we can see that,' said Robbie.

Their words swirled around Zander's mind; he hoped with all his heart they were right.

'CAN you set this on that mat on the table?' Molly handed Zander an enormous tureen of mashed potato. Her phone had just pinged with a text. 'Normally I'd leave that, but I'm expecting to hear from Tom so I'll just quickly check it.'

'Course, no problem.'

Molly clapped her hand to her forehead. 'Arghh! The troublesome old bugger, I wish I'd ignored it now.'

'What's the matter?' asked Zander.

'Well, from that tone, it can only be one person,' said Kitty. 'Granny Aggie.'

'Yep, it's Granny bloody Aggie; up to her usual with the vicar.'

'Sounds ominous,' said Zander.

'You've no idea,' said Jimby. 'What's she said now, Moll?'

Molly sighed. 'You know how she's been feeding that stray cat?'

'Yes.' Rosie looked worried.

'Oh, God, I think I know what's coming next,' said Violet.

'Well, she's only gone and sent Rev Nev a text telling him that she has a lovely pussy and asked him if he wants to go and stroke it. Told him it purrs if he does it gently.'

Zander, had been taking a sip of beer from his bottle and swallowed it quickly to avoid spraying the room. He looked around at the others who were bent double with laughter. 'Please tell me she's done that in innocence.'

Molly snorted. 'Like bugger she has; the wicked old bat knows exactly what she's doing, pretends it's innocent though.'

'She tortures poor old Rev Nev, I'm surprised he hasn't asked for a transfer,' said Ollie.

'Does she say how he replied to her?' asked Rosie.

'Apparently he wasn't keen.'

'Can't say I blame him.' Camm headed to the worktop where a bowl of buttery garden peas were waiting. 'These ready for the table, Moll?'

'Yep, let's get cracking, just stick a lid on them so they keep warm. I need to line my stomach before I deal with that wayward old pensioner and her sodding mischief.' Molly took a breath. 'Grub's up. Come and park yourselves at the table. Young 'uns, you're at that end, big 'uns, you're at this end. Pass your plates down and I'll stick some game casserole on them for you.'

'Talk about a foghorn.' Vi rubbed her ears.

'It's the only way I can get you lot to listen.' Molly grinned at her friend.

Zander tried to imagine Mel fitting in up here. Nope, he

thought, that was never going to happen. Livvie, however, was a different matter. He turned his gaze to her; she was having an animated conversation with Kitty and Rosie, chuckling about something, her nose scrunching up in that cute way that made his stomach flip. He needed to do all he could to show her what she meant to him.

37

LIVVIE

'THAT WAS ABSOLUTELY DELICIOUS, MOLLY.' Livvie leaned back in her chair and rubbed her stomach. 'Thank you for inviting me.'

'You're welcome, hon, I'm just glad you could come.' Molly beamed at her. 'Anyone fancy a tea or a coffee?'

'Ooh, I could murder a cuppa,' said Kitty.

Livvie glanced between the cousins. 'I couldn't tell the other night – for obvious reasons, with the fancy dress and all that – but there's such a strong resemblance between you two and Jimby, and your mum too, Molly.'

'It's the big brown eyes and dark curly hair, isn't it?' said Rosie.

Livvie nodded. 'Yeah, it is.'

'Yeah, and while Kitty's features area all dainty and elfin, I'm like a bloody great carthorse,' said Molly.

'Though no one knows where Moll's filthy mouth comes from, do we, chuck?' Vi giggled.

'Bugger off.' Molly grinned at her friend.

'Molly!' Her mum gave her a disapproving look.

'Could be worse,' said Vi. 'Usually is.'

'Nowt wrong with a hearty dose of Anglo Saxon, if you ask me. It's part of our heritage.' Molly gathered a handful of mugs together and set them on the table to make tea.

Livvie giggled; Molly was a hoot.

'Well, I've heard some excuses for your filthy language, but that's the best so far,' said Vi. 'I'm impressed, Moll, I've never heard it described as being "part of our heritage" before. Inventive, chick.'

Molly curtseyed. 'Thank you.'

'Molly, lovie, while the other children are in the living room letting off steam on the game thingamajig, I'm just going to take this little one for a lie-down; she's looking shattered.' Annie had a drowsy-looking Emmie in her arms. The little girl was sucking her thumb, a finger hooked over her nose.

'Oh, okay, thanks, Mum.' She turned to her daughter, placing a hand on her chubby cheek. 'Oh, you do look like a sleepy little pudding. Have a good nap, sweet pea.' Molly dropped a kiss on the top of Emmie's dark curls which made the tot suck on her thumb with greater vigour.

'Any idea how many swear boxes you've filled this year, and have you worked out what you're going to do with the money?' asked Kitty. She reached into the fridge for the milk, passing it to her cousin.

'Hundreds, I should imagine,' said Vi, dryly.

'Could even be running into thousands,' added Rosie.

'Very funny. I've lost count, actually, but I was talking to Tom and Ben about it, and we've agreed that it should probably go to the Air Ambulance.'

The friends went silent for a moment and Livvie sensed they'd touched on something sensitive but she didn't like to ask.

'That's a good cause; they'll be over the moon that you've

got a gob like a fishwife.' Vi gave Molly a nudge and the mood lightened in an instant. Livvie made a mental note to mention it to Zander; she didn't want to put her foot in it at a later date.

She sat back in her chair, sipping her tea and doing her best to ignore the throbbing ache in her shoulder as she listened to the good-natured banter between the friends. Molly had a wonderful home; the atmosphere was so friendly, welcoming and happy. A far cry from the one Livvie had grown up in, or her sister's for that matter. Poor Ryan, though he could be obnoxious, Livvie felt for her nephew; he knew no better.

'Ooh, that reminds me.' Livvie set her mug down, a twinge in her shoulder making her wince. 'You said you wanted to talk to me about something, Vi.'

'We certainly do, don't we, Kitts?'

Kitty nodded enthusiastically. 'Absolutely.'

'I'm intrigued.'

'Good,' said Vi. 'We're hopeful you'll like what we've got to say.'

Livvie listened intently as between them, Kitty and Violet explained how they were keen to expand Romantique into wedding dresses – not just the occasional one as they'd been doing so far. They'd been inundated with orders and had even had to turn some away owing to Vi's pregnancy and Kitty's family commitments. Mary, Vi's mum, had been a talented seamstress in her younger days and had been keen to help out, but arthritis had cruelly distorted her fingers, making it difficult and painful for her to sew.

'We've been testing the water locally, trying to spread the word that we're looking for someone who can sew, but no one who's applied has the skill level we're after,' said Vi.

'We're just putting it out there,' said Kitty. 'We love

your clothes, the fact you can make your own patterns and your sewing's of an amazingly high standard, plus the fact you work in a wedding gown shop and do the alterations – and this dress you've made is stunning.' Kitty smoothed her hand over the plum coloured midi dress Livvie had made and embellished with beads she'd found in a charity shop.

'What we're trying to say is, we've been having a chat – well, a few actually – and wondered if you'd consider applying for the job?' said Kitty, beaming at her.

'Wow!' Their words tumbled around Livvie's mind. 'I don't know what to say.'

'Yes!' said Vi. 'Just say yes.'

'That would be the perfect answer, but please feel that you can take your time to think about it, you don't have to let us know right now,' said Kitty.

'The only thing is, it's a long way from Rickelthorpe.' Already, Livvie had started to weigh up the pros and cons.

'Jimby's cottage will be available in the New Year. The rent would be very cheap; we've already discussed it. Just saying ...' Vi gave a hopeful arch of her eyebrows.

'But you hardly know me,' said Livvie.

'Ah, but we're bloody good judges of character, chick, and the way you've just slotted in says it all, really.' Molly gave her a wide smile.

'Talking of good judges of character, have you seen Mabel and Alf?' Kitty nodded towards the two Labradors who were curled up together by the Aga, Mabel resting her head on Alf's rear.

'Ah, bless.' Vi smiled across at them. 'They look like an old married couple.'

'Not sure Ethel would be pleased to hear you say that; she was quite taken with him on the night of the eighties do,' said Kitty. 'I reckon there'll be a touch of the green-eyed-monster there.'

'He's such a lady's man is old Alfie.' Zander had joined them. 'I hate to break up a party but it's started to snow, Livvie; I think we should consider heading back.'

'Really?' Livvie didn't want to leave, but if she was honest, she was feeling shattered and, on top of the increasing pain in her shoulder, her headache was creeping back.

'Afraid so,' he said.

'Don't forget what we said, Livvie, and you're very welcome to have a look around the studio, see what it's like, how we work. Just let us know and we'll make sure we're both there.' Vi gave a hopeful smile.

'Ooh, yes, that's a good idea.' Kitty looked equally hopeful, making Livvie giggle.

'Okay, I'll do that.' She liked the sound of having a peek in at their studio; it sounded like an awesome place.

'And you know I said fate was talking to you the other night?' said Molly.

'Yes,' said Livvie.

'Well, it's bloody bellowing at you now.'

Livvie laughed and pulled her coat on. 'Point taken.'

OUTSIDE, the weather was worse than Livvie had expected and giant snowflakes swirled around the car, dancing like feathers in the headlights.

'Did you have a good time?' Zander asked her.

'The best; everyone's so warm and friendly.'

'They are; they're fiercely loyal and look out for each

other, particularly the women, and woe betide anyone who hurts one of them.'

Livvie turned to him. 'What do you mean?'

'Oh, it's just a few unpleasant characters have been less than kind, shall we say. The ladies closed ranks and, Molly in particular, made mincemeat of them – she takes no prisoners, that one.'

Livvie grinned. 'And I love her all the more for knowing that.'

38

ZANDER

ONCE BACK AT Dale View Cottage, Livvie disappeared up to her room to text Bryony. Zander sat at the kitchen table and scooped up his phone; he had a couple of things he wanted to run by Noah and Beth.

He called Noah first. 'Hi, Zander. You've got perfect timing.'

'Hi, Noah. I do?'

'Yep. I was just dropping the kids off at a party and I couldn't hear myself think; your call gave me the perfect excuse to escape. Anyway, how's things?' From the sound of traffic in the background, Noah was walking along the pavement.

'Er, things are good. Well, that's not strictly true, things are actually pretty complicated.'

'Okay, and does this have anything to do with Mel?'

Zander sighed. *Mel and so much more.* 'You could say.'

'Why doesn't that surprise me? Where are you, by the way?'

'I'm at the cottage near Lytell Stangdale; I thought it

would be the best place for me to keep a low profile and get my head straight.'

'I can see the logic in that.'

'The thing is, there's been a mix up with the cottage. When I arrived on Friday night there was already someone here – a paying guest.'

'Oops! How did that happen?'

'I'm not sure, but I think it was something to do with a last-minute cancellation and the website not updating properly.'

'Right...'

'Anyway, to cut a long story short, the guest is ... well, we've really clicked. She's called Livvie, and honestly, Noah, I know it's going to sound crazy, and you're going to think I've lost my marbles, but I've never felt this way about anyone before. And I'm pretty certain she feels the same. Don't ask me to put it into words, cos I can't.' Zander gnawed on his bottom lip, anxious for his friend's reaction.

'Wow! I wasn't expecting you to say anything like that.'

'I know, which makes me really wish I hadn't gone and slept with Mel last night.'

'What? Mel's there, too? I thought she was in London.'

'She was until yesterday; she turned up here last night.'

'And you couldn't resist temptation?'

'That's about the measure of it.'

'Things were sounding so good until you said that.'

Zander grimaced. 'I know. I honestly think it's one of the most foolish things I've ever done.'

'I can think of a few others – namely to do with your dodgy choice in wildly unsuitable women – but this Livvie, well, I've never heard you talk about anyone like this before. Sounds to me like you've got it bad, mate.'

Zander ran his fingers through his hair. 'Like I said, I've

never felt like this about anyone before. I just wish I hadn't made such a bloody stupid mistake with Mel. What can I do to put things right?'

'Obviously, I've never met this Livvie before and I can't begin to guess what she's feeling, so all I can suggest is to give her a bit of time and space. Don't push things or you could run the risk of it having the opposite effect. I can't explain it, Zander, but from the way you've been talking, I've got a good feeling about this. But promise me one thing.'

'What's that?'

'You'll keep away from Mel. That means no texts, no calls, no anything. If she tries to get in touch, ignore her; she's bad news and always has been. There, I can say it now without fear of offending you.'

'Don't worry, I've no intention of having anything more to do with her.'

'I can't tell you how glad I am to hear you say that.'

'There's something else I wanted to talk to you about.'

'My, you have been busy,' said Noah, laughing.

'I'm thinking of relocating to Lytell Stangdale.'

'Does that mean what I think it does?'

'Yep, I'm also thinking of taking Beth up on her offer to join her at the practice in Danskelfe.'

'About bloody time!'

'Really?'

'Yes, really! I wondered how long it was going to take you to accept that you're a country lad at heart. You've always looked like a fish out of water in the city, but completely at home in the countryside.'

Zander sat back and smiled; Noah was absolutely right.

～

B<small>UOYED BY</small> N<small>OAH'S ENTHUSIASM</small>, Zander fired off a text to Beth, asking if he could call her. *Strike while the iron's hot!* He hoped she wouldn't mind him intruding on her holiday, nor take an age to reply. He didn't have long to wait when less than five minutes later his phone pinged and her name appeared on the screen.

His pulse picked up speed, racing round his body as he called her number.

Z<small>ANDER WAS STACKING</small> logs by the wood-burner when Livvie came downstairs. She'd changed into a pair of pale purple and green gingham pyjamas, her stunning hair tamed into plaits that hung either side of her face. His heart leapt; she looked incredibly cute.

'Good idea to get comfortable. I think I might do the same,' he said.

'It's the first thing I do when I get home from work; jump straight into my jammies. Can't beat getting comfy,' she said. 'Especially after a stressful day with Mrs "Dragon" Harris.'

'I can imagine.' He wiped his hands together, dusting away any splinters of wood. 'And how's Bryony? Has she heard anything more from Donny?'

'She's fine and, thankfully, he's kept away.'

'Good.'

'But it's not so good with my family.' A shadow fell across her face.

'Oh?'

'Yeah, I tried to ring them to say I wouldn't be going to Cheryl's for Christmas dinner – I probably should've done it sooner, but I was dreading it, so ended up putting it off; pathetic excuse, I know. Anyway, neither of them picked up, which is nothing new, so I texted them. Both replied straight away.'

'I'm guessing they weren't very happy.' *Why wouldn't they answer her call?* It bothered Zander that their behaviour might make her feel sad; he couldn't imagine his family treating him that way.

'No.' She shook her head. 'But I suspect it's probably because they'll have no one to pick on or to ridicule or to make Cheryl look even more successful than she already is. But that's fine; I'd much rather be here.'

Though she smiled, Zander could see their words had hurt her and, hard as it was, he resisted the urge to pull her into a hug.

He looked down at her, trying to read her expression. 'Tea, coffee, teeny glass of wine?' He demonstrated a small measure with his forefinger and thumb.

'Ooh, if it's allowed, I think I'll go for the teeny glass of wine.'

'It's allowed, as long as you sip it slowly.'

'Cross my heart.'

'Right, you make yourself comfy while I get that sorted.'

'WHAT A DAY,' said Zander, swirling the wine around his glass.

'Just a bit. The afternoon was definitely much nicer than the morning.' Livvie smiled at him, firelight shining in her eyes.

He shook his head in disbelief. 'They seem like two separate days. In fact, these last few days, with everything that's happened, seem like they've had weeks' worth of things squashed into them.'

'Tell me about it. I'm trying to push the horrible things that have happened out of my mind so I can focus on the good things.'

Zander glanced across at her. She looked so tiny sitting there on the sofa, in her over-sized pyjamas, her feet curled underneath her. She was watching Alf who was flaked out in front of the wood-burner, unmistakable affection in her eyes. That now familiar feeling that only she stirred in him tugged at his insides. He wanted nothing more than to kiss her, feel those plump, red lips on his, then take her to bed with him. Reality kicked in, scattering his thoughts. After what he'd done with Mel, that wasn't going to happen any time soon.

'You know, Kitty and Vi mentioned they're looking to take someone on at Romantique.' Livvie's voice broke into his thoughts.

'I wondered what they were talking to you so intently about. And what do you think?'

He watched her expression change as she thought about her answer. 'Well, they said some really kind things about my sewing and the clothes I've made, but it's so far from my home, my family ...' He noticed her voice drifting off and wondered if she was thinking the same as him: were her family really worth staying at Rickelthorpe for? From what she'd told him, their lack of kindness and affection suggested they weren't.

'And you think you should say no?'

She sighed. 'Oh, gosh, I don't know. What they're offering is actually my dream job, designing and making wedding dresses. And if there was a job like it going in Rickelthorpe, I wouldn't think twice about applying for it.' She pressed her hand to her chest, her expression animated. 'But, it's a big step, moving here. Does that sound silly?'

'It doesn't sound silly at all, it just sounds like you're weighing everything up and trying to come to the right decision for yourself.' If only she knew how her decision would help him reach his own.

'What would you do?'

I'd say yes! 'Well, I'd make a list of pros and cons, I find it helps clarify things in your mind if you see them on paper.'

'Hmm. I quite like that idea.'

Zander could see she was hesitating. 'But ...'

'Oh, nothing really, it's just I've got a book of drawings ... I've been doing them for years. Of wedding dresses, I mean.'

'And have you got it here?'

She nodded. 'I take it everywhere with me, in case an idea pings into my head. I haven't done anything with them, though, I've never shown them to anyone. Not even Bryony. In fact, you're the first person I've ever told about them.'

Her eyes looked huge in her face, almost as if they were wearing an expression of relief for sharing something secret with him.

'I don't suppose there's a chance I could have a look at them?'

He watched her mull this over in her mind. 'As long as you promise not to laugh.'

'I'm sure I won't be laughing, but if it makes you happy, then I promise not to.'

Livvie shot up the stairs, returning in a flash. She handed the book to Zander. His eyes roved over the doodles on the front as he opened it carefully. He flicked through it without speaking, feeling her gaze intently on him. 'These are amazing, Livvie, you've got a real gift.' He didn't know much about wedding dresses, but it was clear to see that her designs were stunning. It would be a shame for her to waste such talent.

'Really? You honestly think that?'

'Absolutely. It just makes me wonder why you hesitated when we were talking about making a list and then you moved onto this? Surely this is a positive thing; a reason to say yes.'

'That's what I was a bit scared of.'

'But didn't you say it was your dream job?'

'I did ... it is ... oh heck...'

Their eyes locked, electricity crackled in the air around them, the undeniable connection they shared pulling Zander towards her. He reached out and cupped his hand around the back of her head, his lips tentatively brushing hers, sending his pulse racing around his body.

'No!' She pulled back, her voice startling him. 'Please don't, I can't. Not now. I'm sorry.' She stood up and scurried off upstairs, leaving Zander kicking himself for reading thing so wrong.

Frustrated, he pushed his fingers into his hair. *Jesus! What the hell did I tell myself about taking things slowly? I'm such a turkey! Why can't I stop being so bloody impetuous? I never learn! Arghh!*

39

LIVVIE

Livvie threw herself on her bed, buried her face in the pillow and screamed silently into it. *Stupid me! Stupid, stupid, stupid me! Why, oh why did I pull away?* That gentle brush of Zander's lips had felt soft and delicious, sending a bolt of red hot lust raging through her.

She sat up straight and put her head in her hands, her cheeks flaming and her heart still pounding. Livvie knew the reason she'd pulled away from Zander's kiss: because he'd slept with Mel the previous night and that had changed everything. 'How can he switch from Mel to me in less than twenty-four hours,' she said to herself. 'I know men are supposed to be different to women but do they always have to think with their dicks? Ughh!'

She'd never felt so confused in her life. Here she was, sharing a cottage with a man she barely knew yet felt she'd known forever. To be suddenly taken by this ... this primal attraction, connection, indescribable feeling – whatever you want to call it – that she'd never felt with anyone before. Until now, she wasn't even aware it was possible to feel this strongly for anyone. And, despite what had happened with his ex, she had a pretty good idea Zander felt the same – or at least he was doing a damned convincing act. Livvie pushed her fingers into her hair. 'Arghh!' This was so frustrating! They were both free agents now but she couldn't get over the fact that he'd slept with Mel simply because she was offering it on a plate. That just didn't sit easy with Livvie.

She sighed, feeling suddenly exhausted; her eyes were heavy, her muscles were aching, as was her head but that had the added problem of feeling totally scrambled. She climbed into bed, snuggled down under the cosiness of the duvet and closed her eyes. In moments she was claimed by a deep sleep.

WHEN LIVVIE WOKE it was still pitch black outside. She flicked the bedside light on, the clock telling her it was the early hours of the morning yet it only felt like minutes since she'd closed her eyes. She threw the duvet back and tiptoed over to the window. Outside, the wind was still howling round the cottage, pushing and shoving the branches of the trees. Livvie was pleased to see there hadn't been much more snow. She crept back into bed and closed her eyes, but all she could see was Zander and the expression on his face as he'd kissed her. It made her heart squeeze and stirred the resident butterflies in her stomach. How she wished she hadn't pushed him away.

40

ZANDER

I AM SUCH A KNOB! No, scrap that, I am King of the Knobs! Why, oh, why didn't I wait until Livvie was ready before I tried to kiss her? Arghh! Arghh! Flaming arghh!

Passion, replied the voice of reason loud and clear in his ear. Because you wanted to do more than kiss her. She's aroused every little fibre of your body, and set it on fire; you want her, you need her, more than you've ever wanted or needed anyone before. You're meant to be together. You know it. She knows it. Everybody knows it. If only you'd kept your knob in your boxer shorts last night, everything would've been so very different.

Zander groaned inwardly.

When Livvie hadn't come back downstairs, he'd had one last glass of wine before letting Alf out in the garden. 'You don't know how lucky you are, fella, not having women trouble.' Alf looked up at him and wagged his tail. 'Mind you, the way you've been flirting with Ethel and Mabel, I guess it could be on the cards. Just make sure you decide who's the one for you and stick to it, that's my advice.' Alf shot back into the house, apparently keen to get out of the cold night air, snuggling down in his bed. 'Night, Alf,' said Zander as he turned off the light.

ZANDER'S WAKING thought was Livvie and their almost kiss, wondering how things would be between them that day. He'd hate for his clumsiness to create any awkwardness, or worse, push her away from him.

As he lay there, his mind drifted back to their time at Molly and Camm's the previous day, and it slowly dawned on him that today was Christmas Eve. They were supposed to be meeting the gang for carols round the Christmas tree in Lytell Stangdale. He hoped Livvie would still be keen to go with him; that his actions hadn't put her off.

ZANDER WAS SIPPING coffee and gazing out of the window when Livvie came downstairs.

'Morning,' she said. He turned to see her smiling at him.

'Morning. How are you feeling today ... I mean, after what happened with the car?'

'My head feels much better, but my body feels somehow more achey, if that makes sense.'

'It does, it's par for the course, I'm afraid.' He smiled, relieved that there didn't appear to be any awkwardness around them. 'Can I get you a coffee, tea, hot chocolate, juice?'

'I'm usually strictly a tea drinker first thing, but that coffee smells so good, I think I'll have one of those, please.'

'Coming right up.' He set the machine in motion, the nutty aroma soon filling the kitchen.

'It's hard to believe it's Christmas Eve today.' Livvie sat down at the table, smoothing Alf's head that had suddenly appeared in her lap.

'I was just thinking that. And, by the way, Alf Gillespie, what have I said about pestering at the table?'

'Ah, it's my fault, I encourage him, don't I, handsome?'

Alf's wagging tail bashed against the table leg.

'I suppose I can let him off this once.' Zander watched how content Alf was with Livvie. He'd really taken to her – more than anyone else Zander had known, even Steff. They'd both miss her if – when – she went back to Rickelthorpe.

'At least there hasn't been much more snow,' she said.

'Yes, we do seem to be getting off lightly at the moment, it's nothing like the winters Beth's described in the past. There you go.' He set her coffee down on the table.

'Thanks.'

Was it too early to mention this evening's Christmas carols, he wondered? Would she feel like he was pushing her into something? Would she even want to go with him? He watched her stroking Alf; she was smiling and didn't seem uncomfortable about last night. *Oh, what the hell!* 'Are you still up for the carols round the Christmas tree in the village?'

Relief flooded through him as a warm beam lit up her face. 'Definitely. I'm really looking forward to it; provided there's no more snow of course.'

'The weather here seems to be doing the opposite to what's forecast, so I think we should just play it by ear. It'd be a shame to miss it, from what everyone was saying yesterday.'

'I agree; I just love the community spirit in the village; the way everyone seems to pull together. I mean, it's nice at

Rickelthorpe, but not a patch on this place. I can't believe how welcome I've been made to feel.'

Livvie had just put into words exactly how Zander felt. Lytell Stangdale was, without doubt, a special place.

'While I remember, when we were at Molly and Camm's yesterday, Kitty and Vi mentioned Molly's swear box,' said Livvie.

'Good old Molly, I'd forgotten about that,' said Zander.

'Anyway, she said she was going to donate the money from it to the Air Ambulance, but I could sense the atmosphere change after she'd said it; it was kind of awkward – not for long – but it just made me wonder if there's something I should be careful of saying. I'd hate to upset or offend her.'

'Ah, yes. Molly lost her husband Pip in an accident a few years ago; I believe the Air Ambulance was called out for him.'

Livvie pressed her hand to her lips. 'Oh no, poor Molly and the kids. She's done amazingly well to be so happy and get on with her life.'

'Yeah, she's a tough one, but I think she's got a good support network around her. Incidentally, Granny Aggie – the old lady who sends cheeky text messages to the vicar – is Pip's grandmother and, although Molly grumbles about her, I think they share a similar smutty sense of humour.'

'Oh, I'd love to meet Granny Aggie,' said Livvie.

'Well, if you do, don't go giving her your phone number.'

Livvie giggled. 'Good point.'

THE PAIR SPENT the day skirting around what had happened the previous evening. Zander was desperate to ask if Livvie had thought any more about the job with Kitty and Violet, but held back in case it resurrected the awkwardness of the kiss. He longed to tell her that he thought it was an amazing opportunity for her to put her obvious talents to good use, but he kept quiet for fear she would think he was interfering. After all, it was a big decision for her to uproot from the place she'd lived all her life. No, this time he'd do his best to take things slowly, let Livvie lead the way.

41
———

LIVVIE

'How's it looking out there?' Zander asked as Livvie peered out through the living room curtains.

'Well, it looks pretty frosty but I don't think there's been any more snow which is good.'

'Looks like carol singing's on then.'

'Great. What time shall we set off?'

Zander checked his watch. 'Half an hour okay for you?'

'Perfect. I'll just put something warmer on.' Livvie felt inexorably excited at the thought of standing round the huge Christmas tree on the village green, absorbing the warm community spirit that she'd already come to appreciate was unique to Lytell Stangdale. She'd never done anything like it before and felt an almost childlike pleasure at the prospect. She liked that Zander seemed keen, too. She also liked that he hadn't mentioned their kiss, not that she was trying to think too much about it, but she was unsure how she'd react if he brought it up. She shook the thought out of her head. 'Is Alf coming?'

'Of course, though I'm not too sure about his singing skills.' His smile made Livvie's stomach flip.

LIVVIE AND ZANDER made their way over to the towering Christmas tree, its pine scent fragrant in the frosty air, while its warm white lights twinkled in the darkness.

'Yay! I'm so glad you're here.' Violet pulled Livvie into a hug, planting a kiss on her cheek.

'I'm so pleased the snow kept off.' Livvie hugged her back, being careful of Vi's baby bump.

'Hi, Livvie, so are we, we were hoping you'd be able to make it; it's such a lovely event.' Kitty followed up Vi's hug with one of her own.

Livvie felt a glow of happiness in response to this warm welcome from her new friends. 'Where are Molly and Rosie?'

'Molly's just texted to say she and Camm are on their way and Rosie should be here any minute,' said Kitty.

'Tell you what, seeing as though you're here, why don't we take you for a quick peek at the Romantique studio? The carols won't be starting for another fifteen, twenty minutes.' Vi's eyes twinkled.

'Ooh, good idea,' said Kitty. 'I've got the key right here.'

Livvie's heart started to race. 'I'd love to.'

'Fab! Come on then.' Vi led the way across the green and towards Sunshine Cottage that housed the studio in its back garden.

'Won't be long,' she called to Zander who nodded and, she noted, was smiling broadly.

Inside, Livvie gasped as she took in the stunning bridal gown on the tailor's dummy in the corner, its delicate antique lace and tiny pearls painstakingly hand stitched onto the fabric, the shelves of beads and crystals that sparkled in the lights, the bolts of sumptuous fabrics and the array of elegant sketches on the walls. 'Wow! This is amazing.' She felt like a child in a sweetshop, almost drooling at the scene before her. She could sense Vi and Kitty watching her closely, trying to read her expression.

'Thank you.' Vi gave her arm a squeeze. 'It's a great place to work, the team are fabulous, there's tea on tap as well as a daily supply of Lucy's chocolate dipped flapjacks! What's not to love?'

'No pressure, Vi.' Kitty grinned, turning to Livvie. 'Take your time to think about it; make sure it's right for you.'

Vi batted her eyelashes in an exaggerated way, a hopeful expression on her face that made the other women laugh.

'And what would I need to do to apply?'

'Just come in and construct part of the bodice of a wedding dress; one with fine detailing,' said Vi.

'Have a general chat and show us any designs you have, so we can get an idea if your style matches ours,' added Kitty.

Livvie nodded; in that split second, she'd made her decision, but she'd keep it close to her heart for now.

BACK AT THE village green Livvie found Zander chatting to Jimby and Ollie. 'Ah, here they are,' said Jimby, wearing his habitual wide smile. He threw his arm around Vi and planted a noisy kiss on her cheek. 'Now then, Mrs Fairfax.'

'Hi, Jimby.' Vi snuggled into him.

'We've been showing Livvie the studio,' said Kitty.

'We wondered where you'd got to,' said Ollie.

'And what did you think?' asked Zander.

'It's amazing.' She understood the subtext of his question: *Are you going to apply for the job?*

Before she had chance to say anything further, a voice called to say that the carols were about to begin and before she knew it a harmony of voices rose into the frosty night air. Livvie was taken off guard by the emotion that suddenly surged through her, causing her throat to tighten. She looked up at Zander to see him gazing down at her, the expression in his eyes making her heart leap. She smiled and bit back a tear that threatened to spill onto her cheek.

Halfway through the song, and without warning, Alf threw back his head and proceeded to howl woefully, causing a ripple of laughter to run around the carol singers.

'Alf!' Zander gave him a gentle nudge which stopped him momentarily. 'Sorry,' said Zander, glancing around at everyone. But seconds later, the Labrador started up again.

'He sings like you, Kitty.' Molly giggled.

'Oh, I think he's more in tune than our Kitts,' said Jimby.

'I wish I could argue with you, but you're right,' said Kitty.

'This is dreadful, I don't know what's got into him. I'll take him over there, hopefully he'll stop if he's not in the thick of things.' Zander tugged at Alf's lead and headed away from the green. 'Come on, you little sod.'

'I'll come with you,' said Livvie; she was finding it hard not to giggle.

42

ZANDER

'THANK GOODNESS FOR THAT.' Zander rolled his eyes. 'I thought he was never going to be quiet.'

'It was so funny.' Livvie was still giggling, her nose scrunched up in the way he found irresistible.

'It was horrendous. You won't be invited back after that display, Alfred Gillespie.'

'Has he done it before?'

'No! Never. That's why it was such a surprise tonight. Little bugger.' He looked down at Alf, who wagged his tail, apparently rather pleased with himself.

'Oh, he's so gorgeous and cute; he can get away with anything, can't you, handsome?' Livvie bent to stroke Alf's head.

'Don't encourage him. And what you don't yet know is that while you were looking round the studio, he went and had a good old sniff of Freda Easton – you know, the elderly lady who lives on her own and doesn't trouble soap and water; I think I heard Molly telling you about her?'

'Oh, yes, I remember.'

'Well, he only went and proceeded to cock his leg on her

and empty his apparently full bladder all over her feet. I can't tell you how relieved I was to see she was wearing wellies, and she took it well, bless her.'

'Oops.' Livvie pressed her lips together, struggling not to laugh.

'Still think he can get away with anything?'

'Well, at least the old lady was wearing wellies plus she didn't mind.'

'That's hardly the point.' Zander was treating Alf to a fake stern look when the Labrador threw his head back in readiness to resume his howling. 'Don't even think about it, matey.' Zander gave him another gentle nudge which seemed to do the trick, leaving Alf looking suitably chastened.

'Ooh, is that snow?' Livvie held her hand out as several large flakes swirled around them, one landing on her nose. With a smile, she swiped it off.

Zander felt a tug at his heart. He needed to clear the air, apologise to Livvie about last night. He was desperate to have her thinking well of him once more. *Go for it!* A persuasive voice urged him on, trampling over his resolution to take things slowly. *Oh, what the hell? What have I got to lose?*

He cleared his throat. 'Livvie, I just want to say that I'm truly sorry for what I did; for making you feel confused and upset over my stupid behaviour with Mel. I have no excuse and I still don't know why I did it. You've no idea what I'd give to turn the clock back and change what happened.' His heart was racing but already he was feeling a sense of relief at getting the words out.

'You don't have to apologise.'

What did that mean? Was she not bothered anymore? Would his apology not make any difference? He swallowed. 'I do, I really do. And I want to tell you ... need to tell you, er, what I want to say ... what I'm trying to say is ... oh, God, Livvie, as crazy as this may sound after only knowing you for a few days, well, I'm ... I've fallen in love with you. Head over heels actually, and I've never felt this way about anyone before.' He could feel his face flaming in the icy air.

Her lips parted slightly as she locked eyes with him. 'It doesn't sound crazy, Zander; not crazy at all. In fact, I, er, I feel the same.'

As his brain was computing her words, he suddenly realised that she was on her tiptoes, reaching her hands behind his head and pulling him into a kiss that was making his whole body tingle. Neither seemed to notice the huge snowflakes that were now whirling down around them or that the wind had whipped up and was racing around the village.

Seconds later Zander became aware of a stream of whoops and cheers. He and Livvie pulled apart to see their friends smiling and waving at them. Molly gave a shrill whistle.

'About time,' Jimby called.

Zander looked at Livvie, pulling her close as the pair laughed. 'Well, they sound happy about it.'

'Just a bit.'

He looked down to see Livvie glowing, her eyes shining brightly; he knew she'd been encompassed by these same powerful feelings, feelings that were way too strong to ignore.

'Shall we join them before anything else gets shouted across?' he asked.

'Good idea.'

'I hate to be a party-pooper,' said Jimby. 'But I think this snow is set to get quite bad; you'd probably be wise to get yourselves home, it can change pretty quickly out here.' He gave Zander a nudge and a wink.

'Aye, we've been lucky up to now, but I think the winter's about to catch up with us,' said Ollie.

'Well, after my stint in the snow yesterday, I'd rather not risk it,' Livvie said, looking up at Zander.

Zander noted the look of concern in her eyes. 'Of course, we'll head off. At least we caught some of the carols and the festive atmosphere.'

'PHEW, I'm relieved to be home.' Livvie shook the snow off her hat which despite the short distance from the car to the front door, was surprisingly well covered.

'Yeah, me too.' Zander's heart was singing; he was glad to be home for another reason: to be alone with her, but he'd take things slowly, wouldn't push her, he'd let Livvie set the pace.

'Fancy a glass of wine?' he asked.

'Love one.' She went to dry Alf off with his towel. 'What do you think we should do about dinner, seeing as though we missed out on having a meal at the Sunne?'

'Well, I think we need something warm and comforting on a night like this.' *I don't need anything to eat; I'd just like to take you to bed and spend the evening there with you.* 'I could always rustle up a quick macaroni cheese if you fancy? We should have the ingredients in the cupboards if I remember rightly.'

'Mmm mm. That sounds perfect; comfort food at its finest.' She beamed at him. 'I'll give you a hand.'

Zander poured the wine and the pair took their glasses into the living room. He threw a log on the wood-burner and opened the spin-wheels, flames instantly springing to life, casting a warm glow around the room.

'Oh, I love this cottage,' said Livvie as she flopped onto the sofa. 'I've never been anywhere with underfloor heating before but it's heavenly.'

'Yeah, it's definitely one of the best things I've had done here.' He was struggling to take his eyes off Livvie's delicious, plump lips; he longed to feel them against his again.

She sighed contentedly and sank back. Zander didn't know how to bring up their kiss or the words they'd spoken before it. An idea sprang into his mind and he got to his feet. 'Livvie, would you just pop over here for a moment?'

'What, oh, yes, what's the matter?' She went over to where he was standing.

'Well, it's just that I need to do this...' His voice was husky as he raised his eyes to the sprig of mistletoe hanging from the beam above them.

'Oh.'

Tenderly, he cupped her face in his hands and pressed his lips against hers. She groaned and he felt her melt into him. The feeling was intense and a wave of scorching heat surged through him. He'd never experienced the feeling of love and lust combined but it was intoxicating.

'Wow,' she said when they finally pulled apart. 'You're one amazing kisser.'

'You're not so bad yourself.' His eyes dark with passion, he tried to ignore the throbbing in his groin.

'I wasn't expecting all of this tonight,' she said, heading back to the sofa. 'I feel all of a dither; I need a sit down after that.' He followed and she patted the seat beside her.

'Me neither.' He sat down and threw his arm around her; she rested her head on his shoulder. Instinctively, he reached up and ran his fingers through her thick curls, enjoying their softness against his skin.

'So where do we go from here?' she asked.

Zander knew exactly where he'd like them to go right now, but he'd wait for Livvie to give him the signal.

43

LIVVIE

'I've REACHED A DECISION,' Zander said. They were curled up together on the sofa, Livvie's head resting on his chest.

'Oh?'

'I know my family are based in Leeds and I work with my best mate, but I'm going to take Beth up on her offer; I'm going to join the practice at Danskelfe.'

Livvie could feel her heart begin to race. 'So does that mean you're going to commute or ...?' She hardly dare ask.

'I'm going to relocate; I'm going to move in here full time.'

She sat up and faced him. Did she hear right? 'Really?'

'Yes.' He nodded 'And how about you, have you reached a decision about the job with Kitty and Vi?'

'Yes, I was already pretty certain I was going to apply – the texts from my mum and Cheryl went some way to helping me make up my mind actually, as did Bry moving to London – but seeing the studio tonight and all of the awesome things there, just confirmed it. Plus the fact that Kitty and Violet will be totally brilliant to work with; I'd be mad not to apply.' Excitement was thrumming through her veins; how had her life undergone such an about-turn?

'Well, after seeing your book of sketches, I have to agree and, incidentally, you need to show them to Kitty and Violet, I think they'll be really impressed.'

'Really?' She'd longed for the day someone would say that to her.

'Of course.'

Livvie leaned back into him; she couldn't imagine feeling any happier than she was in that moment, wrapped in the arms of a man she'd fallen head over heels for, discussing how she was going to embark on her dream job. Was it really happening? Perhaps she should pinch herself.

'You're welcome to stay here if you get the job at the studio.'

His suggestion hung in the air for a moment. 'Vi said something about Jimby's place coming up for rent. It might be a better idea if I live there, just while we're getting to know one another. After all, I might have some horrible habits you'd find unbearable.'

'What, worse than Alf's?' He laughed 'Only joking; I doubt you've got any such habits, but I take your point – about us getting to know one another that is. Anyway, I've just realised something: I need to kiss you some more.'

'If you insist.'

'I insist.' Zander pulled her to him, brushing his lips gently across hers before deepening the kiss, his tongue seeking hers.

Oh my days! Livvie wanted nothing more than to rip his clothes off right now and run her hands over the firm muscles she could feel beneath his shirt, but something was holding her back: she wanted him to wait, there was no way she was going to offer herself on a platter like *her*.

'Right,' Zander said. 'I think it's time I started work on dinner.'

As he pushed himself up, Livvie caught sight of the tell-tale bulge in his jeans. Lust was raging through both of them; how easy it would be for her to give in right now. She almost pulled him back down to her, tempted to say, "not yet", but for now, she let her head rule her heart. 'Good idea, I'm starving,' she said.

THE REST of the evening was spent sharing stories from their past, with a generous helping of heady kisses thrown in. Livvie couldn't believe it was possible to feel such happiness.

'Come and see this.' Zander beckoned Livvie over to the back door where he'd let Alf out for his last toilet trip into the garden.

'Wow, that's a whole load of snow.' A good four inches had settled since they'd got home and it was coming down in a dense flurry of fluffy snowflakes. Alf was scampering about in it, leaping up and trying to bite at the snow as it fell, making Livvie giggle.

'It sure is; if it carries on like this, it looks like we're going to be snowed in for Christmas day.'

'I can't think of anything nicer.' She stood on her tiptoes and pressed a kiss to his cheek, his five o'clock shadow prickling her lips.

'Me neither.' He wrapped his arm around her and pulled her close, the warmth of his body seeping through to hers.

'RIGHT, one last kiss under the mistletoe then I think I'll hit the sack.' Zander took Livvie by the hand and led her to the beam where it was fixed.

When they finally pulled apart, Livvie was dizzy with lust; it was taking every ounce of strength she had not to drag Zander upstairs. *Get that idea right out of your head, Livvie Weatherill!*

As she lay in bed, she reached her hand up to her lips, tracing where Zander's had been only moments before. The intensity of his kisses had blown her away, the feelings they'd generated in response made her whole body tingle. She closed her eyes, trying to steady herself but it was no use, she was aching for him; she needed him.

Sex with Donny had been a perfunctory affair, with no great depth of emotion on either part, if she was completely honest. And he'd never stirred up the intense feelings inside her Zander had. Nobody had.

Before she had time to think, Livvie had flung the duvet back and marched into Zander's room, her body pulsing with desire.

'Livvie?' He sat up and flicked the bedside light on. Her eyes went to his broad chest covered in dark hair. She needed to touch it, run her fingers over it, feel his warmth, inhale his masculine scent.

Unspeaking, she walked over to him and climbed into bed beside him. He rolled over and cupped her face with his hand before kissing her harder and harder. She ran her hand over his strong back, up and down the undulating muscles of his arms, her whole body aching for him. His hand reached under her pyjama top, finding her full breast. She sat up and pulled the top over her head before wriggling out of the trousers.

'God, you're beautiful,' he said tracing a line of burning kisses down her neck.

'Oʜ. Mʏ. Goᴅ.' Livvie threw her arms above her head, a sheen of dewy sweat glistening on the surface of her skin, her heart still racing. 'That was amazing. I've never felt that way before.'

'Me neither.' Zander gasped. 'It was mind blowing.' He laughed and said, 'Did that sound as cheesy to you as it did to me?'

'Just a bit.' She giggled and he pulled her close to him, pressing a kiss to the waves of her hair.

'But it was; mind-blowing, that is.'

Livvie thought her heart would burst with happiness. Was this really happening? Was she really lying in the arms of the most drop-dead gorgeous man she'd ever set eyes on, having just had the most – to pinch his expression – mind-blowing sex ever, after he'd told her he was in love with her? She squeezed her eyes shut and wiggled her toes. *Yes, it's really happening!*

44

ZANDER

WHO KNEW that sex with someone you're in love with would be so intensely different, Zander mused as Livvie lay in his arms. He wasn't going to start counting how many women there'd been in his life – he'd certainly been no monk – but tonight had been a first. Wow! That connection, that intensity of feeling, that they were so in tune with one another, had all added together and culminated in something ... well, something pretty bloody fantastic.

He squeezed her close to him, pressing his face in her silky auburn waves, inhaling her delicious fragrance of summer flowers. He felt his heart flip and a twitch in his groin.

Propping himself up on his arm, he glanced down at her, running his finger down her cheek, taking in her creamy skin and the smooth undulation of her curves. 'You're so beautiful, Livvie.' The ensuing blush that stained her cheeks only added to her appeal. He leaned down and kissed her. 'Now, where were we?'

She giggled and wrapped her arms round his neck. 'Hmm. I think I need you to remind me.'

'MORNING.' Zander set a cup of tea down on the bedside table before kissing Livvie gently on the mouth.

'Morning.' Her voice was heavy with sleep. He watched with amusement as her eyes suddenly pinged open and she took in her surroundings. A slow smile spread across her pretty face as if remembering the previous evening. 'Oh, morning! That was quite a night.'

He laughed. 'It was. That's one hot little minx you're hiding under that sweet, butter-wouldn't-melt exterior.'

She laughed and her cheeks flushed. 'You brought it out in me; it's all your fault.' She threw back the duvet and arched her eyebrows, an invitation on her face.

'I think that proves my point.' His eyes roved greedily over her voluptuous nakedness.

Livvie grabbed hold of his T-shirt and pulled him towards her. 'Merry Christmas, Zander.'

'Merry Christmas, Livvie,' he said, his lips on hers as he climbed in beside her.

'I'LL GO and make some coffee while you get your pyjamas on.' Zander pulled his T-shirt over his head. Then we can fess up about us to Alf.' He laughed as he headed through the door.

'Do you think he'll be pleased?'

'I think he'll be over the moon.'

Livvie wasn't long after him. Zander glanced up from splashing milk into the jug, to see her looking cute in her huge pyjamas, the birds-nest of hair at the back a tell-tale sign of how they'd spent their night. The thought set a smile playing over his mouth.

'Morning, Alfie; Merry Christmas.' Livvie stroked his head. 'He seems extra excited this morning; he's obviously taken our news well.'

'He was overjoyed. Though there might be another reason.' He nodded towards the utility room.

She watched as Alf trotted to where the two sledges were propped up. He sat down beside them, his tail sweeping back and forth on the flags, wearing a look of expectation on his face. 'Ah, that explains a lot.'

'Well, judging by the snow, I don't think we'll be going far today, so I thought we could get a bit of sledging in – if you fancy it, of course.'

'I'd love to, and I wouldn't dream of disappointing Alf.'

Zander peered across, feeling his heart squeeze with love for his loyal friend. 'He has way too much personality for one Labrador, that one.'

'But you wouldn't change him for the world,' said Livvie.

'Not for anything.'

Livvie

They'd sledged for a couple of hours, before the unforgiving cold became too much and the snow began to fall heavily once more. With cheeks aching from laughing so hard and fingers and toes numb with the cold, they dragged their sledges back up the field and down the path to Dale View Cottage. Livvie thought how achingly pretty it looked with the lights from the Christmas trees twinkling away; this could be her home one day. Though she was too scared to linger on that thought for too long, not wanting to jinx her new-found happiness.

AFTER A SHARED BATH, Livvie and Zander tumbled into bed, revisiting their passion for one another. Once finally sated, they made their way downstairs where they prepared their first Christmas dinner together.

'This has been the best Christmas Day ever,' Livvie said later that evening as they were curled up on the sofa together, the flames from the wood-burner casting long shadows up the bumpy walls.

'It has, I agree,' said Zander.

'What, even with your amazing family and your amazing childhood?' She sat up to look at him.

'Even with that.'

'Wow.'

'Because it's the first one with you.' Zander paused before pulling a face. 'Sorry, more cheese; I don't know what's happening to me, it's like I've been taking lessons in how to be a cheesy jerk.' He reached up and touched her face. 'But, the thing is, it's true.'

Livvie felt her heart melt into a puddle as indescribable happiness washed over her. 'Let's hope they're all like this.'

'I'm trying desperately hard not to let an even cheesier line spill from my wayward mouth than my last comment, which is proving bloody damned hard, so I'll keep it simple and just add that I'm sure they will be.' They both laughed and Livvie leaned in to kiss him.

Just as things were getting steamy her phone pinged.

'Bugger, I thought I'd turned that off after I texted Bry.'

It pinged again.

'Oh, no.' Since Donny's visit, her heart always lurched to her throat when her phone went off; she still hadn't managed to lose the fear that it might be him trying to get in touch.

'I think signal was down for a while so a lot might come through at once,' said Zander. 'I turned mine off after Skyping Carcassonne.'

'Wish I'd thought to do that.' She went across and picked up her phone, tapping on the messages. In the next second she'd clamped her hand to her mouth, trying to contain her giggles.

'What is it?'

'A text from Molly.'

'Oh, hell, I can only imagine. What does she say?'

'Well, she reckons they can see sparks flying across the dale from here, specifically from one of the bedroom windows.'

'Cheek!'

'Then she'd asked if you've tied a ribbon round your "old man" –as she puts it – and offered yourself to me for Christmas.' Livvie's giggles got the better of her and she struggled to get the last few words out.

Zander threw his head back and roared with laughter. 'I wish I'd thought of that!'

'I'm glad you didn't; I'm not sure me howling with the laughter is the reaction you'd expect.'

'Quite, nor would it be one we could tell the grandkids. "So, Grandpa, tell us about your first Christmas with Grandma; what present did you buy her?" Nope, thinking about it, it's just as well my mind doesn't work how Molly's does.'

His mention of grandchildren made Livvie's heart swell with happiness; it told her that like her, he was in it for the long-haul. She went and sat back beside him, his arm enveloping her as she rested her head on his chest, hearing the loud, strong beat of his heart.

'So the other text wasn't anything to worry about?' She knew he was referring to Donny or her family.

'No.' She shook her head. 'Just a generic one from the network.'

'That's good.' She felt him relax. 'Though, you know, if we'd had more time, I would've bought you a present, whether we were together like this or not.'

'I would've bought you one, too. But, truthfully, I don't need anything; the best present I could ever have is being here with you and Alf. Having this wonderful memory will last forever; I don't need anything more than that,' she said.

Zander squeezed her arm. 'I feel exactly the same. Falling in love with a woman as special and amazing as you; I couldn't ask for anything better.'

A warm fuzzy glow of happiness washed over Livvie and she could feel a huge smile spread across her face. 'Would it ruin the moment if I said, "cheese alert"?'

He replied with a low chuckle.

45

SIX MONTHS LATER

Livvie

'THAT LOOKS AMAZING.' Kitty cast her eyes over the mood board and sketch Livvie had prepared for a client from Middleton-le-Moors who was coming in later that morning. 'I love the detailing here on the shoulder; it's from one of the sketches in your book, isn't it?'

'It is; I thought it would work really well with that vintage lace we picked up last week.'

'Oh, it'll be absolutely gorgeous,' said Vi. She rubbed the swatch of fabric between her fingers and thumb. 'Makes me want to get married all over again.'

'I think the next wedding we go to will be somebody not too far from here.' Kitty gave Livvie a knowing smile.

'Now that's one dress I really can't wait to work on,' said Vi. 'You need to tell Zander to get a wriggle on with his proposal, then we can have a sumptuous Christmas wedding. I can see you in a velvet cloak, a bouquet of winter flowers, Victorian cream leather ankle boots ...'

'Steady on there, Vi, we're not that far on yet.' Livvie laughed. Though, in truth, Zander had been quizzing her about engagement rings the other night, trying –but failing – to be subtle. It had made her stomach fizz with excitement but it was quickly quashed when she thought about what her mother and Cheryl would say if she had to tell them she was engaged: "You hardly know him! You're being ridiculous! It's too soon!" Or worse. There wouldn't be a positive comment between them, that's for sure. 'Though, we have been talking about moving in together.'

'About bloody time, you're hardly ever at Forge Cottage now Zander's moved here full-time,' said Vi.

'Ooh, that's so exciting.' Kitty beamed.

Livvie couldn't believe how things had turned out; she still expected to wake up to discover the last six months had been a dream. It hadn't all been plain sailing, of course. Mrs Harris hadn't taken it well that both Livvie and Bryony had handed their notice in, making the four weeks they had to work as unpleasant as possible, finding any excuse to make snide comments and bullying every step of the way. But Livvie had borne it well, watching the light at the end of the tunnel grow bigger and brighter with each passing day. The only downside was saying goodbye to Bryony who had packed up and moved to London straightaway; she'd miss their get-togethers and putting the world to rights sessions. Thank goodness for Skype, she thought.

There'd been no good luck wishes or kind words from her family, but though Livvie had hoped for them, she hadn't been expecting them. And the day she pulled the door to her flat shut for the last time felt ever so slightly surreal. The removal van had gone ahead with her small collection of furniture, crunching through the miles to

Lytell Stangdale where Jimby would be waiting to let the removal men in and set out her belongings.

After his visit to Zander's cottage, Donny had thankfully made himself scarce and Livvie hadn't seen nor heard from him since that day. It still didn't stop her from bolting the door every time she was in the flat; she wouldn't be sorry to say goodbye to that little undercurrent of fear.

Meeting Zander's family had been amazing. A week after their return from Carcassonne, Steff had organised a Sunday lunch get-together and Livvie was invited. She'd been a bag of nerves as she drove to Leeds. *What if they don't like me?* She'd tortured herself all the way there, unable to get the niggle of how much they'd liked Clara out of her mind. *At least Zander will be there; he'll make everything alright.*

As it turned out, Livvie had nothing to be worried about. As soon as she stepped through the door, she felt at ease. His family welcomed her with open arms, apparently thrilled to see how happy she'd made Zander. Steff's house reminded her of a more suburban, less rustic version of Molly's with its cosy atmosphere, happy noise and evidence of family everywhere. Zander had been attentive until he realised there was no need to remain glued to her side and she'd chatted animatedly with Steff and his mum, Toby's wife Jo, too.

If anyone had told Livvie a year ago that her life would turn out like this she would have laughed in their face. But it had, and she was deliriously happy.

Zander

The last three months, living at Dale View Cottage with Livvie had been the happiest of Zander's life. They'd slotted into an easy routine and he couldn't remember feeling so utterly content. Waking up with her in his arms was the most amazing feeling; he wanted to stay this way forever. Indeed, his time at the practice in Leeds seemed like a lifetime away now and he hadn't had a moment of regret.

It had been strange to think he wouldn't be working with Noah anymore, Zander had mused as he'd left the surgery for the last time, after working his three months' notice. But there hadn't been a single doubt in his mind that it was the right thing to do. He'd been looking forward to making a fresh start in Lytell Stangdale; that village had grown to mean more and more to him with every visit and Livvie had more than a little to do with that.

With Steff's help, he'd packed up his personal belongings in readiness for the arrival of the removal van the following day. He'd left most of his furniture since his replacement at the practice had been keen to rent his house while he got a feel for the area. It was an arrangement that suited Zander.

He'd only seen Mel once since Christmas. She'd turned up with a woman he'd never met before, the pair of them giving him dirty looks and making snide comments as they'd disappeared upstairs and noisily scooped up her clothing and make-up, slamming the door behind them as they left.

Introducing Livvie to his family was something Zander had looked forward to and had no qualms about doing; he knew instinctively they'd adore her. And they did. He'd been thrilled that she'd felt at ease with them, seeing her happily chatting away, particularly with Steff and his mum.

'She's delightful, Zandie,' Steff had whispered in his ear. 'And look how Alf loves her.'

'I can see why she makes you so happy, Zander darling,' his mum had said.

After their keenness with Clara, he knew they were mindful not to push things, but this time they'd be justified. Livvie was, without doubt, "the one".

AFTER ENJOYING a delicious meal at the Sunne where Bea had excelled herself with the most mouth-watering lamb tagine and aromatic bejewelled couscous, Livvie and Zander were enjoying a steady walk back to the cottage with Alf trotting along beside them. It was a languid, balmy evening, the heat of the day's sun being thrown back from the land. 'What a view.' Zander stopped to take in the bucolic vista of the dale that was bathed in a mellow light from the fading sunset, glowing in muted shades of gold, apricot and peach. Birdsong had all but silenced as the perpetrators had gone to roost for the night in the leafy hawthorn bushes or trees that dotted the fields or edged the meandering sliver of ribbon that was Swang Beck. The occasional hooting of an owl floated by, adding an ethereal quality to the late evening. In the distance, the low thrum of a tractor making the most of the burst of fine weather, hurrying to get the silaging done, could be heard from the fields at Tinkel Bottom Farm. It was punctuated by the odd bark of a stag from the woods near Danskelfe Castle.

Zander inhaled deeply, the heady scent of wild honey-suckle that scrambled over the hedgerows, mingled with the sweet smell of freshly-cut grass, drifting by on a barely-there breeze. 'What a stunning evening.'

'It's perfect.' Livvie sighed, following his gaze.

He glanced down at her, his heart leaping at how beautiful she was with the sun's warmth illuminating her face, making her eyes sparkle. She was wearing a loose-fitting vest top and floaty ethnic skirt, with bracelets that jingle-jangled on her arms.

He swallowed; an idea had been circling his mind for the last couple of weeks, growing and gaining momentum each time he thought about it. Before he knew what was happening Zander had taken Livvie's tiny hand in his and he cleared his throat.

'Livvie.' He pulled her close to him, kissing her gently. She looked up and smiled at him, making his heart melt. 'Livvie, I've got something to ask you.'

'Oh?'

'I know we haven't know each other long, but I adore you with all my heart and feel like I've known you forever.'

'I feel the same.' She beamed up at him.

'And we've both said we feel we're meant to be together.'

'We have.'

'Livvie.' Zander cleared his throat again and, despite feeling a little silly, got down on one knee, watching as her expression changed. 'Livvie, would you do the honour of marrying me?'

Livvie clasped her hands to her chest. 'Zander! Oh, wow! I'd love nothing more in this world than to marry you.'

His heart soared; the pure happiness shining in her eyes matched his own.

'That's fantastic!' He got to his feet and scooped her up in his arms. 'Woohoo!' He swirled her round making her squeal with joy. Alf joined in the excitement, leaping around giddily, giving the occasional bark.

Still laughing, Zander set her down and pulled her close to him. 'You've just made me the happiest man in the world.' He pressed a kiss to her lips.

'And you've just made me the happiest woman in the world.'

'Who'd have thought a mix up with a holiday booking could result in this?' he asked.

Who indeed?

THE END

AFTERWORD

Thank you for reading A Christmas Kiss, I hope you enjoyed it. If you did, I'd be really grateful if you could pop over to Amazon and a leave a review – if you just google the link below it will take you right there:

A CHRISTMAS KISS – ELIZA J SCOTT AMAZON UK

A CHRISTMAS KISS – ELIZA J SCOTT – AMAZON US

It doesn't have to be long – just a few words would do – but for us authors it makes a huge difference. Thank you so much.

If you'd like to find out more about what I get up to in my little corner of the North Yorkshire Moors, or if you'd like to get in touch – I'd love to hear from you! – you can find me in the following places:

Amazon author page: Eliza J Scott - UK or Eliza J Scott - US

Blog: www.elizajscott

Twitter: @ElizaJScott1

Facebook: @elizajscottauthor

Instagram: @elizajscott
Bookbub: @elizajscott

ALSO BY ELIZA J SCOTT

The Letter – Kitty's Story (Book 1 in the Life on the Moors Series)

You can get it here:

UK: Eliza J Scott – Amazon UK – The Letter – Kitty's Story

US: Eliza J Scott – Amazon US – The Letter – Kitty's Story

The Talisman – Molly's Story (Book 2 in the Life on the Moors Series)

You can get it here:

UK: Eliza J Scott – Amazon UK – The Talisman – Molly's Story

US: Eliza J Scott – Amazon US – The Talisman – Molly's Story

The Secret – Violet's Story (Book 3 in the Life on the Moors Series)

You can get it here:

UK: Eliza J Scott – Amazon UK – The Secret – Violet's Story

US: Eliza J Scott – Amazon US – The Secret – Violet's Story

YORKSHIRE DIALECT GLOSSARY

The Yorkshire dialect, with its wonderful elongated, flat vowels can trace its roots back to Olde English and Old Norse, the influences of which can still be found in some of the quirky words in regular use today. As a few of them crop up in The Secret – Violet's Story (as well as The Letter and The Talisman), I thought it might be a good idea to compile a list of them for you, just in case you're wondering what the bloomin' 'eck I'm going on about. I do hope it helps!

Aud – old

Aud mucker – old friend. Used in greeting i.e. 'Now then, me aud mucker'.

Back end – autumn

By 'eck – heck

Champion – excellent

Chuffed to bits – very pleased, i.e. 'I'm chuffed to bits with my new coat'.

Diddlin' – doing – i.e. 'How're you diddlin' means, 'How are you doing?'.

Ey up – hello/watch out

Fair capt – very pleased

Fair to middlin' – fine (in answer to the question, 'How are you/how are you doing?)

Famished – hungry

Fettle – fix/put right

Fizzog – face (used as slang throughout the UK, not just in Yorkshire)

Fower – four

Gander – look, i.e. 'Have a gander at this'.

Goosegog – gooseberry

Hacky – dirty

Jiggered – tired

Lops – fleas

Lug/lug 'ole – ear/ear hole

Mafted – hot

Mash – brew, as in a pot of tea

Mucker – friend

Nithered – very cold

Now then – hello

Nowt – nothing

Owt – anything

Raw – cold, in reference to the weather

Reckon – think

Rigg – ridge

Rigwelted – word used to refer to an animal that has fallen over and got stuck on its back

Rum – odd/strange

Snicket – an alleyway

Summat – something

Yat/yatt – gate

Yon side – on the other side

ACKNOWLEDGMENTS

It's been great getting to know two new characters in the Life on the Moors series; I don't know about you, but I think they fit in with the other residents of Lytell Stangdale rather well. I love how the mystical powers of fate brought Livvie and Zander together and gave them the happy ending they deserve. Could there be a wedding story to follow I wonder...? Of course, I could hardly forget to mention Alf, Zander's adorable black Labrador; he's a real character who's guaranteed to make everyone smile with his waggy tail and mischievous ways.

I'd like to take this opportunity to thank the people who've helped towards publication day of A Christmas Kiss. Here goes ... (deep breath!) First of all, I'd like to thank my family for being my cheerleaders; your support means the world to me – as do the cups of tea and ginger biscuits you keep me plied with while I'm writing! Hopefully, my writing room will be ready soon, then I won't have to keep hogging the dining table (sorry!).

Special thanks must go to editor Alison Williams. I really enjoy working with Alison and feel I learn more and more with every manuscript. Her warm words of encouragement are always a welcome boost.

Huge thanks are due to Berni Stevens for designing yet another beautiful book cover. Getting Berni's cover ideas back is always an exciting time and one I look forward to like a child waiting for Christmas! I think she's captured the essence of Christmas on the moors perfectly.

As ever, I must thank the very calm and organised Rachel Gilbey of Rachel's Random Resources. Rachel's amazing publication day blog tours are the perfect way to launch a book; they've certainly helped get mine out into the big, wide, book world, and introduced me to some wonderful book bloggers along the way. Thank you, Rachel!

I'd like to say an enormous thank you to the fabulous book bloggers who have been involved in the Publication Day Blog Tour for A Christmas Kiss – I nearly fell over when Rachel told me how many of you had signed up for it! Thank you for taking the time to read my book and reviewing it on your awesome blogs; it's very humbling and I'm incredibly grateful.

Finally, I would like to thank the warm and welcoming book community – I know I mentioned you in the dedication at the front of the book but, just in case you missed it, I thought I'd mention you again! It's been lovely getting to know you; your support and kind words always brighten my day.

THANK YOU!

ABOUT THE AUTHOR

Eliza has wanted to be a writer as far back as she can remember. She lives in the North Yorkshire Moors with her husband and two daughters. When she's not writing, she can usually be found with her nose in a book/glued to her Kindle, or working in her garden, battling against the weeds that seem to grow in abundance there. Eliza enjoys bracing walks in the countryside, rounded off by a visit to a teashop where she can indulge in another two of her favourite things: tea and cake.

Printed in Great Britain
by Amazon